S0-AMR-600

Brother of the Third Degree

Will L. Garver

Brother of the Third Degree

A Cornerstone Book
Published by Cornerstone Book Publishers

Cornerstone Book Publishers
New Orleans, LA

www.cornerstonepublishers.com

ISBN: 1-887560-43-2
ISBN 13: 978-1-887560-43-6

MADE IN THE U.S.A.

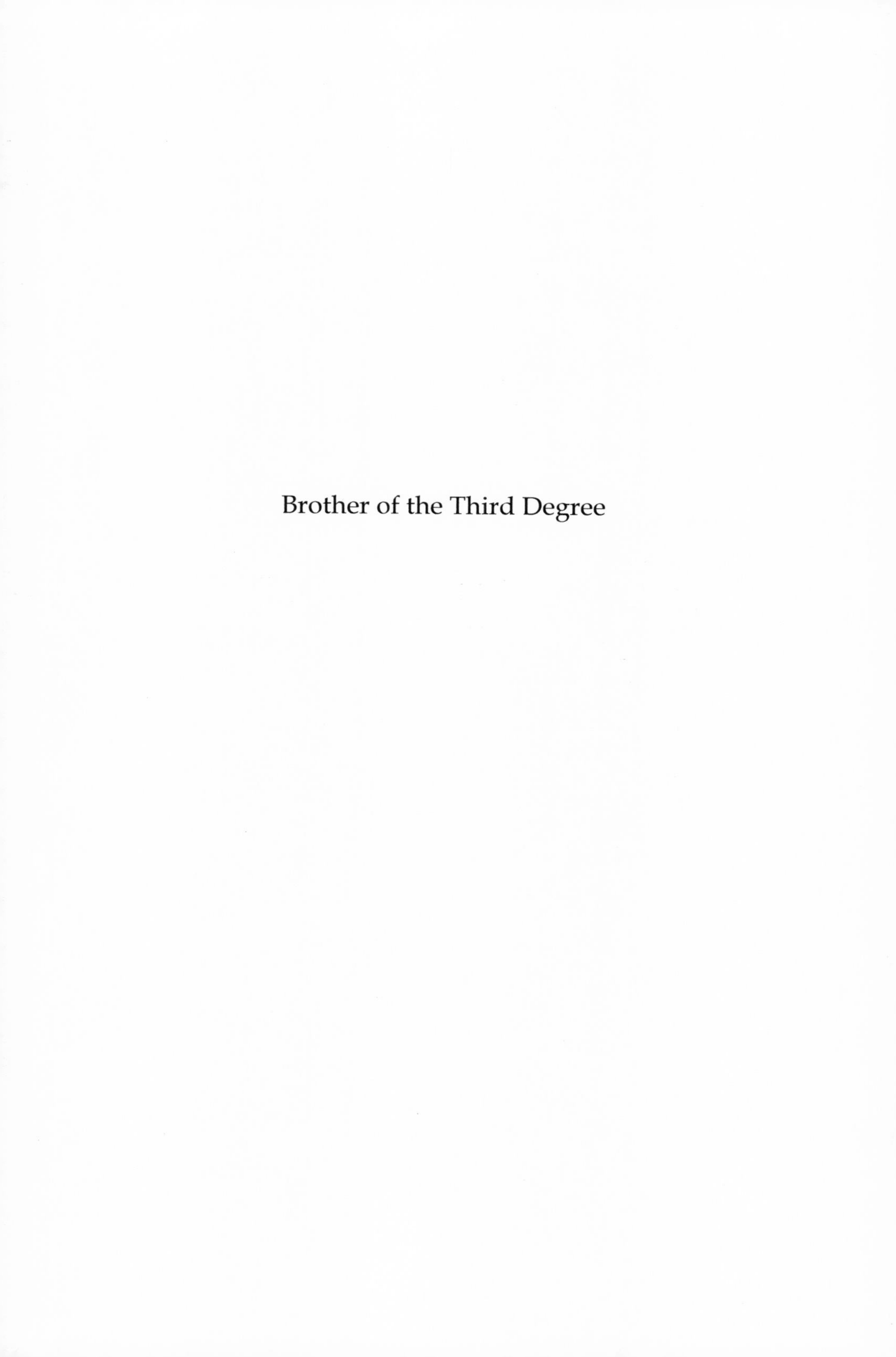

Brother of the Third Degree

CHAPTER I
CHILDHOOD

There is a principle, proof against all argument, a bar against all progress, and which if persisted in cannot but keep the mind in everlasting ignorance-and that is, contempt prior to examination. —PALEY.

Accept nothing that is unreasonable; discard nothing as unreasonable without proper examination" —BUDDHA.

MY name is Alphonso Colona. I am a Mexican of pure Spanish descent, but was born in the city of Paris. I am the only son, but had a beautiful sister, Esmeralda, three years my junior.

My father, Ferdinand Colono, was a direct descendant of the Colonos of Granada, who traced their ancestry back to the time of the Moors, and who were known throughout the Hispanian peninsula for their skill as physicians. My mother was of the noble Vesta family of Seville, who were likewise most skilled physicians.

Father and mother first met while they were students in Paris. After ten years of the purest and most studious companionship, and after they had both graduated with highest honors, they were married; and I am the first offspring of that union. After my birth my parents moved to the City of Mexico, where my father's parents had located early in the nineteenth century.

There had always been a mystery connected with their schooling; a mystery I did not understand until late in life. They were two of the most learned people of their time, and strange to say, they came from the very center of materialistic thought deeply imbued with mystic ideas.

Upon his return to Mexico, father immediately commenced to practice as a physician, and soon became known far and near for his wonderful success and skill.

In fact, his fame became so great that it was not confined to Mexico alone, but extended throughout the entire west; and he was offered almost fabulous salaries by the governing powers of the South American states.

All these he respectfully declined, and remained in the city administering to the rich and poor alike, never refusing the low or the high. As a result he was known and beloved by all, and exerted a powerful influence both in governmental circles and among the masses.

Mother, scarcely less learned, and most highly accomplished in art and music, possessed an influence equally as great as father's, but, except on special occasions, spent most of the time at home as the instructor of sister and myself, considering it here special duty to be our tutor.

Our home was beautifully located upon a hill in the suburbs of the city. A two-story building with a classical exterior in stucco, and a large interior court beautifully paved with many-colored pebbles and made pleasant by a sparkling fountain and tropical plants and trees.

Many years have passed away since mother sat here in the cool of the evening and pointed out and explained to sister and I the starry constellations which shine so brightly in the clear sky of all tropical countries.

Still do I remember with most vivid clearness those evening lectures. She did not consider the starry hosts as mere shining lights to dispel the gloom of night, but thought like her ancestors of Moorish times that all were filled with life, the dwelling places of gods and spirits, and had a most intimate relation with the children of earth. Many years have passed away, many vicissitudes and the bright sunny days when my beautiful mother would take Esmeralda and me to the neighboring mountain peak, and cultivate out tastes for nature's beauty as we gazed out upon the placid mirror of the gulf, and far away to the blue and misty mountains 'round about. I still remember the pleasant lessons in geology and natural history we received upon these journeys, for many were the curious stones, plants and animals we here found joy in studying. I still recall the loving light that shone from mother's dark, bright eyes as she cautioned us not to harm the little creatures, as all life was sacred and from God; that these small insects were in existence for a purpose, and we could learn more by studying them in life than by pulling them to pieces in death.

After frequent journeys to the mountain, even the birds seemed to learn we were not like most beings of our kind, and became kind and friendly, lighting on our shoulders and perching on our hands. Even now I see Esmeralda, with her long, dark curls floating in the wind, laughing and talking to the redbreast on her hand.

Ah! These recollections made me sad for many yeas. I loved my beautiful mother and sister with a pure and holy love, and I often wished I was a child again to enjoy the unalloyed happiness of those hours. But now I know this was not wise. You see, dear friends, what I have lost, but do you know what I have gained? Great were those joys, but still greater are those that come from the full unfoldment of our spirit natures. And then, it is not wise to dwell upon the past beyond recall, except in study that may better guide our footsteps in the future.

Father, while almost constantly administering to the sick, never lost an opportunity to be at home, and frequently accompanied us upon those mountain journeys or talked with us beside the fountain in the court.

Mother and lie would talk for hours upon philosophy and science, and Esmeralda and I, though young in years, sat by and took deep interest in their conversations, which, while we did not fully comprehend seemed, by some unknown and interior intuition, strangely familiar. The child knows more than we are wont to give it credit. Knowledge does not come from the intellectual mind alone; the pure, uncontaminated heart dwells close to the spirit wisdom and reflects its light.

In addition to his professional duties, father taught what I at that time thought to be a school of medicine. In his laboratory, on the second floor, he never allowed us to enter; its only door of heavy oak was locked with a peculiar and strange looking lock, and its windows were covered with iron bars. Every Wednesday evening a number of men called and repaired with father and mother to this room. This number I noticed to be almost invariably twelve, and they generally came and went alone. During these Wednesday evening meetings sister and I remained with a tried and trusted servant, who saw that we retired at the proper time. Thus things continued for eleven years, and I was fourteen and sister eleven. All was love and kindness, and year in and year out was a constant but pleasant school. Mother was an exceptional linguist, and I, while only fourteen, had become proficient in Spanish, French, English and Italian, and was well along in the natural sciences, philosophy and art. Esmeralda was fully my equal, but music was her forte; and when her voice rose in song, crowds of peons gathered in the street and listened in silent awe to the perfect beauty of her voice. Both of us were accomplished artists upon many instruments, and while she played the harp I would accompany her upon the violin. These family concerts, in which father and mother often joined gave them much pleasure, as also the wonderful resemblance we bore to them, I becoming every day more like my father, while Esmeralda was the perfect picture of her mother.

One evening father returned earlier than usual, and he and mother took seats beside the fountain and were soon very earnestly in conversation. Sister and I were playing with a large collection of fine sea-shells beside the court, and, ordinarily, would not have paid more than passing attention to their conversation; but the absence of father's usual kiss and play, together with the sad look upon his kind and handsome face, attracted our attention, and we stopped our play to listen.

"Nina," he answered, kissing her, "I have been thinking that our love-life must soon come to an end and give place to more serious duty. And, while I would not for a moment shirk the task laid down for us, it fills me with unusual sadness to know that we must part."

"You forget, dear husband, that while we may appear to separate, our souls are always one. Our twenty years of pure love and unselfish labor have bound us inseparably together in our interior natures, and unfolded our higher faculties until we are now fitted for a still more noble work. We love as only pure, unselfish souls can love; but we must not neglect our duty to those who all these years have overshadowed us with their loving protection. Neither should we forget that all things here on earth are fleeting. Nothing but the real endures. We have been instructed in the science which leads to the eternal, and for twenty years have enjoyed the highest happiness of earth to aid us to a dim perception of a still higher and eternal joy. Shall we now, for thoughts of self as separate from the All, renounce our blessed privilege and neglect our higher duties?"

Mother's face was radiant, and a halo of light shone around her head, while her eyes were bright with a wondrous beauty.

"My darling wife," responded my father, "you nobly represent the Masters; you do full justice to the noble Vestas; you recall me to my duty. Truly, how uncertain is this earth's existence! When all is bright, a cloud may be overhanging. Today we live in peace, happiness and love; to -morrow death may desolate our home, fortune change, and wealth give place to rags. We, truly, by being pledged to Masters, have been overshadowed by their protecting love; and we shall not now allow the joys that are but fleeting to lead us from the path of duty and the bliss that is eternal."

"Well spoken, husband; now both are strong - what is the news your face bespeaks?"

"I have this day received special news from France; Santos has passed his initiation and will be here before long to relieve me of my charge. He will be accompanied by Albarez, the meaning of which I know not; but we may be sure it portends change."

"True, husbands, this is significant; yet use not the word portend. IT implies evil; and we may be assured that the presence of one so great can mean naught but good. But, if this is the case, it is time to give our children more advanced instructions."

"Yes," answered father, "their knowledge, together with their intuitions, will enable them to now understand; I will join you and them in a ramble over the mountain tomorrow, when we can speak with freedom on the subject which we have guarded for so long, yet which will be of vast importance in their lives."

With this, their conversation drifted into other channels; and by and by, sister and I tiring of our play, got our instruments and all four joined in an evening concert.

The next morning lunch was prepared in anticipation of a whole day on the mountain. The sad look on the face of father the evening before had disappeared, and he joined with lively interest in our rambles. All the morning our geological hammers broke the rocks, and many were the flowers and plants we analyzed. The mountain-top was covered with many sea -shells, and father took advantage of our inquiries concerning them to give a talk upon the ancient world, when what is now land was then the bottom of the sea, and what is now sea was then the home of vast and mighty civilizations long since lost to history. After partaking of our noon lunch, and when all were seated upon the great porphyry rock that marked the summit, father commenced the following talk:

"Children," he said, as mother took her sent between us, " the full meaning of what I have to tell you will be made clear as you grow older; and, as it is surrounded with considerable mystery, and what cannot at present be fully explained to you, I must trust to your innate knowledge to make it pain.

"Your mother and I are members of a secret Brotherhood, all of whose members are pledged to devote their lives in labor for mankind. Not only we, but our parents and ancestors for many ages before us were, or are, identified with this secret order."

Esmeralda and I were now paying the closest attention, and father's words had a strange fascination for me.

"This Fraternity," he continued, "has many degrees or grades of membership, extending from those who work unselfishly in the humblest walks of life, to hose who mark the highest possibilities of human development. Each degree has its peculiar duties and obligations, and your mother and I belong to what is called the fourth degree. As members of this degree, and before we can pass on to the exalted 'Third Degree," we must raise, in pure love and through all the paths of virtue and goodness, two souls to take our places in the world when we pass on.

"You, dear children testify to the fulfillment of that duty, and we trust and believe that you will be fully competent and willing to do your part as you grow older. In addition to this duty, we must live a loving and unselfish life for twenty years as ordinary members of the world, during which time we are to teach and train you until you are able to proceed by yourselves.

"If these duties are faithfully fulfilled, if for all these years we are a living example of all that is pure and good, it is our privilege to become members of the exalted 'Third Degree,' rise superior to the bonds of death, and live immortal in the purest love."

"Children, our twenty years have now almost expired, and

the only unfulfilled condition is that you should be fit to fill our places. We know, for our life of study has not been for naught, that this is only a matter of time, and that you both will be our superiors.

"We tell you these things, dear children, because we have reasons to believe changes are soon to call us to new duties, which may necessitate a sundering of the ties of love.

"In explanation of this seeming cruelty, we would say that while the love which has been ours is blissful, it cannot compare with a still higher love which marks a higher life. And remember, children, that whatever may come to pass, if love-bonds are broken and you appear to have no friends, you are, by right of birth and the Brotherhood's adoption, surrounded by protecting powers that defy all opposition.

"So long as you live a life of purity and goodness, and adhere strictly to the path of duty, the Great Ones, called Protectors, will protect you from all harm."

Grand and noble were the words of father as he continued upon this subject which seemed to possess his entire soul, but still more so were the beautiful and eloquent words of mother who followed him with a description of the great souls who were members of the "Third Degree." With full confidence they outlined the possibilities that now lay before them and us, their children, and when they had finished Esmeralda and I, although young in years, were filled with an enthusiasm like their own.

"Now, children," said father in conclusion, "we have taken you into our full confidence that you may in the future more fully understand our actions; and while we impose no solemn pledge upon you, you will keep secret all we have spoken until it is permitted you, by proper authority, to reveal."

Mother's description of the members of the Brotherhood, with their great knowledge, powers and wondrous beauty, filled us with desires to be like them and to know more of their relations with our parents.

Evening having now arrived, we returned to our home, Eameralda and I walking on ahead with the Brothers the sole theme of our conversation.

Nothing unusual occurred until next Wednesday evening, the

regular night for the meeting in the laboratory, which meetings we now know from father's talk were of a Masonic lodge of which father was Grand Preceptor.

Upon this evening father returned accompanied by a stranger.

He was a tall, lithe, agile-looking man, with brown curly hair, rather long, and thin curly whiskers and mustache of the same color. His eyes were of a steel blue, wide open and very penetrating in their look. His features were pale and somewhat angular in contour. His form was almost completely enveloped by a long indigo-colored cloak which hung loosely from his shoulders to his knees. Upon his hands he wore gloves, which I noticed he never removed, and he always spoke in a low, suppressed tone which seemed to have a power unknown, as it sent shivers through us when we heard it. I noticed, also, that the stranger avoided personal contact with any one, and immediately upon his arrival he proceeded to the laboratory from which he never departed, not even for meals, which were prepared especially by mother and delivered in person.

Upon the arrival of this stranger, mother came to us and said that she and father had a very difficult work to perform that night and we must not be alarmed if they did not come down until late the next day. Then kissing us good-night she repaired to the laboratory, father remaining below until the usual time. About eight o'clock the weekly callers arrived, but this time they were all in a body and led by another stranger. Esmeralda and I were now left with Juanita, the maid, and father, with the others, proceeded to the laboratory.

After retiring to my bed the mysteries of the last few days commenced to crowd upon me, and it was only after a long and restless evening that I fell asleep.

Sleep, strange mystery, who knows thy meaning and the wondrous powers that in thee find full play? I fell asleep to dream I was carried far off into a wild and mountainous country, where, on the steep and rocky side of a lofty range, encompassed around by peaks of snow, was a large, monastic-looking building. Next, by the marvelous transformations which characterize the dream, I found myself in an interior court, surrounded by cyclopean columns and thronged with white-robed priests. Upon a large white cube, which served as a throne, at one end of the court, sat a robed figure in a chair of pearl or ivory. His head was uncovered, and he wore long golden curls; his face was young, his eyes mild and blue. As I looked his form became surrounded with a halo of light, and as I gazed more intently I saw tat his form was transparent like crystal, and a golden light emanated through the light blue robe of gauze that enveloped it. Then his features changed, and from the kind and gentle look that had at first marked his face, it became stern and violet scintillations filled the air around, with eyes fixed in awe and wonder on the scene, I saw the whit-robed throng draw back, and twelve figures, transparent, but not golden like the first, robed in gauze of yellow, come forward and stand in a circle around the throne. Then I noticed for the first time a golden zodiac upon the whit e marble floor, around the throne, and each figure stood within a sign. The court was flooded with radiant light from no apparent source, and now, behold! Twelve figures, robed in indigo, lead forward another figure in like ferments. A beautiful form of pearly-white shines through its transparent folds, and lo! as I gaze I recognize my mother. Upon her broad noble brow, now ivory-pearl color, shines with brilliant luster a five-pointed golden star. Oh, how beautiful her face! How calm and grand her features! Her twelve robed conductors separate in front, six take each side and join behind to form a triangle around her. She advances. Then a fog came over the scene and I became lost in deep and dreamless sleep. O soul! Untrammeled by the chains of matter, where did you in this sleep wander?

On the following morning I learned from Juanita, that after having been in session the entire night, all had left before dawn except the mysterious stranger who was still with father and mother in the laboratory. "And," whispered the maid, with a scared look upon her face, "the court started to return to my room, the full moon lighting up the court showed it full of white figures."

I said nothing in reply, but could not help but relate her strange statement with my dream, and determined to ask mother concerning it.

Nine o'clock came, and father came down with a pale and

careworn look upon his face.

Noon came' father took a light dinner with us, but in answer to our questions only said, "Mother will come down later."

Three o'clock came, and at last mother appeared. On, how supremely beautiful was her face, now a pearl-white in color, and radiant with divine love. She came to us, and as she kissed me her touch thrilled my entire being. A delightful fullness filled my heart; I never felt so happy.

In answer to our questions, she said that the stranger was great Master, and that by his aid she had gone far away and seen many of the mysteries of the higher life. When I told her of my dream she smiled happily, and, kissing me, said:

"My dear son and brother, you are wiser than you know, and w ill some time know more fully the meaning of your vision,"

The stranger did not appear until evening, when he walked into the court where we were all sitting together, and, coming up in front of me, uttered some strange words which had a wonderful effect.

A white mist formed in a cloud before my eyes; the vapor, vibrating rapidly, took form, and a panoramic view spread out before me. I saw a smooth, mirror-like body of water surrounded by mountainous hills and containing many islands; a bright blue sky, filled with floating banks of snowy clouds, was reflected on its placid surface; then a vast feet of ships full of armed men appeared, and the land also became black with a surging mass of shielded warriors. How, I knew not, but I seemed to recognize the scene, and the words Xerxes, Persia, Greece, formed in my mind. Then the mist took new shapes, and I saw a plain covered with hosts of dark-faced, turbaned men, with short, curved swords, mounted upon Arabian steeds. Opposite this swarthy host was an army of men of giant size, with long, yellow hair, immense battle-axes and suits of mail. I saw the turbaned hosts rush forward wit loud cries. The two sides met in wild, tumultuous battle, and I saw the words – Martel, Poitiers. Then the mist faded away, and I heard the strange man say:

"Brother of yesterday and tomorrow, your course is fixed." Then turning to Esmeralda he gazed at her long and intently. As he gazed her features became fixed, and her eyes took a far-away look; but I could see no mist. Then he uttered the words: "Child-sister of the Orient in western form, thou, too, shalt return." He waved his hand, and sister started up with a look of surprise upon her face as she turned inquiringly to me.

This strange performance had, taken only a few moments of time, and father and mother had been silent witnesses.

As the stranger stepped back from Esmeralda, he turned, and with a peculiar gesture and knowing look, departed.

We both plied father and mother with questions; but they had seen no mists or scenes. They had only noticed our steady gaze and heard the words of the stranger, whom they now said was a great adept named Albarez; and that he had the most wonderful powers, such as belong to all exalted men among which was that of recalling temporarily to others their past existence.

"For," said father, "the soul is eternal and uncreated, and passes from life to life and country to country. No doubt what you beheld were scenes in your past existence, and if you join the Brotherhood and pass through its higher courses, the vast knowledge that is concealed within your soul from many lives gone by will be revealed and become a part of your consciousness. This is in reality the secret of the Masters' knowledge of whom we have so often spoken, and it is within your power to become like them, for they are but men passed on to higher planes of being."

"Yes, children," added mother, "you are spirit-souls dwelling in bodies for the time being. When you have purified, trained and perfected your bodies and made them fit instruments for the manifestation of spirit, it will bring to you all knowledge, for it is the knowing power in man."

Thus you see my early training. From childhood my life had been full of mystery; and, at the early age of fourteen, I had formed ideals of perfect men called Masters, like whom I wished to be. If my life has been different from most men's this will help explain it. These mystic teachings of my parents, together with my strange experience with Albarez, made the Brotherhood a constant subject of my thoughts. The presence of the adept, Albarez, had evidently caused a change, for the next Wednesday evening there was no lodge-meeting. In answer to our questions, father said his duty had been performed and his charge had been transferred to others.

CHAPTER II
SEVERED TIES

Two weeks after the departure of the adept, Albarez, father entered the court with a letter which he handed to mother as he took a seat beside her near the fountain. Having broken the seal and read, she handed it to father, at the same time calling Esmeralda and me to the seat beside her.

"Ferda," she said, as father laid down the letter and we approached, "it is all for the best, and we must show no sign of weakness." Then turning to us she said:

"Dear children, we have lived long and happily together, but the time has now come when we shall have to separate. Alphonso, Esmeralda and I must leave on the first steamer for Paris. I have been called there to perform a duty, and will take Esmeralda along so she can complete her studies. You have still much to learn which father can best teach you, and when you have become sufficiently advanced to be prepared for teachings higher than he can give, you will also came to Paris and we will be together again. Now, children, we will have our family concert for the last time, as I understand that the Altata leaves Vera Cruz the day after tomorrow, and sister and will have to take that steamer."

Father acquiesced in everything that mother said, and I, fully confident of the superior wisdom of my parents, willed to take things as they came. Nevertheless, it was not without a feeling of sadness that Esmeralda and I went for our instruments, and tenderly we caressed each other on the way.

"What mother says is for the best, brother," said sister, "and while you are learning to be a great doctor, I will become a great artist, and then we will meet again in Paris and be all the happier because of our separation. For, if we were always to be together, we would not realize the darkness that comes from separation; and, no doubt, after being away from each other for some time, we will love more strongly when we meet again. Then observe how much father and mother love each other, and they bear it all in calmness. We, too, must be like them, strong and brave; and by and by we will become members of the Great Brotherhood.

"Do you know, brother, I believe mother's sudden call to Paris has something to do with this great Brotherhood about which they have talked so much?"

"What do you think, sister?" I asked.

"Why, I think mother is advanced, and is much greater than we know or think. In fact, I think neither of us fully knows our parents. I believe bother are great members. And, brother, I believe that when the great adept, Albarez, was here, he found out that mother is advanced, and he has now sent for her. Anyhow, we will write often, and you will tell me all about father and I will tell all about mother."

We had now returned to father and mother in the court, and, once started, continued our concert until late at night.

Father and I played our violins, and sister and mother played the harp and flute.

Sudden though the announcement had been, there was no delay; and father and mother, taking everything in a calm and systematic manner, were ready for departure the next day.

We all took the train for Vera Cruz, where mother and sister board the Altata for New York on their way to France.

Father had all along mastered his emotions, but I noticed tears in his eyes and heard his suppressed sobs as he kissed his loving wife and daughter "good-bye."

I hung around my dear mother's and sister's necks until the order was given to return, then with father I kissed them a sad "good-bye" and descended into the boat to be rowed ashore.

Mother seemed to be possessed with a marvelous calm, and this fact undoubtedly strengthened father. This was not because of her supreme control over all her part, but because of her supreme control over all her feelings and emotions. 'Tis only now, after many years of toil, labor and experience, that I begin to realize the exalted nature of my mother. 'Tis only now, when I know the full meaning of that parting, that I can appreciate my father's strength of character. Truly was their love of duty great when they would sacrifice a life of happiness to work for mankind's good.

Father and I were rowed back to the landing, and there stood and watched the black hull of the Altata as it grew smaller and smaller upon the waters of the gulf.

A long cloud of black smoke rose from the steamer's stack and circled across the clear blue sky, that gave no toke of a coming storm. The birds were chirping in the trees and the air was full of the busy hum of insect life. The many colored plants and trees, fresh from the morning dew, made the world around a land of beauty, and everything in happiness seemed to try to soothe our sadness.

That day we domiciled at the hacienda, home of Don Ignacius Martenez, a great scholar and physician of the city who was a fellow-student in the occult and a particular friend of my father.

When he learned of the departure of mother and sister, he shook his head gravely, and said: "Senor Colono, I would not cause you any unnecessary fear or uneasiness, but you must have neglected to look at your charts before this action."

"Truly, Don Ignacius," replied my father, "I have not noticed the planetary aspects for some days now, although I never neglect that knowledge when practicing, as I deem the influences and substances that are symbolized under the names of the planets to e most intimately related to disease. Like Hippocrates, I hold that astrology in its true sense is the very foundation of therapeutics. But, Don Ignacius, what are the indications:"

In reply, Don Ignacius took us to his study, where he called our attention to a large celestial globe of some transparent material, and having the constellations thereon in colors; while within, and capable of different adjustments, was our solar system with the sun in the center.

"You will notice," said the Don, "that the planets portend a storm, and that upon the water; Saturn and Uranus, both maleficent planets, are in conjunction, and the Moon, Venus and Mars are in the same sign, the sign that rules the gulf. This is evil; and while I hope no harm will come, I prophesy a change ere long."

Father evidently fully understood the remarks of Don Ignacius, and agreed with him in his conclusions; but, in reply simply said he had obeyed orders and could believe only for the best. I had been an attentive listener, and although I myself had some confidence in astrology, as I looked at the clear blue sky I thought their wisdom this time must certainly be at fault.

But my conclusions proved erroneous, for few hours later, with almost incredible swiftness, the sky became overspread with dark and ominous-looking clouds. The wind arose, and the blackness of night usurped the day.

Then came a short gust of wind, a slight shower of rain, and then a calm - a dreadful calm - oppressive in its stillness. Then a storm - a terrible storm. The wind roared and the trees snapped before its awful force. The very timber of the building screeched and trembled beneath the blasts. The heavens seemed a holocaust of fire, and the thunders contested with the roaring winds in awful din of terror.

In an hour all was over. Only an hour - yet, O God! What devastation it had wrought! What violence it had done! What changes it had brought!

Throughout the storm father had sat with a stern, far-away look in his eyes; and now, when all was over, I noticed a change had come over his features. No more that happy smiled of yore, but a stern and inexpressible sadness.

"My dear brother," said the Don, taking my father's hand, "I feel with you, and would give what strength I could in this hour of doubt and trial. It seems impossible to think the steamer could survive that storm, but all is for the best. We cannot lament over that which some call death, for we know that with her it would be but the commencement of new life. You have lost her from this life, but your loss is her gain. And when we recall the facts as they really are, it is even you gain, for while you have lost her in the visible, she will be constantly present in the invisible; and what looks like separation is in reality a closer union. Then remember, brother, that you acted in accordance with Masters' orders, and they are wiser than we. And when we look at it in this light, we must remember that if she still had duties in this world of form, she was guarded by those against whom not even this tempest could prevail."

Don Ignacius' words had a strengthening power, and father shook his hand and said: "My dear brother, you speak words of truth; I have loved my wife until that love has become selfish, and, no doubt, this is brought to recall me to my duty and direct my love to man. I will be strong and never more forget my true labor as a man. I obeyed the Masters' orders; I have full confidence in their superior wisdom, and from henceforth I dedicate my life to humanity and truth."

As father spoke he arose, the very picture of self-control; and his sad, whit face became lighted up with a noble calm."

"My son, Alphonso," he said, turning to me, "remember the words that have here been said; impress them well upon your mind and heart. Your mother is not dead. There is no death. Through that act or process so called we pass from prison-forms of flesh into the universal light and love.

"In all probability your loving mother and sister have passed from our kind of life into higher planes of joy and labor. "

"Tis left for us to continue in our labors here and earn the right to join them in the higher brotherhood of love. Will you follow me in this great effort? Will you join with me in efforts to reach this end?"

I seemed to imbibe my father's strength, a new life pulsated through me, and an inner voice said: "On! On!"

With a determination and enthusiasm I had never shown before, I answered, "Yes."

Father kissed me, and Don Ignacius grasping my hand said:

"You are a noble son and destined for great work; great wisdom will you have and pass beyond. Go with your father; study well; he is most competent to teach. Be pure, be good, and full of love for man; and thy end is fixed and certain."

We remained with Don Ignacius still another day. The papers giving an account of the storm said it had swept the entire coast and gulf, and all vessels on the water were undoubtedly lost.

Following was a list of the passengers on the Altata; and after Senora Nina Colono and daughter was reference to two unknown men who had embarked just as the boat was pulling anchor, and whose names had not yet been registered.

The next day father and I returned to the city, and from that time I became his almost constant companion. The old laboratory was opened, and I was taken through a thorough course in chemistry, and everything that pertains to medicine was made a subject for investigation. Father became more assiduous than ever in his attention to the sick, and I accompanied him on all his visits, listening to his lectures on the way. As time went by, and my knowledge increased, he spoke with less reserve, and, pledging me to secrecy, told me much about the occult theories of medicine. The science of signatures and correspondences were broadly outlined, and he told me more fully of his schooling in Paris.

Mother and sister were not banished from our thoughts or conversations; we talked of them often, and although it was with sadness, we controlled our feelings and did not waste time in unprofitable longings for what was past.

Speaking one day of his success in medicine, father said:

"I do not treat disease as many suppose, and my success does not come from the titles that follow my name, nor from the diploma which I have from one of the world's most celebrated schools, but from the knowledge that I acquired in certain secret schools, in which I was a student when in Paris.

"These schools," he continued, "have existed unknown to the public from the time of Mesmer and St. Germain, who taught far more than they are credited with by the uninformed public. These schools are closely guarded, and none but the deserving can obtain admittance, for the knowledge they reveal would be an awful power for evil in the hands of selfish and malicious persons. I hope, my son, to secure you admittance into this school when you become of age, no one being allowed to enter under the age of twenty-one.

"In the meantime you must graduate as a regular physician, for in this age of superficial knowledge and much for, you could not practice openly as you are therein taught. Therefore you must cloak your practice under the title of a regular, as I do. This title, but at the same time using means which, if know, would be branded as superstitious and make me a charlatan."

When questioned if this secret school was in any way related with the great Brotherhood, he replied that it formed a part of a semi-esoteric section, and that all fourth-degree members sent their children there to get the benefits of both esoteric and exoteric schools.

"Remember, my son," he said, "the members of the fourth degree must seek power and influence in the world; not for their own selfish ends, but in order that they can thus be more potent instruments for good. Each candidate for membership must be a master of the three great professions, medicine, law, and art.

"This will be more fully explained to you when the proper time comes."

"Was mother, and are women admitted to this school?" I asked.

"Mother was a member, and women are admitted; but while they are exempt from professional practice if they so desire, they must stand all examinations the same as men.

"Mother was a high graduate in art and music, was most skilled in the preparation of drugs and the diagnosis of disease, and was my constant advisor in all difficult cases. At the same time she was acquainted with the laws of nations, the principles of government, and when it came to law in its philosophical aspect had few equals. Remember also, Amphonso, that it was here that I met mother; and in explanation of our remarkably sympathetic natures, I would say that all fourth-degree members of the Brotherhood send a son and daughter to this school, and this practice our brothers before us did for many centuries in the past, wherever their schools might be. The knowledge of the laws of generation imparted in this school enables all who go there from to bring suitable members into their households, each father and mother raising a son and daughter; and thus is the organization perpetuated as the older members pass on to higher degrees where marriage is unknown. With me at Paris was an only sister who married a fellow brother, and from whom I have not heard for twenty years.

"Likewise mother had a brother, who did not marry, but took and exceptional course and passed on. Concerning this I can say no more, but hope you go to Paris you will, like me, find a soul clothed in the feminine sex that will be responsive to your own and full y worthy of your love."

"But," I said, thinking of my lost sister, "How are the gaps filled when there are deaths?"

"That, my son, belongs to the secret s of initiation, which I am not at liberty to give; suffice it to say, there are councils who regulate these matters. And aside from those who are entitled to become members by right of birth, there are those who become such by adoption."

Seven years thus passed, with me a constant student under my father. Nothing had ever been heard of the Altata from the day of that fateful storm. Not a word concerning mother. Whenever I broached the subject to father he persisted that she still lived, and so far entered into the "Third Degree" whose members were superior to death and lived immortal. "But if this be true," I urged, "why do we not hear something from her?"

"My son, you do not understand," he solemnly replied. "Those of the 'Third Degree' know not the ties of husband, wife, or parent. No individuals, as such, can claim their love, for it is boundless and universal, and belongs to all mankind."

I was now twenty-one years of age, and far advanced in medicine and science.

My love for knowledge had become almost insatiable; but, notwithstanding my intense application to study, I had not been allowed to neglect the requirements of social life.

"For," said my father, "so long as your field of labor is in the social world, you must know its forms and usages. And it is not necessary to sever your studies, but only that barren farce, society without mid, where vanity, frivolity and fashion have shriveled up the heart, and forms conceal the defects of the soul." This participation in the social world was productive of good results: I commenced to analyze its so-called pleasures, and found them all illusions and unsatisfactory.

While participation in them as a matter of form, knowledge, and a desire to solve to some extent, at least, the mysteries of the universe, became my sole ambition. One day we returned home and found a visitor whom, at first sight, from the manner of his dress, I took to be Albarez, whom I still remembered; I soon found he was another man with a similar style of dress and cloak, but black instead o f blue.

Unlike Albarez, he greeted father with a cordial handshake, and when father introduced him as Monsieur Garcia, from Paris, he immediately commenced a pleasant conversation.

A month passed, and Monsieur Garcia, being almost constantly with me, had become a most intimate friend. At this time father, in a long conversation upon occult subjects, informed me that Monsieur Garcia was a student of the secret schools of Paris, and would in a few days return; and I, being now of age, should go with him, and try to obtain entrance into the school in order that I might have more light thrown upon my studies by learning secrets which he was not allowed to communicate.

"And remember," said my father, "while as the son of an older member you are entitled to consideration as a candidate, you can enter only upon your own worth and merit, and must stand many tests and examinations before you can be admitted into full membership, even in the lower degrees."

The day having come for Garcia's departure, father took me into his study for his farewell lecture.

"Alphonso," he said, after he had dwelt long and eloquently upon the grandeur of brotherhood and love, and outlined the organization which sought to make these universal, "Monsieur Garcia is an advanced member of the secret Esculapian School and worthy of your full confidence. He come with credentials from high brothers, and will leave you in good and trusty hands.

"Recall what I have told you concerning students of this school. None but he pure and good are admitted, and to all others their existence is unknown; none but the elect can find them. 'Tis your privilege to be among those who can lead you to their benefits. Respect this privilege, and maintain the utmost secrecy with regard to everything pertaining to them. Beware of the glitter of the world and avoid all sentimental love and follies. Let your love be pure, strong, and without measure for all that is good and true. As regards the other sex, marry not unless you find a soul fully sympathetic to your own, and a mind devoted to the same great end. First seek admission into the school, for it is there you will find those whose hearts and minds beat in harmony with your own. There, among your brother sisters, you will no doubt find one worthy of your love and best suited to aid you in your advancement.

"Choose her for your fellow-student, cultivate for her a pure and holy love, and when knowledge entitles you to again appear before the world, wed her in true wedlock and perform your duty to your brothers and world.

"Ever remember that this life is but the necessary probation to a life still higher, and never allow the exalted pleasures of this most happy period to lead you from the path of final duty.

"Pure love for wife and children will expand the flame within your heart. Pure devotion will unfold the hidden spirit that dwells within your inmost being, and lead you to more beautiful and still grander heights of love.

"My son, learn to love, for if you learn not here you cannot hereafter.

"Let your whole soul be ravished with the divine flame; but never for one moment allow it to be sullied by an evil thought or lost in selfish separation.

"Love your wife that you may the better love mankind; love your children that you may the better love all God's children, and then will the universal love illuminate your mind soul and bring to you all wisdom.

"And now, my son, be strong and brave; be true and patient, and ever labor for the good. Farewell! We may never meet on earth again! Farewell!"

My father spoke with voice full of love and tenderness, and a halo, like that which used to surround mother when speaking in like manner, shone around his head and face.

His words had a strange, strengthening power, and, while my love for him was as strong as ever child's for parent, I controlled my feelings, and suppressing my tears, bade him a kind farewell and left with Garcia for France.

CHAPTER III.
PRINCESS LOUISE.

WE crossed the Atlantic, reached Liverpool, and took the train for London without incident of note.

Garcia was a most interesting companion, possessed of extensive knowledge and well informed in the ways of the world.

As though to stimulate my aspirations, he talked much of the mysterious Brotherhood to which he and my parents belonged.

Many were the stories he told of the exalted wisdom and wonderful powers of the members of the higher degrees.

Nothing was more interesting to me, as I had now become fully imbued with occult ideas and had determined to do all within my power to learn and master the mysteries of the hidden side of nature.

I noticed, however, as with my parents, all information was strictly confined within certain limits, beyond which he would never go, and he always diverted the conversation when thus pursued. At London we stopped three days, during which time an incident happened which increased the mystery that already surrounded me.

Garcia was well acquainted with the streets, and was taking me over the city. On the evening of the second day we were walking along in the neighborhood of Trafalgar Square, when a sudden commotion attracted our attention.

"'Tis a runaway!" he exclaimed. And as the crowd drew back, I saw a royal carriage drawn by two black and fiery steeds come dashing with terrific speed along the thoroughfare.

"My God!" cried a hundred voices, "it is Princess Louise, the Queen's most favored daughter! She will be dashed to pieces! Give them the road! Don't turn them! God, what nerve! See how she holds them!"

Pale as death, a beautiful woman with braced feet pulled on the reins with all her power, and with wonderful presence of mind kept the frightened animals in the middle of the street. But her strength would not suffice to stay them, as, covered with foam, their iron-shod hoofs struck fire upon the granite paving.

"Can't some one stop them? My God! They go right toward the monument! Oh, horror! 'Tis death!"

Just then a tall cloaked figure stepped hurriedly from the frightened crowd, and rushed out directly in front of the flying steeds. I felt a tremor run through the hand of my companion and a suppressed cry came from his lips. At the same time a strange, thrilling sensation ran through my form and my heartbeat quick and fast.

"Stand back!" cried many throats. "No human power can save her. 'T will be your death! Take care! Rash man ?"

Straight toward the daring man, now standing calm and erect, dash the frightened steeds and carriage. Will they trample him under their grinding hoofs? Now they are no him? no. Quick as thought he stands aside, a whit misty vapor fills the air, enveloping coach and horses. It clears away. And now, what strange and wonderful mystery! The fiery steeds have changed, and, trembling in every limb, press back upon their haunches to stay the carriage which comes to a stand just in front of the monument. The mysterious stranger, who had followed the carriage, stepped in beside the now fainting princess, and before the astonished multitude could realize what had happened, seized the reins and turned into a side street.

I was no less dumbfounded than those around, and stood speechless, a strange sensation pervading my being. As the crowd commenced to recover itself, Garcia grasped my hand hurried me along to escape it."

"What does it mean?" I asked. "Are not the days of miracles over?"

"Miracles," he answered, "there are no miracles; but this means much."

"What?" I asked.

"That man was an adept," whispered Garcia, "and as the lady was the queen's favorite daughter, we may expect great changes in governmental circles.

"The Masters do all within their power to aid the world in its upward evolution, and, working through human instruments, seize all opportunities for the accomplishment of this end. It is only on the most exceptional occasions that they would use the powers here demanded."

In reply to my further questioning, he said:

"A wait developments, and then my explanations will be more intelligible."

On the following morning we started for France. As w boarded the cars for our station I bought a Daily Times; and there, in full-face type, side by side upon the front page, were the headings:

STRAGE AND MIRACULOUS ESCAPE! PRINCESS LOUISE BY SOME MYSTERY OF MAGIC SAVED FROM A MANGLING DEATH. Princess Louise, who, as all know, is a most skilled horsewoman and an expert with the reins, while taking her usual after noon drive behind a pair of untried steeds, lost their control, they being frightened by an accidental explosion on the street.

With her usual coolness and presence of mind she held the fiery animals well in line, but was not strong enough to stay them. Along the street they dashed, faster and faster, wilder and wilder. The heavy steeds would have trampled any human to pieces, and the only hope was to keep a clear road. It seemed that all was lost and death was inevitable when it was seen that they were bearing directly toward the monument in the center of the street.

A cry of terror a rose from the crowd as they saw the danger; women fainted and men turned away to shut out he awful scene, when a tall, unknown man, with a long indigo-colored cloak stepped out directly in front of the flying steeds, and with a coolness that looked like madness calmly awaited their approach. Two deaths seemed inevitable, but when the horses reached him stepped quickly aside, and y some strange mystery of magic, we know not what, covered coach and steeds with a white, vapory mist, which in some still stranger manner seemed to change the entire nature of the animals, and brought them in trembling terror to a stand just in front of the monument.

Before the crowd could recover from its astonishment, the mysterious stranger stepped in beside the fainting Princess, and, seizing the reins, turned the horses into a side street and disappeared.

Who the man was cannot be ascertained. He was not with the Princess when she arrived at the palace, and the Princess will not talk and refuses silent, and the indications are that his identity will remain a mystery. But the wonderful nature of the occurrence, together with well-known fact that the Princess is a deep student of the occult, led us to investigate in that direction.

A reporter called upon Hager, the celebrated hypnotic animal trainer, and asked his opinion on the subject.

Hager says it was not done by hypnotic or magnetic power, as that requires the animal's attention and a fair, square look into its eyes, which was evidently impossible under the circumstances.

At the headquarters of the occult section of the Theosophical Society, very little satisfaction could be obtained, although it is known that Princess Louise is a frequent visitor there. Sankya Rao, the Hindu adept now there, hinted in vague terms about Akasic ethers, elemental vortices and Kri yasakti powers, etc., but gave very little information.

Whoever the stranger was, and whatever his powers, the occurrence will remain a nine days' wonder and give the charlatans and pretenders to secret wisdom another harvest from the multitude of dupes who now throng the city in search of the occult.

The second heading, no less conspicuous, read as follows:

WILLIAM HERBERT MORLEY APPOINTED PREMIER;

WHICH MEANS THE END OF ENGLISH POWER IN THE EAST.

JNO. CLARK RUSSELL LEAVES AS SPECIAL ENVOY FOR INDIA, AND THE NEW PREMIER TAKES HIS SEAT TODAY.

Then followed a lengthy account of startling and unexpected political changes.

Garcia had also bought a paper and read the articles. Seeing my inquiring looks, he glanced searchingly around and commenced in a low tone as follows:

"My brother, do you think the material world is ruled by law and the social world is left to chance? Do you think that human evolution has no guidance, or that it is ruled direct by God? If the latter, you are in error. God, the Infinite Spirit, while pervading all, is far beyond all earth affairs. But between us and the Supreme are many grades of beings? superior men, heroes, demi-gods and gods? and each host of these works through those below. Kings, Queens, Presidents and Rulers are not always so by chance; they never are in periods of transition, when great changes are impending, for they are but instruments for higher powers, a nd work unconsciously for predetermined ends.

"Warriors, statesmen and great religious teachers are thus overshadowed by superior beings and are often even conscious of the fact, as Socrates who had his Demon; Joan of Arc, who had her Voices. Mohammed, Cromwell, Napoleon and all great men who have thought themselves the instruments of fate for the accomplishment of some great end, have thus been overshadowed.

"This is the secret of what some call fate. Men make themselves fit instruments through which these powers can act and work to bring about some lawful end. Men thus used shine with great genius, but when the end is brought about, the real powers, who are unseen, forsake them, and they sink again to the common grades of men. You are themselves to blame, for they abuse the privileges they hold, and, thinking these powers their own, commence to work for selfish ends and assume divine prerogatives.

"Then they must fall; for, in the words of Hugo, 'they displease God,' and must become once more but men.

"These men are sometimes evil, but evil men are often, in the end, unconscious instruments for bringing good."

"And do you relate all these remarks to the occurrence of yesterday?" I asked.

"Yes," he replied in a suppressed whisper, "indications would seem to say that the throne of England is thus overshadowed; but the invisible workers veil their activities by working through what seem natural channels."

Just then a stranger took a seat ear by, and Garcia immediately changed the subject of conversation.

We crossed the strait and proceeded on toward Paris. The crowd prevented further conversation, but I was busy thinking. The brother hood had now become the almost for an opportunity to learn more concerning their mysterious powers and society.

CHAPTER IV.
PARIS? MOTHER!

ARRIVING at Paris, Garcia hailed a cab and we were driven rapidly across the city to the palatial residence of Monsieur Durant, an old-time friend of my parents, and for whom I had a sealed letter from my father.

M. Durant, an elderly gentleman of about sixty years with a military looking beard and mustache slightly sprinkled with gray, met us at the entrance in person, and, grasping my hand and speaking most cordially, led the way to is private reception-rooms.

After some time in pleasant conversation Garcia arose, and, saying he would see me again, departed, leaving me alone with M. Durant to whom I now gave the letter from my father as he had instructed.

As he broke the seal and opened the letter a casual glance showed me it was written in hieroglyphics.

M. Durant read its contents in silence, then turned, and setting his dark, piercing eyes on me, held them there for several seconds as though trying to read my inmost thoughts. At last, evidently satisfied with his inspection, he kindly remarked that I would be his guest for some time; and, as I was no doubt tired, he would accompany me to my room. Reaching a nicely furnished room upon the lawn, he told me to rest and make myself perfectly at home; and he would call in the course of an hour and accompany me to tea with Mme. Durant and their daughter Camille.

An hour later M. Durant returned, and we proceeded to a private supper-room where I was introduced to Mme. Durant and Camille. Madame was a rotund woman of medium height with a broad, motherly face, black eyes and hair, and very kind and agreeable in her manner. Camille was a stately brunette with broad, whit brow and lustrous eyes, that spoke welcome as she shook my hand and took her seat beside me at the table. The pleasant manners of all soon made me feel as one of the family, and I soon cast off all reserve.

The lunch was very light, and consisted solely of fruits and nuts, Mme. Durant remarking by way of explanation that their rules were to have only two regular meals a day a light repast for supper.

I assured them that it was no hardship for me, as I had been raised from childhood on a strict Buddhist diet of only two meals a day and no meat. After a half hour's conversation Camille and I were fast friends, and, with the smiling consent of her parents, we started on a tour of the mansion.

Camille's education had evidently not been neglected, for as we walked along the richly furnished halls and up the marble stairway she talked with equal fluency and show of thought upon art, science and philosophy. Her mind seemed to glide by instinct into the channels of my own, and our sentiments were nearly one on almost every subject. How pleasant it is to converse and be with those whose thoughts are in harmony with your own. Over an hour was spent in the magnificent are t gallery and not a word was foolish of frivolous in its nature. When at last we parted for the night, a carriage drive over the city was on the program for the morrow.

On the following morning M. Durant met mw in the hall and said he wished to have a talk with me before my drive with Camille. So immediately after breakfast we proceeded together to his private room. Having closed the door he offered me a seat opposite him at a center tale; then leaning forward on his hands and looking me fixedly in the eyes he said:

"Alphonso Colono, your father informs me by his letter that you desire entrance into certain secret schools that exist in Paris; and he further vouches for your preliminary training and knowledge. Now do you earnestly desire to enter these schools? If so, what motive prompts your desire?"

"M. Durant," I replied, "from a child I have been fond of knowledge, and knowledge is now ambition of my life. The information that the outside scientific world can give me does not satisfy; it can tell me nothing concerning the real nature of things, and its knowledge consists of a mass of unexplained facts and phenomena only. But from the teachings received from my father, I am led to believe that there are those in the world whose knowledge is not confined to such narrow limits, that they will aid me to reach real knowledge, and it is them I seek."

"Do you realize the serious nature of true knowledge? Do you know the requirements necessary to its possession? Do you know the immense responsibilities and duties that it brings?"

"These to some extent I know and realize; and these I am ready and willing to meet and assume."

"You speak bravely and with confidence, but I fear you know not all. Nevertheless, I believe your motive pure, and will try to find some one who is associated with this school and tell him of your desires. In the meantime you are not to speak or talk with Camille upon this subject; and, furthermore, you are pledged to silence. Do I hear your pledge?"

"You do," I answered.

"Now, referring to your knowledge: Your father says you are well advanced in medicine, art, and law; this is well, for these are indispensable requisites for an active life for mankind. He further says you have not as yet received the formal and superficial titles that are deemed so essential in this world, the great majority of whose people never look beneath the surface.

"Therefore I advise you to enter the exoteric schools and institutes, and get diplomas and certificates in these three professions. Your knowledge will enable you to carry on all three subjects at the same time. And while they can give you no real knowledge, they can teach you much that will be of advantage in the world. In art, they can teach you skill with the hand; in law, diplomacy and forms; in medicine, they can teach you surgery, and give you confidence in yourself from the ignorance they show.

"Then, further, you will form acquaintances, gain influence, and, if you are accepted as a candidate for the secret schools, be ready for consideration without delay, for these qualifications are necessary to all who would enter therein. Now, be silent; for the present may go."

I left the room, and, proceeding along the hall, met Camille and accompanied her in a pleasant drive over the city.

As on the evening before, she again demonstrated her ability as a conversationalist and entertainer, and when we returned our friendship was established.

Thus time passed, and Camille and I were almost constantly together. She was a student of art at the Ecole des Beaux Arts, and, at her request, and in accordance with M. Durant's advice, I also matriculated. At the same time I entered two of the most celebrated schools for instruction in medicine and law.

Through the Durants I gained entrance into the highest social circles of Paris, forming many strong friendships with her beautiful and intellectual women, and becoming closely associated with many men of serious and studious minds. Although surrounded and in almost constant association with the beauty and intellect of the French metropolis, I had not, as yet, found my ideal love. Camille and I were closely attached to each other, but only as brother and sister, and we called each other such.

I often recalled the remarks of my father about my sympathetic soul, and questioned myself if my ideal of love was not too high. Born in purest wedlock, taught from youth to view love in its purest beauty, I pictured it in most exalted form. I found great pleasure in dwelling upon ideal conceptions of the beautiful and good; and, as this habit continued, my ideals grew stronger and purer, until perfect man and woman and perfect civilization were constantly uppermost in my mind. Father corresponded regularly, and his letters were always filled with words of loving tenderness and god advice. He urged me to prosecute my search for knowledge, and learn patience, so as not to be discouraged by the apparent slow manner in which true knowledge comes. "For," he wrote, "knowledge is a growth, and not an external acquirement; and all enduring growths are slow. As your faculties unfold and your organism becomes perfected, true knowledge, which ever dwells within, will find the instruments necessary for its manifestation, and come forth."

Garcia, without a word of explanation, had altogether disappeared; and, trusting M. Durant to attend to my application for membership into the secret schools, I settled down to business an concentrated all my energies upon my studies; and this without divorcing myself from social life, for the keynote of my father's teachings was concentration. I had so cultivated this power, that while in my study I was all student, elsewhere, I was in harmony with my surroundings.

Father's letter contained not a word concerning mother and sister, and, notwithstanding his peculiar remarks to the country, I had concluded they had perished in that fateful storm.

This conclusion soon received a startling contradiction.

It was on the night of the fifth of September, one year after my arrival at the Durant mansion, and Camille and I occupied a box at the Grand Opera House where Mlle. Vivani, the world-renowned prima-donna, was to appear that evening.

The house was filled to its utmost capacity in expectation of the great event, and the *elite* of the city were out *en masse*. The hour had arrived for the performance to commence, and the audience was eager with expectation, when the manager appeared before the curtain, and, with a low and courteous bow, addressed the questioning audience:

"Ladies and gentlemen," he said, "it is with mingled feelings of sorrow and pleasure that I have to make an announcement.

"Mlle. Vivani has contracted a severe cold and will not be able to appear this evening."

A shuffle of feet and murmur of disappointment ran through the audience, when the speaker continued:

"But I am pleased to announce that another will appear in her place, who, while not known upon the stage, has a right to be ranked with the highest who are, and who will surely meet and gratify our highest expectations. It is my pleasure, ladies and gentlemen, to present to you Mme. Nina, the unknown queen of song."

As he spoke a beautiful and stately woman, dressed in a Grecian costume of purest white, appeared upon the stage.

A thrill ran through my form, my limbs trembled with agitation, a suppressed cry escaped my lips; I leaned forward with a startled look, and as Camille, dumfounded by my actions, laid her hand upon my shoulder and asked my what was wrong, I uttered the one word ? "Mother!" Yes, there upon the stage, in all her queenly beauty, her broad white brow and dark lustrous eyes now more beautiful than ever, was my mother. Mother, or her living image?

As though the intensity of gaze attracted her, she turned, and her eyes met mine. A momentary pallor came over her face and she gripped her hand; then, as if by a supreme effort of will, turned her eyes to the audience.

Now her voice rises in song. Yes, it is the same sweet voice I had listened to so often, but, if anything, more sweet than ever.

With wondrous power her voice rises and falls in almost celestial harmony as she sings that great love song, "Utopian Lovers," each word carrying with it the power of a virgin heart. Under its soul-soothing power I forgot my agitation, and, entranced, was only aroused as the last words died away, followed by a deafening roar of applause.

"Oh, Camille!" I cried, as she disappeared, "that is my long-lost mother, whom for years I have thought dead. I cannot be in error. I must see her."

"Alphonso, what ails you? Your mother died eight years ago. 'Tis only a resemblance; don't be so agitated."

Again she appeared, and, as though she knew me, her eyes again met mine in kind and loving look.

And ? was I deceived? I hear the words as though coming from within my ears: "Be calm, my son, be brave and do your duty; all is well." "Camille, did you hear that?" I asked.

"No; hear what?"

Then her voice again arose in the deep and soul-thrilling words of "The virgin Wedding." A death-like stillness seized the audience; an all-pervading calm seemed to hold each being. Never had Paris been so entranced before.

For several moments after she had ceased a hush pervaded all, as though too sacred for applause, and then ? a heavy breath, as from a thousand souls at once, was followed by a deafening roar. Tears had come to many eyes; not tears of pain, but tears of suppressed emotion.

Souls that had never before given thought to beauty and love, were thrilled by the all-pervading love stirred by that heavenly voice and soul.

It was the last appearance.

"Camille," I said, "it is my mother. I must speak to her; I must see her. Let us to the stage entrance."

"I don't know what is the matter with you," she replied, "but lead the way; where you go I follow."

Quickly we hurried to the stage entrance most convenient, and, pushing open the door, entered but to be confronted by a tall, cloaked figure.

"Albarez!" I exclaimed, for I could never forget his face.

"Alphonso Colono," replied the adept, "away and do your duty; when that is done then can you meet your mother. All is well? away!"

"And then she is my mother?"

"She is or was, now she awaits you in the Brotherhood where alone will you ever meet her. Away!"

And, as though I could not disobey, I turned, and hurrying with Camille to a cab, returned home all agitation and excitement.

CHAPTER V.
MORE MYSTERY.

THAT night sleep was a stranger to my agitated soul; vainly did I try to control my restless and wandering mind, but all of no avail. What mystery surrounded me! Mother alive! What of Esmeralda? And this mysterious man, Albarez. She awaits me in the Brotherhood. What did it all mean? Twelve chimes told the beginning of another day. One ? two ? three, and still I rolled and tossed, my mind run wild ? beyond control. Four. At last I sank into a troubled sleep; and, as though to add still greater mystery to that already around me, I dreamed, as eight years before I had of monastery court among mountains wild. But this time it was my father who was led by monks in robes of indigo before the Radiant One. And, as before, a fog came over the scene and left the end unknown; and I was lost in sleep. I awoke somewhat refreshed, but filled with a restless agitation. I was all on fire with an inward energy.

"She awaits me in the Brotherhood; then will I meet her," I said, with a determination that brought my teeth together. What is the meaning of this dream? Has this mysterious adept anything to do with it? He was present when I had the other. Thus I continued to soliloquize. For one year I had patiently waited in silence without hearing a word from my application. M. Durant vouchsafed no information, and in answer to my question replied aphoristically ?

"Everything comes to those who wait." But I had waited long enough; and, having now received first-grade certificates in law and medicine, I would know the reason if I waited any longer. As I paced up and down my room, I only grew more restless. Something seemed to say,

"You are right; you are right. Go on! Go on!" filled with these thoughts I went down to breakfast, fully determined to have an interview with M. Durant immediately it was over.

By a kind of tacit consent they said nothing of the events of the night before, Camille complimenting me on my excellent graduation grades. After breakfast, and before I could ask for an interview, M. Durant said he wished to see me in his study. Having reached his study and entered, he closed the door with his usual caution and motioned me to a seat opposite him at the center-table. Then without a word he handed me two letters, all the time scrutinizing my features.

The letters were postmarked ? City of Mexico, and one was in the handwriting of my father, while the other I did not recognize.

As it was unusual for me to receive strange letters from Mexico, I opened it first.

It contained a newspaper clipping, a bank certificate of deposit, and a written sheet which read as follows:

CITY OF MEXICO, MEXICO,
August 15th, 18? SENOR ALPHONSO COLONO,

DEAR SIR:

Your father, Ferdinand Colono, you will see from the enclosed clipping, has mysteriously disappeared. Where he has gone or what has gone or what has become of him no one knows. The day before he disappeared he sold his property for cash, and deposited the proceeds, together with all other available assets, amounting in all to 500,000 francs, with us, requesting that we transfer it to your credit in the Bank of France.

In compliance with this request we herewith send you a certificate of deposit for said amount. Trusting everything will be found satisfactory, and that you father will soon return, we respectfully solicit your business in this part of the world in the future.

Respectfully,
CARLOS SANDOL Y CIA,
BANKERS.

Nervously I took up the clipping and read:

MYSTERIOUS DISAPPEARNACE.

Don Ferdinand Colono, Government physician and one of the most prominent men in Mexico, has mysteriously disappeared without any apparent cause, and without leaving a word of explanation, but evidently with aforethought and premeditation; for on the day before the one on which he was last seen, he sold all his property. And transferred everything he possessed to his son, now in Paris.

Senor Colono was learned, wealthy, influential, and highly respected; and these facts, together with his almost universal popularity, would not lead us to suspect foul play.

So far as can be ascertained, he was last seen near the Hotel Iturbid, in company with a tall, cloaked stranger.

It is said by those who appear to know, that Senor Colono w as a member of some mysterious Occult of Masonic Brotherhood, and that his disappearance is in some way connected with this organization; but nothing can be learned concerning it.

Ever since the departure of his son, over a year ago, Senor Colono has been frequently seen with a cloaked stranger, but who this man is, no one knows.

Any information concerning Senor Colono will be thankfully received by his many friends in this city. We hope his absence is only temporary, and that he will soon return.

"The mystery deepens," I muttered between my set teeth, as by a mighty effort I restrained my feelings.

I handed the clipping and letter across the table to M. Durant, and as he took them opened the letter from my father. It read as follows:

MY DEAR SON AND BROTHER, ALPHONSO:

I have at last, after years of waiting, been given an opportunity to pass on. Eight years ago your mother passed; but I, for certain weaknesses, failed. Now it is my privilege to join her in the higher ranks. We shall never meet in this world again, unless it be in the Brotherhood, which, in the degrees where I go, is not of this world. When you receive this, I will be with your mother and far away—

I jumped up; I could not contain myself any longer.

"What does it mean?" I cried. "Join my mother, whom I saw here last night, in Paris, and yet far away. I do not understand it," I exclaimed, pressing my brow in excitement.

"Read on," said M. Durant coolly, "distance is not a thing of miles. The prisoner in his cell is far away from the flowers that fill the lawn around him. That which seems farthest is in reality, the nearest."

Surprised at seeing M. Durant thus cold and unsympathetic, in marked contrast to his usual nature, I took up the letter and continued:

Remember the teachings of your youth, and work with all your energies for the higher life.

Remember the unsatisfactory and delusive nature of all things earthly, and seek only the eternal.

My son, I see dark clouds now hanging around you, but it is necessary that it should be so. For, if thou wouldst join the Souls who love, thou must pass through trials, for it is only thus that strength is gained.

The time will come, yea, even now is near, when uncertainty will wrap you in the gloom of night, and doubts and fears harass your soul. Then be patient, and rely upon the guide that never fails if thy motive be but pure—that is the Spirit Self.

When all forsake thee, and thou knowest not whom to trust, go to thyself. Fast, seek solitude and meditate; then, if thy soul is pure, the light will surely come.

Trust those who would lead thee to the Brotherhood; show no fear; suffer no

delays and we will meet again, brothers of that Universal Band whose members live in the Eternal. Farewell! My son and brother; though far away, ours and the Masters' love surrounds thee! Farewell!

Thy father—brother, FERDINAND COLONO. ?

As I finished the letter, all the tender memories of my loving parents rushed upon me, tears welled in my eyes, and a deep sigh broke from my lips. But I had never seen M. Durant so cold before; he seemed cruelly unsympathetic and severe.

"Control yourself," he said, "the wise restrain their feelings."

I looked at him reproachfully, but his piercing black eyes never winced; when, having read the letter, which I handed him, he spoke as follows:

"Alphonso Colono, son of Ferdinand Colono, high initiate, if you would follow in the footsteps of your most exalted parents you must master and control your feelings. For, cruel as it may seem, in the Brotherhood into which you seek admission, joy and sorrow, pleasure and pain, happiness and misery are one. Where is your strength?"

He spoke with a coolness I had never heard before, and his tones goaded me to desperation, I bit my tongue, and with gritting teeth answered: "I have all strength; I am controlled."

I thought I detected a gleam of satisfaction in his eyes, but his face remained as impassive as a sphinx. Reaching into his inner pocket he handed me another letter.

"There," he said, "don't open that until you get to your room. I have done as you requested and had your application presented. That is, in all probability, your answer. What it contains I know not; but whether it be much or little, I now demand of you the most inviolable secrecy as to its contents and everything you may hereafter learn that pertains to the Brotherhood."

"You have it," I replied, with hand raised as if to swear.

"Very well," he answered, "take this as a memorandum; if you are accepted, they will want to know the day and hour of your birth. Your parents, knowing the great truths of esoteric astrology, preserved this information in a register kept for that purpose, and I there obtained it."

He handed me a slip of paper on which was written—

"June 5th—7:45 A.M. 18— Leo--"

"Now you can go; maintain secrecy and consider yourself free to act without any explanations to us."

CHAPTER VI.
THE WOMAN IN BLACK.

THE manner of M. Durant had served to some what allay my agitation, and when I reached my room I drew the sealed letter from my pocket without delay.

The envelope was made of linen, and could not be torn, while the sealed portion on the back was covered with a wax stamp bearing mystic characters—the interlaced triangles with an Egyptian tau in the center, and surrounded by a serpent with a Chaldean swastika at the meeting of mouth and tail.

Breaking the seal, I drew forth the following note, written in a small feminine hand:

Sir,

Your application has been favorably reported. My carriage will call for you this afternoon. If you wish to proceed, accompany without question, and bring this note with you.

MADAME PETROVNA.

The signature was written in a peculiar manner, and was covered with a perforated, five-pointed star, as though to prevent alteration, while the paper was so light and delicate no erasures could possibly have been made.

"At last my opportunity has come," I muttered.

"There must be crises in men's lives; here in the last twenty - four hours I have found my long-lost mother, lost my father, and received word from the mysterious Brotherhood which seems destined to control my life."

I re-opened the letter from my father, and now for the first time the triangle which followed his signature attracted my attention.

It was not like the other writing in color, --it was not writing! I stepped to the window and rubbed my finger over it, looking at it closely. It looked like a kind of carbon substance built up or embossed upon the paper, yet it would not rub off. As I stood gazing and wondering if it could be a precipitated sign, to my utter astonishment it commenced to fade away, until it had entirely disappeared.

"My God! Am I a victim of magic?" I cried, as I stared at the now blank space. "Am I surrounded by powers invisible? Are they good or evil?" Then I recalled what I had read in an occult book, that a ma n is surrounded by powers and influences corresponding to the thoughts he thinks.

"My thoughts are pure, my motives all unselfish," I said. Then it seemed as though an inner voice said:

"Then you have naught to fear, naught to fear, naught to fear."

I placed the letters carefully away in my pocket, and went down to the lawn to enjoy a morning walk, all the time filled with eager expectancy for the evening.

I had not been walking long when Camille, seeing me, came down, and laughingly remarking that I was thinking too much, insisted that I take a drive with her.

Thinking a little recreation would do me good and aid in preparing for the coming trials that I now pictured in my mind, I accepted her invitation, and we were soon flying along the beautiful boulevards and enjoying the fresh morning air of the great city of art.

An hour later, having driven until our horses were a little warm, we stopped at the Louvre. Entering the great picture gallery, our attention was immediately attracted by a large crowd standing before a picture that had apparently only recently been placed on exhibition.

As we approached, a tall, Oriental-looking man with an orange-colored turban on his hand, left the crowd, and as he passed us I heard him soliloquize:

"Dangerous; the sacred truths must not be thus revealed. 'Tis rash, ?"

Turning to the picture, which was of exceptionally large size, the first thing that attracted my attention was the predominance of mystic symbols. It was entitled "The Dawn," and was signed by a combination of the five and six-pointed stars.

Fastened in the center at the top by a golden, five-pointed star, two magnificent curtains in red swept to the right and left.

That on the right was held back by a young man in all the beauty of Apollo. Holding back the curtain with his left hand, in his right he held a golden wand made like a winged Caduceus, while upon his forehead was a golden sign of Mercury.

The figure on the left was a woman, a Venus in all her beauty. The golden sign of Venus on her forehead seemed to scintillate, and the winged globe, sky-blue in color, that rested in her hand seemed to be a thing of life.

The foreground in front of the curtain was black, and in the vapors of a smothering smoke were hosts of horrid creatures overshadowing three groups, representing war, pestilence and famine.

Back of the curtain all was filled with a golden light, and rich fields and beautiful cities, thronged with happy, joyous people, festooning, as on a holiday, stretched far away to the blue but snow-crowned mountains which formed the horizon.

In this golden light, and occupying the center of the picture, were five figures whom I recognized as the five great religious teachers of the world ? Zoroaster, Confucius, Buddha, Christ and Mohammed.

In the center, on a mighty lotus, sits the meditating Buddha; on his right leans forward Christ, radiant in loving beauty, to crown the sage with a wreath of lotus flowers; on his left Mohammed, his sandaled foot upon a broken sword and his Arab face lit up with a smile of love, reaches forward to crown the crowning Christ.

Zoroaster and Confucius, one on the right and the other on the left, look smilingly on, and, with rolls of parchment which represent the law, point to the fields of happiness beyond. Over these five great teachers, and beheld with admiring looks by those who held the curtains, was a central figure ? the wonder of the whole. Its meaning then I knew not, but, even in my ignorance, it had a power that made strange feelings in my soul. An oval sphere of misty vapor that seemed alive with motion and marvelously rendered in a sacred color.

Within this sphere, like those around, five-pointed and radiant with a golden light, a "star."

Spell-bound we gazed, our soul's mysterious powers interpreting, and became enraptured as in a mystic charm.

We were suddenly aroused by voices, some speakers approaching in very earnest conversation.

Turning, we saw the Oriental with the director and four distinguished-looking men.

"Yes," said the apparent leader to the director, "the picture must be veiled at once, and it will be removed this evening. See to it, Monsieur, have it done without delay."

The director immediately left, while the newcomers conversed in low tones.

In a few moments the director returned, accompanied by some aids carrying a large covering, which they immediately put over the magnificent picture, the men standing by until it was accomplished.

As they turned away I heard the leader say to the Oriental:

"Yes, it was an unusual indiscretion on the part of Aerol to place that here. A man with the most fragmentary knowledge would, with an hour's study, learn enough to be dangerous. Hereafter he must let us inspect such productions."

Camille and I, both being connoisseurs, appreciated the work, but could not understand the action of the men in thus concealing it. As we left the gallery she said the spokesman was Gen. Careau, Secretary of War, and his companions were all prominent officials of the government.

Who the Oriental was, she did not know; but from his remarks, which I had heard when entering, I knew that he had influence and was the cause of having the picture veiled and ordered removed.

My stuffy of symbols and recent experiences gave me an idea I could throw some light upon the subject; but remembering my pledges, I kept silent.

It was now noon, and we returned home. The not had said this afternoon, at what hour I knew not; so thinking it was best to be ready at any time, immediately dinner was over I repaired to my room.

Now my thoughts returned to the picture gallery. Evidently

the painter was a mystic. The symbols used plainly showed that fact. But who was Zerol? I had never heard o him before, and I nth last year I had made it my business to get acquainted with every reputable painter and artist in the city. And were the very powers of the government associated with this secret organization? Thus my thoughts continued to dwell upon the mysteries surrounding me until nearly four o'clock, when the hall-boy brought up a card with the initials, "M.P.," and said the sender was waiting for me in a carriage at the front gate.

Proceeding to the gate a cabman opened the carriage door, and as I enter a woman moved over to give me a seat beside her. She was dressed in black and was closely veiled; but as the carriage moved away the pair of beautiful whit hands that lay exposed upon her lap told me she must be young. At the same time an indescribable feeling of restfulness and ease came over me.

"And is Monsieur dissatisfied with the knowledge of the colleges, that he seeks Madame Petrovna?" asked a sweet, musical voice, that caused a thrill of pleasure to run through me.

"Yes, Madame," I replied, inferring immediately that it was the Madame herself whom I was talking to, "the knowledge of the colleges is all very well so far as it goes, and as long as it is confined to facts as they exist without explanations; but their knowledge is only superficial and does not satisfy the mind that would know the true nature of things in themselves."

"Ah!" and that same tingle of pleasure again went through me, "then Monsieur is of a philosophical turn of mind, is he?"

"From my childhood, Mademoiselle," said I, changing the form of my address in the hope of getting some clue to her identity, "I have been taught in a philosophical manner, and, therefore, naturally look at everything in that light."

"It was very fortunate for you, Monsieur, that you should have had such teacher; very few have that privilege nowadays,"

Thus no clue to her identity was given as the conversation continued and the carriage rolled rapidly along.

But every word uttered by my unknown companion filled me, nevertheless, with a never-before-experienced feeling of pleasure, and I drank in each musical word as some delicious beverage. So absorbed was I with my companion that I took no notice of the route we were traveling. Once she was looking at the palm of her fair white hand, and I took advantage of the opportunity and asked:

"Does Mademoiselle believe in palmistry?"

She closed her hand quickly, and turning to me replied:

"Is not the palm of the hand, if protected, one of the most sensitive parts of the body, and does not the Scriptures say that the hand is all covered over with light? Let me see Monsieur's hand."

I held out my open hand, and she took it gently. Oh, what means this great joy that steals around my heart? What pleasure in that touch! Did I mistake? Her veil was double and I could not see her face, but I thought I saw a tremor shake her form and there was a slight quiver in her voice as she said:

"Monsieur has never loved ? that is," she added quickly, "not in this life."

"And does Mademoiselle believe in past lives?" I asked. Without answering she continued:

"But the lines and mounts say, Monsieur, that you will love deeply when you do love; and that you will meet her in your twenty-second year, or very near that point. May I ask your age, Monsieur?"

"I am twenty-two," I answered, with what was to me unusual warmth. And did a secret feeling make me wish that what she said was true? Just then the carriage stopped, and as she dropped my hand I looked out.

We were in front of a granite arch which marked the entrance to a palatial residence, situated in the middle of a large lawn surrounded by a high iron fence with granite posts.

Glancing up, a group of statuary surmounting the arch attracted my attention. A huge bronze tiger, the very picture of subjugated humiliation, was held in chains by a winged cupid standing on a golden egg. Whoever these people are, I thought, they understand the secret of art. It is evident that group has a meaning and value which comes from other than a mere skill in execution.

My companion had noticed my admiring glances, and, as the iron gates swung open, as by a secret order, and we passed through, she asked:

"I see you have an artist's eye; do you understand the meaning?"

"I might mistake; will you explain?" I answered.

"The group, *with the egg*, comprehends, in its entirety, a great deal; but to explain briefly, the tiger symbolizes man's animal or tiger nature ? the beast which is subjugated and chained by love, which, according to the Mystics, comes from a golden egg."

There was a soul-stirring tenderness in her words as she thus answered, and for the first time in my life I felt the thrillings of a newborn love.

"Beautiful thought," I answered; "if one can judge these people by their art, they must be pure and good."

"They was," she replied.

We were now driving along the gravel road through the carefully kept lawn. The velvety sward adorned with flowers and trees reflected the rays of the afternoon sun in all of nature's beauty.

Truly, I thought, if this is the way I am to be initiated, it is anything but that which I had thought. I had pictured terrible ordeals and blood-curdling tests, and here I had been met by a woman who, while I had never seen her face, I knew must be beautiful, and everything seemed bright and joyful. Then I thought, perhaps this is the calm before the storm; and so thinking I braced myself to meet it. My companion had become silent as we approached the mansion, a model of classical architecture and built of polished marble. Arriving at the steps that extended up to the Corinthian portico, and which had two magnificent groups of statuary at the ends, the cabman opened the door and I courteously assisted my companion to alight. Leading the way, she entered a hall which was a masterpiece of art. The walls were hung with the most magnificent paintings, and the Corinthian pilasters along the sides were polished like mirrors.

Without saying a word, she conducted me to a large parlor to the right; then, saying she would return in a few moments, left me. I had hardly time to take in my surroundings, when she returned and motioned me to follow her. Along the hall and up a marble staircase we proceeded, until we arrived in front of a door which she opened without knocking, and, I having entered at her motion, closed it behind me. I found myself in a room finished throughout in a light-blue color. At a table draped around with blue silk, covered with mystic symbols, sat a heavily built woman of about sixty. Her face was broad, and its wrinkles made it appear rather coarse at first glance; but, I soon learned, it was capable of almost instantaneous changes of expression. The eyes were the chief characteristic of the woman, and seemed to read the very soul. As I entered she motioned me to a seat, and, without saying a word, set her steel-blue eyes upon me and kept them there for fully a minute, when she said:

"You have a mote?"

I handed her the mote I had received in the morning. She placed it in a drawer in the table and continued:

"Your name Colono?"

"Yes, Madame," I answered.

"Well, young man, what do you come here for?"

I thought her tome and manner of speech somewhat brusque, bur answered:

"To seek entrance into the Brotherhood."

"What are your motives?" she asked, her piercing eyes never leaving mine.

"I desire knowledge. Knowledge is the end and aim of my life."

"For what do you want this knowledge? Is it for any personal ends or selfish purposes?"

"No selfish purpose prompts me," I answered. "It is an inborn desire within me. Every since I was a child, I have longed to know the real meaning of things; and the mystery of life has had an irresistible fascination to my mind."

"And you think there is a Brotherhood that can assist you to this knowledge, do you?"

"I know there must be those who know more than the outside world concerning the essential nature of things."

"Where did you get this knowledge?" she asked abruptly.

"My parents have always taught me so," I answered.

"Oh! And is that all the foundation you have for your affirmation?"

"My parents being members of this Brotherhood would know, and they would not deceive me; furthermore, I have an inner consciousness which tells me this Brotherhood exists; and that among its members are exalted me and women who possess wondrous knowledge, powers and God-like wisdom."

"Ah! You believe in an inner consciousness then, do you?"

A momentary softness came over her face, and I thought I detected more of the woman in her tone.

"I believe man is a temple of the Divinity, and that within him are divine powers and possibilities," I answered.

"Man is not only a temple of the divinity ? man is the Divinity? Perfect man is God," she replied, with a vehemence that forbade contradiction.

Then, suddenly changing the subject, she asked:

"What do you think of the present social condition of the world?"

Now, while I had been raised in the midst of wealth and aristocracy, I was what some over-conservative, people would call an extremist; and I answered accordingly:

"I believe it is abnormal, monstrous, and contrary to the divine intention. A social state where altruism and industry are made the victims of greed and sloth cannot long mock eternal justice, and its end draws near."

This strange woman, by the supreme power of will controlled her features; but I could see from the brilliant light in her eyes that I had voiced her sentiments.

"And how will it end?" she asked.

"That depends on man. If in time the moral sentiment becomes sufficiently strong, the present lamentable condition of things will give place to something higher; but, if this moral change is too long delayed, then, like all civilizations of the past, we will sink into the chaos of an awful night; and then, from the shattered fragments of what is left, through years and centuries of toil and pain, build up again."

The restless activity which always came over me in moments of great earnestness, commenced to rise within. I could hardly sit still, and moved restlessly from side to side.

"And what would you do to aid mankind to avert this awful doom? Or have you any interest in the matter?'

"Madame, I would do all within my power; but what can I

do? I am but one little insignificant man; and look how much is to be done."

"You, as an isolated and separate man can do little, but as an instrument of the Infinite, much."

I was about to reply, when she again abruptly changed the conversation by asking:

"Have you the exact hour and date of your birth?"

Remembering the dates given me by M. Durant I answered accordingly.

Without evincing any surprise at the exactness of my knowledge as to the hour, which is very seldom know, she wrote it down in a small book. Then opening a drawer she drew forth and handed me a card, saying:

"Report at that address tomorrow morning at nine o'clock; keep the card for presentation, and, without informing any one, go alone. You are now excused."

My veiled conductor was awaiting me in the hall. Without a word she led by a different rout to the hall below, where another surprise awaited me. The side-hall through which we were passing was covered with finely executed portrait paintings of men and women. All the great nationalities of the earth were represented ? Hindu, Chinese Turk, Greek, Egyptian, and all the modern nations of the West. As I was giving them a hurried glance, while passing along the hall, a cry broke from my lips as my eyes fell upon the life-size portraits of my father and mother, hanging side by side. Portraits not of youth, but of recent years. My companion, who was little in advance, stopped, and as I fain would have lingered to question, silently motioned me to follow. Out through the marble portico to the carriage which was still waiting, we proceeded. The driver opened the door, and to my pleasure my companion entered with me. Not a word was spoken until we passed the arched gate, when she broke the silence by asking:

"Why did Monsieur utter the cry in the hallway? Did he recognize some one among the pictures?"

"No one less than my father and mother," I replied. "Oh, Mademoiselle, how did they come there? And so natural!"

"All high-degree members of the Brotherhood are there," she answered. "Would you like to have your picture there?"

"It will be, if it is in the power of man to put it there."

"Monsieur knows not the meaning of his words," answered that same sweet voice, every word of which thrilled me no less than it did on the previous drive.

"My parents did it, and so can I. All men can attain to the same great end if they but will. They trust me to do it, and I will. But, is Mademoiselle's picture there?"

"Ah! How could a poor, weak woman like me become so great? Do you know, Monsieur, that none can have their picture there who harbors thoughts of love? Then how can woman who is born to love ever reach that end?"

My heart was now throbbing in my throat; it seemed to me her words had a secret meaning, and it was all I could do to regulate my breath, as I answered;

"But my mother loved, and she is there."

"Then she had to sacrifice that love."

Now did the words of my parents once more steal across my memory? Again did I recall the sad parting of my mother on the fated steamer? Then all the mysteries of the last few days crowded on my mind, and I was once more about to loss my self-control, when my companion, seeming to divine my thoughts, said:

"There are three great steps in man's progress to perfection, and these are all included under the one word ? self-control. Separately they are ? control of body, control of mind, control of heart. Great is he who controls the body, still greater he who controls the mind, but greatest of all, he who controls the heart."

Most truly, I thought, as each word set mind on fire. Oh, how I did long to see the face behind that cruel veil of black! Now I thought of my father's words about my sympathetic soul. Surely this is mine, I thought; I will ask her of the doctrine.

"Mademoiselle, talking of love, do you believe in sympathetic souls?"

She turned half around, and I surely saw her hand tremble and heard her voice quiver a she answered:

"Yes, I do."

I, too, was trembling now, but steadying my voice, I asked:

"What is the teaching, Mademoiselle? Does it mean that all souls have their mates and no others?"

"No; that may be the popular idea of the doctrine, but it is erroneous, the true teaching is, that there are souls ? not all ? who have become inseparably conjoined because of a harmonious union in lives gone by. These cases are rare, but they do exist."

I was about to question further, when the carriage came to a stop in front of the Durant mansion. "Are we here already? My! How short the drive!" I remarked, as the driver opened the door.

Did she see my lingering action and the wistful look in my eyes? I knew not; but she at least extended her fair white hand to say "good -bye." I could not control the impulse, and raised gently to my lips. Oh, what magnetic tie was in that kiss!

"Good-bye," she said, as she closed the door, and I half mechanically turned toward the mansion.

"She is gone," said I; then the full truth came upon me, and I muttered: "I'm in love. In love, and with a woman I do not know, and whose face I have not even seen. Not even her name do I know; married or single, old or young. My God! What insanity is this? But she must be young, her hand said so. But then old people sometimes have young hands. And that voice and mind! Well, Colono, you are a freak; you went to get crucified an fell in love."

Thus pondering, I entered the house just in time for the evening lunch.

Camille and the Durants were again as of old, and asked no questions to embarrass. After a light supper and a pleasant chat at the table, I took a stroll with Camille.

Now here was a girl who was finely educated, beautiful and accomplished, with whom I had been for a year, and with whose parents I was on the most intimate terms; yet there was nothing like a feeling of love, or at least nothing like the feeling I had experienced when with the unknown stranger.

Was I one of those rare souls she referred to? Was she my sympathetic mate?

What a mystery is life! How many puzzles it contains! Whatever of truth there might be in the idea, the thought gave me pleasure, and I found myself constantly recurring to it.

CHAPTER VII.
MEMBER OF THE FIFTH DEGREE.

THE card I had received from the Madame read M. Raymond, Rue Notre Dame des Champs, and then several lines of writing in what I took to be Sanskrit. While not a Sanskrit scholar, I knew the alphabet and simple word-combinations; but this writing I was unable to decipher. Repairing promptly on time to the address given, I was met at the door of an unpretentious residence by a small, nervous-looking man with a black pointed beard and well-waxed mustache. Upon presenting the card he looked at me keenly for a moment, and then invited me in and motioned me to a seat.

"What is your name, please?" he asked, quite pleasantly.

"Alphonso Colono," I replied.

"Well, Monsieur Colono, you have been sent here for me to find out how much you know; do you wish to proceed with the examination at once, or do you desire time for preparation?"

Although this was a little unexpected, I determined to lose no time, and answered: "If it is convenient for Monsieur; yes."

"No inconvenience," he replied; "we will proceed at once. When a thing is to be done, it should be done, come into this room."

He led the way to an adjoining room which looked like a university condensed. On the walls were blackboards, maps, charts and drawings, while globes, terrestrial and celestial, chemical appliances and laboratory apparatus were on numerous tables. The work commenced at once, and for seven days I was subjected to the most rigid and thorough examination upon every elements to the highest studies of science and philosophy. The title man seemed to possess almost universal knowledge, and took everything in a systematic and orderly manner. On the afternoon of the seventh day, without a word or hint to let me know my standing, he gave a card written in Sanskrit and told to go to my home and await developments. Not a word of encouragement, not a sign of either commendation or otherwise.

I returned home, thinking that I was as much as ever in the dark, and apparently making very slow progress. Another week passed, and still no information. On questioning M. Durant one day when I met him alone, he answered that he had done all he could, and that from thenceforth I must trust to the fates and rely upon myself alone. On the evening of the fourteenth day I received a note through the mail, requesting me to call at the rooms of M. Raymond. I did so without delay; in fact, I was becoming slightly impatient.

M. Raymond met me at the door and ushered me in and along the hall to a rear room, where, upon entering, I found myself in the presence of four other men who were seated at a center-table. Each had his face entirely concealed by a black mask, sufficiently long to conceal whiskers. At a sign from M. Raymond I took a seat beside him near the end, when one of the men handed me a paper across the table, at the same time all keeping their eyes fixed intently upon me. Opening the paper I found it to be a pledge with blank spaces for signatures. It read as follows:

I, Alphonso Colono, son of Ferdinand and Nina Colono, do most solemnly swear and affirm, in the name of my parents and my sacred honor, and in the presence o my living soul and Almighty God, to maintain inviolable secrecy until death as regards all teachings and instructions that may be given me in the Secret Hermetic Schools; and I likewise swear and affirm never to divulge or reveal anything concerning persons, things or places which knowledge may come to me through connection with these schools.

"Will you sign that?" asked the man who had handed it.

"I will, with one qualification," I replied.

"And what is that?" he asked.

"That my ideas of God may not be misunderstood or misconstrued, I would have the words ? the Infinite and All-pervading Spirit ? inserted after the word God. I do not believe in God as many men give meaning to that word."

The four men looked at one another and then at M. Raymond.

"Very well," said the leader, "we will insert the clause."

He took the paper and made the insertion, handing it back when he had finished.

Again reading the pledge, I signed. Then each of the four signed as witnesses and handed it to M. Raymond. As the latter signed, I noticed that each had put a different and peculiar mark after his signature.

"Now, M. Colono," said the spokesman, as he took the paper, "you are an accepted member of the fifth degree of the Fourth Degree. The Fourth degree has seven sub-degree; you were born in the third sub, and have for eight years been unconsciously a member of the fourth. You pass to higher degrees as your growth and knowledge permits. Men are frequently members of the lower degrees when they know it not. Admission does not consist in the possession of a certificate, but in compliance with rules. Those who obey the rules and lead the life are members, though they know it not. In this degree the watchwords are ? Study, Patience, Knowledge ? and all advance depends upon the efforts of the student and the purity of the motive that prompts his desire for knowledge. At the start know that all depends on you, and on you alone. Ask no advice, but rely upon your inward strength. Now you are excused. Next Thursday night there will be a masquerade ball at the residence of M. Careau; a party will call for you, and you will please attend." As he finished, he motioned toward the door. Ushered through the hall by M. Raymond, I departed, wondering what possible connection there could be between a masquerade ball and a school of occultism. Then I recalled the name Careau. Careau, why that was the name of the secretary of war, who had ordered the removal of the picture from the Louvre.

I had not learned much that was definite in its nature, but he isolated incidents were becoming more connected.

"A party will call for me ? I hope it will be my unknown friend," I muttered. "But will she be masked, and will I never see her face?" thus thinking and soliloquizing I returned home, and applied myself with still greater diligence to my studies.

Thursday evening came, and I had robed myself as a monk and was awaiting my expected caller. It was something after seven o'clock when a cab drove up to the front gate, and to my disappointment a man got out, and, proceeding to the entrance, rang the bell and sent me this card. Joseph Henry, I read, awaits you at the carriage at the carriage. The sender had returned to the cab, and, adjusting my garments, I soon joined him. Where the Careau mansion was I had not as yet learned; but the carriage started directly toward the center of the city.

"Have you the card given you by M. Raymond?" asked my companion in pure English.

"I have," I answered.

"Then it will not be necessary for me to accompany you; and as I have some other very important business to attend to, I will give you my carriage and leave you to proceed alone." Before I could answer, he continued:

"When you arrive at the ball-room entrance present your card, and when admitted answer all questions that may be asked and obey al commands that may be given."

"I shall do as you have instructed," I answered, at the same time thinking this was a strange proceeding for obtaining entrance into a ballroom.

As the stranger vouchsafed no further remarks, we drove on in silence until we reached the Madeleine, when he got out the carriage, which immediately turned about and proceeded rapidly away. Along the brilliantly lighted thoroughfares, the sidewalks of which were thronged with crowds of gay and careless people, the driver hurried until we came to a boulevard less brilliantly lighted. We continued along this at a rapid pace for about thirty minutes when we drove up to a gate in front of a brilliantly lighted residence some distance from the street. After a brief stop we passed through and drove up to the front portico. As I got out of my carriage a veiled woman in black left a cab just in front of mine. Seeing me, she turned as though about to speak, when a tall cloaked figure passed between us, and I heard the words ? "four plus three." The woman immediately turned and hastened up the steps, while the man disappeared around a pedestal. The same happy sensation which I had experienced when in company with the unknown woman in black some weeks before again ran through me, and I felt certain that this was the same party. I hurried up the steps and entered a crowded hall just in time to see her disappear through a side door. There was evidently some delay in obtaining entrance into the ballroom, as the hall was full of masked people. Pushing forward to the entrance, I found that only one was admitted at a time, and the door was closed for several minutes after each entry. Somewhat mystified at these proceedings, I took my turn and presented my ticket. After a careful scrutiny by the masked doorkeeper, it was returned and I was admitted, the door closing behind me.

A blank wall was in front, but turning down a narrow passage to the right, I found myself in a small, square room filled with a green light from a chandelier in the center, and containing two occupants. At a table at my right sat an aged patriarch, whose long, white hair, beard and shaggy eyebrows gave him indeed a venerable appearance. At my left, at another table, sat a black-robed woman, whose youthful features were only partly concealed by a black mask across the eyes, which, black and piercing, sparkled like coals of fire.

"Your name?" asked the patriarch.

"Alphonso Colono," I answered.

"Are you sworn?" asked the low, penetrating voice of the woman.

"I am," I answered.

"Let us see your card."

I handed it to the woman, who, after examination returned it with a bow and motion for me to also hand it to the patriarch. Bowing affirmatively to the

woman, he returned it and asked:

"Your place and date of birth?"

"Paris, June the 5 th, 18?."

"The hour?"

"Seven forty-five A.M.," I answered.

"Pass to the left," said the woman, who had taken down each answer. As though by some secret signal a door opened at the left, and passing through I found myself with another masked man in a room corresponding to the first. "Brother," said the man, motioning me to a seat, "all these preliminaries which you have gone occasion like this, and I will therefore explain: Those who participate in this ball are our chosen sons and daughters, the flowers of al lands. It is but right that we should protect them from the wolves who, under the polish of a smooth exterior, desecrate and soil. The lives they lead make them extremely sensitive to every evil thought and influence; and we must there fore exercise great care. Brother, it is your privilege this night to associate with world's purest and most perfect men and women. Higher, indeed, there are, but they are not of this world. We hope and believe you are worthy of this privilege. Your presence here constitutes your introduction to all. Formalities and conventionalities, so necessary among the shams and deceptions of the outside world, are here unknown. All are brothers and sisters. Enter! Enjoy life in its highest aspect, where heart and mind unite in harmony with the body's rhythmic motion, and purest love is queen."

He opened a door, and I found myself in a brilliantly lighted ballroom. The sweet strains of a waltz filled the room, and rich perfumes were fragrant in the air. For a moment I stood at the door, surveying the hall, in the hope of seeing her who wore the black dress; but she was nowhere to be seen.

"Does the father grant to woman equal rights with man?" said a low feminine voice at my side. Turning, I found a pretty peasant girl beside me. Wondering what could be the purport of such a question at such a time, I answered as I thought:

"Sex should be no bar to rights; hearts and brains should determine these. In things of heart the woman should have every right and be supreme; in things of head, the man."

"Ah! Then the father does not think that woman is equal to man when it comes to mind?"

"Not as a rule; exceptions there most truly are, but exceptions only."

"Well, father cannot consider the dance a thing of mind, so I ask him to join me in the waltz."

The incidents of the last few days had not been of a nature to stimulate the frivolous in me; the sudden appearance of my mother and disappearance of my father, together with my examination and studies, had made me of a very serious turn of mind; but I could not refuse, so we were soon gliding over the waxed floor in the swaying movement of the dance.

Get any body of people to do the same thing at the same time, no matter how simple or insignificant it may be in itself, and you unite them, as it were, in a common unity. I soon felt myself as a part of the pleasure imbibed from these free, gay hearts. My companion was a graceful dancer, and hung like a fairy on my arm. The feeling that filled me was not, however, like the heart-thrilling sensations that had been caused by the woman in black, but in the pleasure of the moment she was forgotten. The waltz ended, and once more I was my individual self. Serious thoughts again stole on my mind, and, recalling that I was a monk, I determined to take advantage of the character.

"What if the bishop of your diocese had seen you just now, gay monk? Where would be your charge?" questioned my fair companion with a merry laugh.

"Father forgive me, I will never do it again," I solemnly replied. "Oh, that I should for one moment have allowed a beautiful woman to tempt me thus!"

"Another case, my father, of Adam and Eve and the weakness of poor man, said my gay companion with a mocking laugh.

"Yes, the devil subtly tempts us under the guise of beauty," I answered, preserving my character with all its dignity.

"But, my father, where would Adam's children be to-day had it not been thus? Poor imbeciles, blind fools, without mind or sense; innocent but devoid of knowledge. Blessed be Eve who tempted man to eat of the tree which bringeth wisdom," said my hitherto simple peasant girl, becoming serious.

"With subtle sophistries thou triest to defend thy erring mother; beware of heresy, my child."

"Heresy! Do not the Scriptures themselves so say? Did she not temp him to eat of the tree that brigheth a knowledge of good and evil, and makes men as Gods? Who can criticize so high and noble an aspiration?"

"Child, child, confess thy sins before God's wrath shall damn thee," I said, wondering if all here were like her.

"God has no wrath; the Scriptures say that God is Love."

"Child, who taught thee thus to misconstrue the sacred words of Scripture?"

"Misconstrue! For two thousand years monks like thee, with biased minds, have perverted truth and filled men's minds with errors; and dost thou now thus question me?" Her eyes sparkled with the fire of enthusiasm and indignation. Evidently her whole soul was in the augment. Things were getting interesting, I was about to be cornered, but I must maintain my part, so I answered:

"For this men are themselves to blame, not us. We veil forms and under symbols the sacred truths, and men, not using reason, take the shell and lose the kernel, feed on husks and see not the corn."

"But why not teach the plain pure truth? Why thus deceive by forms?"

"It must be so; to cast our pearls before swine, to trample under feet, would be but waste and loss of time and woefully indiscreet."

"Ah! does the father hint at occultism in the Church of Rome?"

"Hush! Talk not so loud; the walls have ears. What knowest thou of occultism?"

"A thumb's length," she answered quickly and mystically; and as I answered not, she looked surprised. Evidently I was caught ? there were passwords here.

"Ah! I comprehend," she said. "Come with me and I will show you what we know." Now deeply interested, and wondering what was next, I followed.

I now noticed that a series of doors lined the hall on each side. Leading the way across to the left, she knocked upon one of these four times. It was immediately opened we entered.

The sides of the room were surrounded by shelves full of books, and the green walls had a frieze of mystic symbols. At a number of tables were groups of men and women, apparently engaged in study. These groups were invariably six in number, with a seventh who was evidently a teacher. In the center of the room, at a table which almost surrounded him, sat a middle-aged man whose features were only partly concealed by a black mask across his eyes. Approaching this man my companion said, "A new student." Turning to me the man said, "Let me see your card, please." After inspecting the card he returned it, and addressing my conductor, said: "The groups are completed to-night; but if Mademoiselle will leave him in my charge I will attend to his instruction."

My companion bowed and was about to retire, when I asked if it would be out of order for me to see her after the ball. "I will await the father at the entrance," she smilingly replied, and departed. "Monsieur," said the man, motioning me to draw up a seat near him at the table, "Your card from M. Raymond, E.E. (Exoteric Examiner), says you have passed a very creditable examination and are competent to receive further and more difficult instructions. From now on your study will be that great but wonderfully neglected mystery ? an, including all that pertains to man, socially and individually, but, first of all, man as a being. Now to come closer to the point, you, yourself, are a man and therefore your study is yourself. Your presence here implies that you are comparatively free from bias and ready and willing to look your own nature, good and bad, squarely in the face. Is this correct?"

"It is," I answered, thinking I was on the right track at last.

"Very well, then know that every man is dual in his nature ? male and female elements make up your constitution. Now you are a man, the male element predominating; the female element is in you, but subservient. The first thing for you to do, the first great step in all occult initiations, is to bring these two elements into a state of equilibrium. Man must be conjoined with woman; mind must be conjoined with heart. Mind, unchecked by heart or the intuitions that come therefrom, but leads to blind materialism and cold dead forms, the riddle of the universe it cannot solve. Heart, divorced from mind, leads but to blind, fanatic faith, where reason is unknown and fancy runs the imagination wild. To reach supreme enlightenment, reason and conscience must go hand in hand, indissolubly united. Now the method we pursue to bring this end so much desired is very simple, but its simplicity may lead astray; do not mistake; mark well my words. To every male we join a female in the lawful bonds of love. You, through her, unfold your female nature, she, through you, her male; and thus is brought that equilibrium so indispensable to light. This is the meaning of this ball. Unlike the monks of old, we cultivate that flame called love, but only in its purest form. Bear this in mind, and know that your growth depends upon your union with a female soul. Among our sisters you will find those who are worthy of your highest love. If one you find whose soul is sympathetic with your own, choose her to be your mate; but do not choose unless your heart so bids, and ever you're your thoughts be pure."

I thought of the doctrine of sympathetic souls and my parents' early teachings. And here it was that my father met my mother; was I here also to meet my fate? My thoughts drifted to the woman in black, and I was anxious to meet her again and know more of her.

"Now," continued my teacher, "we will consider the signs, veiled words, and allegories of the mystics, in particular those of Hermes Trismegistus,

Paracelsus, Jacob Bohme, Elephas Levy, and the much misrepresented and little understood Madame Blavatsky. You are supposed to be somewhat familiar with the published works of these teachers, but only the few find the hidden teachings in their books." Now followed two hours of instruction upon the doctrines of these teachers, and for the first time the veil commenced to be pulled aside. The works of these great mystics had been in my father's library, and we had often studied them together; but while father had often hinted at the esoteric meaning of many parts of these books, he had never divulged it, saying I must learn it in the regular way. Now it appeared the opportunity had come.

All this time each group had carried on its studies in low subdued tones, and my instructor spoke in like manner. Suddenly a single chord of music vibrated though the room and all study ceased.

"The time has com for unmasking and the after converse," said my teacher. "We meet every week, but in order to avoid undesired attention, alternately at the home of another member. In the meantime prosecute your studies. Obtain the works of these writers at M. Callio's, being careful to get only those which have a peculiar mark on the page, and then dwell long and earnestly upon the italics."

We were now in the hall which, masks being removed, was thronged with beautiful, refined and intelligent-looking women and handsome and serious-looking men. No introductions were necessary, as the man at the entrance had said, your presence being sufficient. I now found myself in society as it should be, where men and women were true brothers and sisters and mind and heart dwelt upon the loftiest aspirations and the most profound questions. And what was my surprise and pleasure, here was Camille and many of my social friends. They all crowded around, congratulating me upon my advance.

"You now see," said Camille smiling, "that a woman can keep a secret if she chooses; but from now on we can talk a little more freely." "But where are Monsieur and Madame Durant?" I asked.

"They are not members of this section, they belong a still higher degree, I believe," she answered. A curly-headed Frenchman now claimed her attention and turned seek my peasant sister. As I was vainly searching to find her, the veiled woman in black came out of a side door just as I was passing. That same thrill of pleasure ran through my frame, the same panting breath; now is my time, I thought, I must speak to her.

"Mademoiselle," I said, "we meet again."

She turned, but even under her veil her face was masked.

"Have we ever met before?" she asked in English.

The voice was not the same, but perhaps this was because of language; before she had spoken in French, in which language I had addressed her, and which she therefore understood.

"Does not Mademoiselle remember the carriage drive?" I asked, still persisting in using French.

"What carriage drive?" she replied, equally persistent in English. I recalled my pledge of secrecy and was hesitating whether or not I could speak more full, when we reached another door, and with a low bow that meant dismissal, she left me.

What meant this cold reception? Her actions were unlike the others. She did not even deign to speak as friend. Could my heart have made mistake? No, it must be her; I felt her absence. Now I noticed that a number of people were still masked. In the hope of extending my acquaintance I was about to address one of these, when I was surrounded a group and carried into a discussion on medicine.

Another hour passed in most interesting conversation, when a small, white hand was placed upon my shoulder, and, looking up, I saw my peasant sister, but she was still masked.

"I am about to leave, my reverend father," she said with a mocking smile, "and will bid you good-night."

"May I not act as escort?" I asked, rising and accompanying her toward the door.

"With pleasure, if you so desire," she answered, and together we passed the entrance. The two inner guards were gone, but the doorkeeper was still on duty.

"If you go with me you must grant one request," said my companion, as we descended the steps.

"It is already granted; what is it?" I replied.

"That I see you home in my carriage," she answered to my surprise.

"Why this not leap year," I ventured, half protestingly. "Never mind, no jokes, my request is granted."

"Very well, if you insist," I answered, as we entered her carriage and were quickly driven toward my home. As we drove up in front of the Durant mansion a most interesting conversation ceased, and as the carriage stopped I got out and thanked for her kindness in taking me to my teacher and thus escorting home. In reply she said:

"Had you persisted in the dance, sober monk, you would not have had the opportunity again for a long time. You stood your first and unsuspected test well, and chose the serious and not the frivolous. I congratulate."

"Well, dear sister, I thank you and bid you good-night, hoping soon to meet you again when I may see your face. Why do you and the other few thus hide your faces with masks?"

"There are those who deem it best to hide their identity even from their brothers; as you advance you will no doubt know the reason why. Goodbye." I thought I detected a change in her voice, and, strange to say, that never-to-be-forgotten thrill ran through my frame and a joyous pleasure filled my heart. But she was gone; what did it mean? Was my dream of sympathetic souls naught but a dream? Did I have two loves? Thus pondering I sought my room.

CHAPTER VIII.
IOLE.

ONE year passed by; fifty-two lessons had been taken. Every week, under the cloak of a masquerade ball, we met together for mutual study and improvement. Camille and were still great friends ? brother and sister; likewise a strong attachment had grown up between me and my peasant sister who, while often dressed in different costumes, always kept her face concealed. In vain were my solicitations; she checked them in no uncertain tone.

"Camille, who is she?" I asked one day.

"Know the rule," she answered, "those who keep masked must be unknown."

The veiled woman, who never dressed in anything but black, was a greater mystery than ever; more so than my peasant sister, for while the latter concealed her identity, she was my best companion. The woman in black, however, seldom gave me an opportunity for conversation, but when she did, strange though it may seem, I was the happiest of men. I had become after the first night a member of a student group, and the peasant girl was my sister student.

I made rapid progress, for, as my teacher had said, my preparatory training had been the best. The blanks and gaps of materialistic science were filling up, and its superficialities and guesswork becoming every day more exposed. But this increasing knowledge only made plainer and more evident certain missing links upon which I questioned and pondered in vain. The main teacher, who had given me my first instructions, gave a lecture at the opening of each session. These lectures were pregnant with significant hints upon which he refused to answer all questions, telling us to think and work it out.

When upon one occasion I showed signs of dissent, he said:

"Knowledge is not to be communicated, but evolved. Knowledge does not come from within. All your study of books and things is but to establish the instrumental conditions by and through which the knower can break forth and manifest."

I thought much upon this, and commenced to dwell and meditate upon this Knower. The results were wonderful; I commenced to acquire knowledge in a manner I knew not how, and often spoke with a wisdom that surprised me. Now, after a year of study, it became evident to me that I was as yet only in a semi-esoteric and comparatively outside group. With this conclusion in my mind I formed a determination to advance, and went to the first meeting of the second year with this resolve in mind. I recalled that when I had signed my pledge the spokesman had said my advance would depend upon my growth and fitness, and could not be obtained in what some people cal dreams. Upon the night mentioned, after going through the accustomary opening dance, I entered the study room, and approaching the chief teacher whispered something in his ear.

"Where did you get that?" he asked quickly, looking up with surprise on his face.

"I never got it, I know it," I answered, seriously.

"Well, don't communicate that here," he said, and without another word he took a book from his pocket, and drawing forth a card wrote some mystical characters upon it. Then handing it to me he said: "On next meeting night present that card to the right hand inner guard; now proceed with your studies and say nothing."

It was the fifty-fourth night, and I entered and handed my card to the veiled woman at the right. She took the card, and having read it motioned me to hand it to the patriarch on the left. After careful scrutiny, he nodded as in affirmation and, as I received the card back, made a sign to the woman who said;

"Enter at the right and await our coming."

Heretofore I had always turned to the left, but as she spoke a concealed door opened near her, and I passed through into a small room finished in pure white. I took a seat upon a whit e divan, and had waited some time when the patriarch and woman entered.

"Brother," said the woman, taking a seat in front of me, while the patriarch seated himself as a table near by, "your presence before us demands that you give us your unqualified confidence.

The Esoteric Examiner tells us you have information which belongs only to members of the sixth sub. Where did you get it?"

"By meditation and inward concentration upon the Spirit," I answered, almost before I thought, and was then surprised at my answer. They looked at one another and the patriarch drew nearer.

"Don't you know that such practice is dangerous to those who are unprepared?" questioned the patriarch in very serious tones.

"In my unselfish desire for knowledge I deem myself prepared," I answered.

"Is your life pure and free from taint? Are you free from even a shadow of selfish ambition?" he again questioned.

"My life is pure, from childhood it has been thus," I replied.

"Why do you seek knowledge?"

"Because it is the soul's true nature so to seek," I answered.

"Will you ever use your knowledge for evil purposes or selfish ends?"

"I will not; the self is dead." As I said this I was startled at the intensity of my answer. My companions looked at each other and the patriarch continued:

"If this knowledge brings you power how will you use it?"

"For my fellow-men and truth," I answered, as an inspiration grew upon me. "Not otherwise nor indiscreetly?"

"Only for the good and with certainty of right; not otherwise."

"Have you learned the power and do you possess self-control?"

"I think I have," I answered, as I thought of the woman in black. "Your words imply a doubt, where is your weakness?"

"I would not be too positive; there may be conditions under which I might lose control of heart; although I have been sorely tried." I was thinking of my parents and the possibility of love. As though she divined my thoughts, the woman asked:

"Have you ever loved?"

"As child for parent, yes; as brother for sister, yes; as..." and I hesitated.

"And not as lover?" asked the woman.

"I am in doubt, the word to me has uncertain meaning, but, I must confess, an unknown sister here affects me strangely."

"Who is she?"

"I know not; she is always dressed in black and never is unmasked.' The two looked at one another, and the conversation was abruptly changed by the patriarch who asked:

"How did you learn that man is seven minus two?"

"All the afternoon in deepest thought I had dwelt on man's mysterious constitution. So deep in thought was I, the supper hour went by and in my chair deep sleep came over me. Suddenly I arose in space and was carried over the ocean; unburdened by a form of weight I passed in thought's swift motion to the East. I saw the Snowy Range deep in the blue of heaven high above the clouds. Then by some miracle of change of which all dreams are made, I found myself a student over a book in some unknown and isolated crypt. Here many mysteries, many things of wonder did I read. Long did I study, much did I learn; and then a blank. Oh, that I could recall this knowledge! But when once more I awoke, naught but this one fact and the memory of the dream remained."

That strange inward activity which at frequent intervals throughout my life had stirred within me had once more arisen, and I spoke as one inspired. My questioners, who had been watching me with sparkling eyes, now both spoke at once:

"We welcome thee, now art thou a member of the Sixth Degree; and she shall be your teacher!" I was about to speak again, when the patriarch pressed his finger to his lips in token of silence and spoke:

"Two paths start from the Sixth Degree, both leading to the Seventh; and thou must wear a mask until thy path is chosen. Let no one see thy face while here assembled unless permit is given. Now to the hall; a friend awaits you."

As the patriarch finished speaking a door opened, and at his motion passed through into the hall. The second waltz was in progress, and I, this time masked and attired like a knight, was about to seek a partner, when a nun, veiled and robed in purest white, laid a fair, white hand upon my arm. The same thrilling sensation of pleasure ran through me, and my heart beat violently as in a sweet, musical voice she said:

"In the name of peach and love, Sir Knight, discard thy arms.

Dost thou still sanction war, most cruel war? Or is thy dress a mask on man of noble heart and honor?"

"Fair nun," with beating heart I made reply, "If all women had the power of thy sweet voice the world would soon have peace and all who fight would love. But, fair nun, thou dost wrong the knights of chivalry who ever fought for virtue an for love."

"Ah, that this, indeed, were true, but my memory says ? not so. Well do I remember when in past life knights, claiming honor, fought for and stole poor nuns?"

"Thou canst not be thus old, fair nun; what dost thou mean?"

"The age of form is not the age of soul. You and I have both lived on earth many times before."

What strange feeling was this stirring in my heart? What strange ecstasy of joy within my soul? I could not change this conversation for a dance; she was bordering on the greatest question of life, the deepest subject of my thoughts. With a never-before-experienced feeling of pleasure I urged her on:

"If we have lived before, and thou rememberest, why not I? Perhaps I am the knight of yore who stole thee; but, if so, it was for love. And if I loved thee once, I love thee still; for I am one who never loves but once."

"Be not so bold, thou warrior armed and mailed, thou mayest unknowingly speak truth, at least in part; but if thou art interested in this subject, let us go where we can be alone."

"Most gladly," I replied, as she took my arm and led the way to the right side of the hall. Angel of love, I thought, she must have changed from black to white. Her voice was the same as that of her whom I had first met on the drive to Madame Petrovna; but how different from the woman in black whom I had met in the hall. Could they be the same? If so what meant this sudden change?

I had never been through any of the doors on the right-hand side of the room, and as we now passed through one, I found myself in a room finished in whit and trimmed with gold. She closed the door and motioned me to a sofa; taking a seat beside me she removed her veil, saying as she did so:

"Will not the knight unmask his face?"

For a moment I was speechless, the marvelous beauty of her face surpassing anything I had ever seen. At the same time strange memories crowded through mind. Where had I seen that face before?

Large brown eyes filled with a light of love, windows, truly, of a mighty soul. Long, regular lashes, shapely brows, and a mouth of exquisite form. A face of pearl white with a healthy tint of rose upon the cheeks; but, above all, her facial expression, which made her a perfect picture of divine beauty. No wonder she wore a mask to avoid attention; no one could see that face without a pause.

Without dropping her wondrous eyes, and apparently unconscious of my admiration, she repeated her request. Only a short time before I had been warned by the patriarch not to sow my face, and, recalling my pledge, I with hesitancy replied:

"I am pledged to remain masked."

"We are alone," she answered; and I was on the point of yielding, when, with a long-drawn sigh, she put on her veil and motioned me to desist. Now I saw it was a trial, and she had seen my weakness. They had told me of a friend and teacher, but nothing of a tempter.

"Sir knight," she now said, "we were talking of past lives, and you asked why you did not remember such. First, the brain memory, which experiences of this life; past lives have their records in the soul. Training brings the soul to consciousness, and with this consciousness all memories of the past preserved therein. Now, if you will kindly listen I will tell you a story; please let your soul awake."

Again she removed her veil, and taking a seat directly in front of me, looked me fixedly in the yes, and continued in a low, musical voice:

"It is a bright spring morning. A light breeze is carrying golden -colored clouds across the azure blue of heaven. The fruit trees are covered with wide-open flowers and blossoms and the air is fragrant with their wetness, while the happy birds sing everywhere. The mountain-bordered horizon on one side, and the silver rivers flowing through fields of green to the placid mirror of the sea upon the other, shows that we are in Ancient Greece. Two figures are journeying along the pathway that winds across the foothills. One, a young man in all the glory of his strength and beauty, with features and half-exposed form the like of which has seldom been seen since Greece has passed away. At his side a beautiful woman, a Grecian woman, such as Phidias would have sought for a model.

"They are going to the Games, the Olympian Games; he in full confidence of this ability and skill, she happy in the thought of his sure victory. With hands clasped and swinging arms, they go joyfully along the way. Picking wild flowers, she makes a wreath and crowns his golden curls, and, in token of appreciation, he stops to caress her and kiss her rosy cheeks. Thus with joyous song they go merrily along. It seems that the gods, nature, and men have united for once in love and peace. But now a courier, rushing up behind, o'ertakes them.

"Xerxes is coming! Men are needed to guard the pass. All true Greeks join Leonidas at Thermopyla. Do your duty!" And he rushes on. With hastened footsteps the couple hurry along to the outskirts of the crowd that surrounds the Games. The word goes forth that the Games cannot be neglected, even though the host is near; but among the crowd they find a company preparing for an immediate start to guard the pass.

"The youth enlists to join them, and his fair companion, with tears restrained, combs his hair in the careful style of those who fight till death, and with a parting kiss says, ' For Grecian liberty I give you.'

"His name was Cleomedes, and with Leonidas his body lay upon the path that wound o'er Ceta's mount. That night Iole, Cleomedes companion, was searching for her lover's form among the slain. She finds him, his face now cold and white, but beautiful with a noble calm. Yes, she will take one golden ringlet from that noble head to ever keep his love in mind. A looting soldier of the Eastern horde thus finds her, and seeks her virtue to betray. What monsters sport as men! She fights; in rage he stabs her, and she falls with bleeding wound upon the body of her lover. With mingled blood she dies, and night comes o'er the scene."

She paused for a moment, but I was in a spell; some magic power had seized me. Every word brought pictures to my mind, and all were scenes most strangely familiar. Seeing me thus silent, she continued:

"More than a thousand years have passed, and vast changes have been wrought. The Roman world has come and gone and civilization's night is on. The scene is now in Gaul. A youthful monk, ever bent on deeds of charity and love, is bending o'er the mangled forms that fill the fields of Poitiers.

'Tis night, and the pale moon stealing from behind the clouds seems to give forms to specters that hover o'er this awful field of blood. All unmindful the monk works on; with bandages he bin ds the wounded, both Moor and Gaul alike. Morning finds him following in the wake and administering to the fallen Moors. He gives no thought of heathen, he works for man alone.

Journeying on he comes to a convent among the Pyrenees. Tired and worn out from travel without food, he stops to rest. A youthful abbess meets him and gives him kindly welcome. He stays. The abbess is deeply versed in occult lore; so is the monk, and even now is secretly on his way to Seville to get instructions from the Moors. Their souls in sympathy and strangely drawn together, they fall in love, and, contrary to their vows, live as man and wife, bound only by the ties of love. For a time all goes well and they live happily together. But who could then escape the spies of Tome? They were found out. He was cast into a basement cell, and for many weary years he lingered, until death, kind friend, relieved him. She, poor nun, persecuted by those who knew not honor, sought relief in flight; but knights return her captive and she dies in the cell beside her lover."

She had finished, and her white hands, which by some magnetic attraction had drawn to mine, were trembling as I held them. Her soul-consuming eyes were still on mine, and I was speechless. By some unknown power the present had become linked with the past. Lost memories indeed now filled my soul, and the meaning of her stories came to me like a revelation. An impulse came over me to enfold her in my arms and claim again my long-lost love, but second thought prevailed and with trembling voice I gasped:

"My God! And is this our past life history? Has love, eternal love, once more brought us together?"

With wonderful self-control she answered: "My brother

knight, be calm; pure love is indeed eternal. What does your soul say?" "My soul is clouded, my spirit vision bedimmed by this flesh encasement, and through the smoke I see but indistinctly," I answered. "Well, my dear brother," she said, pressing my hand, "in the nest degree all becomes clear and the past yields all its knowledge to you."

"And do you belong to this degree?" I asked, now recovered from my spell.

"By right I do; by choice I am here," she replied. Then almost before I thought, I said:

"Then let us join our forces and push on together." Looking me in the eyes she clasped my hands, and in eager and serious tones replied: "Do you mean it? Have you the strength?"

"I do, my love, my soul; with you I have all strength." My love would out; and on the impulse of the moment I had spoken. Still holding my hand and with a wonderful tenderness in her voice, she asked:

"Do you know the first condition?"

"No, but if you go with me it shall be fulfilled." She now dropped my hands, and drawing back, in a calm, serious voice said:

"Well, we shall see; but you must first pass through the sixth degree. Much will be required of you and I will commence as your teacher at the next meeting. But it is now getting late and you must meet my other sixth-degree brothers and sisters."

As she spoke she arose. Be it confessed, for the first time I was selfish; she called me like the others, simply brother. I wished for and thought our past relations entitled me to a dearer term.

"Be a knight now," she said, as we again entered the hall. The study hours had passed some time and the hall was alive with the informal group conversations, which always followed. I looked around for my peasant girl, but of course only as a matter of interest.

"Whom do you seek?" asked my companion, noticing my glances.

"A peasant sister who has been kind to me," I replied.

"The peasant has become a nun," she replied in the voice that my peasant sister had made so familiar to my ears. In astonishment

I looked at her.

"What!" I exclaimed, "you and she the same?"

"The same, yet not the same; I played a part and evidently with success," she answered.

"And where is the black-veiled nun?" I asked, wondering if she too had played her part.

"Black is a somber color and partakes of earth; she must have been in mourning. I hope she mourns no more," she replied, in tender and what I thought significant tones.

"And have we sadness and mourners even here?" I asked.

"Ah, yes, my brother; is there a place on earth where sorrow does not find its way? All bound to earth have sorrow, more or less, and there are come who are by right above the earth, who, for a lingering brother still tarry. But, brother, you have learned enough to-night; and as I am to be your teacher, we still have many nights to learn together; now let us meet our friends."

My companion and my mask seemed to bring me closer to the others who were masked and who had heretofore been somewhat distant.

"We all assume new names here," said my companion, as we approached a group of masked brothers and sisters.

"My name is Iole, and I suggest that you take Cleomedes; will you?"

"Since what you have told me, none could be more agreeable, my dear sister, if such I must still call you; and as I take the name, so will I ever cherish in my memory the glimpse you have give me of Ancient Greece." As I spoke I pressed her hand and she returned the pressure.

A gypsy girl leaning upon the arm of a stalwart Turk now attracted my attention.

"Let me make you acquainted with a subject of the Sultan," said Iole, as they approached.

"El Arab, this is Cleomedes," she said, addressing the Turk; and as he answered and bowed with Oriental salaam, she continued: "And this is Rahula, Cleomedes." As I took the small, gypsy hand, unusually whit for one of her tribe, a strange agitation seized me, and I noticed that she trembled and seemed likewise agitated. She bowed in silence to my address, and drew her shawl more closely around her neck and head. Somewhat surprised at this unusual silence, I was eying her more closely than I should, perhaps, when Iole called me away to another group. Thus time passed until the hour for adjournment arrived.

"And will the nun permit a knight to escort her to her convent?" I asked, as we approached the entrance.

"Believing you, Sir Knight, to be unlike the knights of old, I accept your company with pleasure." We passed the entrance; no one but the outer doorkeeper was on duty.

"You must take my carriage; no other are allowed within the convent grounds," said my companion.

"It seems the ladies run things here, but, if you so request, I must," I answered.

The carriage rolled rapidly away, I sitting close beside my companion; but some restraining power repelled and further demonstrations of affection. Her presence was sufficient, and for some time not a word was spoken ? I was happy in a silent joy. Did she likewise fell the joy I felt? I thought so, and on we rode in silence. At last the carriage stopped, and looking out I beheld the arched gate surmounted by the tiger held by Cupid's chains. This entrance I had never been able to find since the day of my first visit, when the veiled woman had cast such a glamour over me. But now doubt was dispelled, and I said:

"Art thou, white nun, my sister Iole, she who was in black?"

"The same, Sir Knight; and thou art the father priest whom I refused to know."

"And why were you so cruel?"

"You were not then of my degree, and had no right to know me. We have rules as strict as castes, but all can enter who are worthy; you will learn more as you progress." The carriage now drew up in font of the great Corinthian portico, and I was thinking I was some distance from my home, when she said:

"This time my carriage will take you home." I was preparing to assist her our, when she motioned me to keep my seat, and shaking my hand, said:

"We will meet again next Thursday night, and take more serious teachings. In the meantime study well, analyze thyself and learn the art of self-control, for you may be sorely tried. And remember what I told you on our first drive ? 'Great is he who controls the body, still greater he who controls the mind, but greatest of all he who controls the heart.'" Turning, with a kind "goodbye," she was gone; and the carriage turned about and took me toward my home.

"Ah God!" I cried when now alone. "Control the heart! What superhuman effort that must take! And why should I control my heart? I love with purest love and what can ask for its suppression?" Yes, after years of ideal dreaming the pent-up love within my heart had broken loose. What a torrent these accumulations made! But for the strange controlling power her superior will changed the tempest into calm and made my passion peace the peace of love supreme.

That night I dreamed of Iole; and all the following week naught filled my thoughts. Where was my study now? where my self-control? I argued, why should I crush out this love, so pure, so strong? And, deeming my argument unanswerable, I determined to know the reason why before I did it.

CHAPTER IX.
LOVE.

THURSDAY night came again, and I, filled with the expectation of meeting Iole, once more passed the doorkeeper. I had again dressed myself as a monk, but contrary to the usual garb, had taken the orange robes of the Buddhist. Some slight accident with my driver had made me somewhat late, and I found I was the last one to enter, the guard closing the outer doors as I passed. As I appeared before the inner guards, the woman said something to the patriarch in Sanskrit, with which I was comparatively familiar. The words were not distinct enough, however, for me to catch their meaning. Presenting my card, they bowed in acknowledgement, and the woman arose an accompanied me into the white room at the right. Motioning me to a seat she took one just in front of me. For several minutes we sat facing each other in silence, her piercing eyes never leaving my face. Presently the patriarch entered, and, taking a book from his robe, seated himself opposite us at the table.

"Alphonso Colono," began the woman, in her low, penetrating voice, "when you first entered here we had cast your horoscope and found all things favorable." She paused an instant and her voice became very stern as she continued: "But recent developments have caused us apprehension, and fearing some mistake in hour of birth, our conclusions must be verified. We must protect our darling daughters and debar all unfit from the sacred chambers; and unless you can pass the test you must go back to earth until your time. None but the pure can associate with those who wear robes of white."

A fear commenced to steal over me; what had I done? Then a conviction of purity came to me, and I grew firm and strong, reaching out her hand the woman said:

"Let me see your palm."

Ah! I thought, they are going to check my horoscope by the science of chiromancy.

Leaning over my hand she gazed at it long and intently; then taking my other palm, she pressed the palms together, straightened them out and seemed to compare them with great care. Then with a peculiar instrument, not unlike a compass, she gauged the length of my thumb and finger joints; then, having taken a measurement as though for a standard, followed carefully along the line of life. At last she seemed satisfied, and rising, said to the patriarch:

"'Tis well; there is no conflict; his hand is strong and has marks of special favor. A halo on Apollo's mount, a long, deep, jaggy, but continuous line of heart with branches high up on and over Jupiter's mount. This means great glory and strong and freely given love. Saturn's line of fate plows straight through. The line of head, broad, deep and of good color, is torn from that of life ? he is unselfish. No Venus girdle, no crosses that bring lasting ill; and Luna strong, but not to excess, gives occult mind. A double square, distinct and plain on Jupiter, declares that he is doubly protected. All signs indeed are good; he can be trusted. If she can but divert his heart from on to all, there are promises of a Master."

The patriarch, who had noted down each item, now put up his book, and as she dropped my hand pointed to a door at the side of the room and said:

"You may pass."

As I arose to leave the room, the woman said: "Brother, guard well heart, your greatest strength and yet your greatest weakness. It must be controlled, otherwise your mind will be unsteady. Allow not thoughts of pleasure, brief and short, to keep you from wisdom that leads to the Eternal. Now enter!"

The door opened; and, as though by some secret signal or understanding, as I stepped through, the whit-robed nun stepped up beside me.

"A heathen monk! and in Christian land!" she exclaimed, with well-simulated surprise.

"The Buddha was no heathen, nun, he taught the morals of thy Christ and three of the grandest doctrines that ever man has taught."

"Ah! Since when? What were they, monk?"

"Since five hundred years before thy Christ Buddha and his

true disciples have taught the doctrine of Enlightenment, Law, and Evolution, to perfection."

"What! Enlightenment in that benighted country?" she said mockingly, apparently in an altogether different mood this evening.

"How long benighted? Only since the sword of Allah usurped the throne; only since he British Christians robbed and plundered; only since the iron rule of might has usurped Buddha's teaching of gentleness and right." While my garments were assumed this speech was not, and, as I finished, she answered:

"Thou hast most firmly-set convictions, monk; what of the law?"

"The law that every cause has its effect which again reacts upon its cause; and that all things upon the earth are bound by this eternal law, immutable and certain."

"But what of evolution? That is a modern doctrine; Buddha taught no such."

"The materialistic evolution of the West ? no Mind cannot come from cold, dead matter; life cannot come from lifeless form; but the endless evolution or unfoldment through manifestation of an invisible and all-pervading Essence ? yes."

"But the Buddhist is an atheist."

"Not so; thy priest has taught thee wrong. The Eastern idea of God, I must confess, is very different from that held in the West; no form -clothed personality can they conceive as present everywhere, but an infinite and all-pervading Brahma they do proclaim."

"Well, we will not quarrel, Christ and Buddha both were good; and this is very serious conversation for a ball-room."

Speaking this with her usual tenderness, she took my arm.

"Shall we not reliever our minds by participation in the dance?" I ventured, as the music struck up a waltz, and I remembered I had never danced with her.

"To think," she answered, "that monk and nun should dance. No mind can dwell on serious thoughts that drifts thus to the frivolous."

"Not so," I answered; "the master minds can dwell on different times; but others mix all things at all times, which brings confusion, never wisdom. Now, when the dance is over, we will concentrate our thoughts in study and the recreation will have refreshed us."

"You reason with wisdom, monk, and, listening to you, the nun, against her rules, will dance."

Ah, hitherto a formal handclasp, now like a fairy on my arm! Could this be the peasant girl? Ah, no! There she had by power of will kept soul restrained; here she was her real self, her heart alive with fire. Now her head leans on my shoulder; now I fell her beating heart. Souls attuned to subtle music blend in unison on earth.

Oh, happiness! What joy! Our souls are one. What! The music ceased already? How short! How delusive is that thing called time!

She was the first to return to consciousness. For the time she had given herself to me, but now, again individualized and separate, she spoke:

"Come, my monk, we must waste no more time, but get to our studies."

"Waste time!" I protested, as we started toward the study door.

"Yes, waste time," she answered cruelly, and then added earnestly: "That was but a temporary union; there is a union which is eternal."

We had now entered the study-room, and, to my surprise, she took a seat in front of me and asked:

"What have been thinking of since last we met?"

"Sister," I answered, with some hesitation on the word, "my thoughts have been mostly of thee."

"A very poor subject for thought," she answered; and before I could reply continued:

"You spoke with wisdom prior to the dance; is it a fact that you can concentrate and control you mind?"

"I had attained some success in that line prior to our meeting," I answered honestly, trying to draw her into the channel of my thoughts.

"Then you have not been so successful since meeting me?"

"I must confess I have not," I answered, hesitatingly.

"Then I have exercised a bad influence on you, have I?" There was a tone of sadness in her voice, and I quickly answered: "No, no bad in fluence, only my heart has become stronger than my head. My love has become master. Iole, my long-lost love, I love you."

I stretched forth my hands, and, with heart on fire with love would have caressed her, but with a look that almost consumed my soul she motioned me back, and with a voice most wonderfully under control, answered:

"Have all thy past existences been for naught? Has all the pain and suffering we have endured been productive of no results? Must we, bound down by earth desires, still dwell in this vale of misery? Did we die on Cetas mount, did we languish in convent cells for naught? No! It was but to exhaust the evil dues that came from lives still prior. It was but to teach us the uncertainty attached to all selfish loves. And now, with Karmic dues exhausted, with all these experiences registered within our souls, must we still linger, through weakness, in this vale of night and death, the victims of rebirth?"

She leaned forward as she spoke, her veil thrown aside, and her expressive brown eyes were luminous with a spiritual fire. Far from repelling me her words entranced, while they held me checked in action as I answered:

"Thou hast recalled the memory of my love for thee in times gone by, and that, added to the present, only makes it stronger; but know, my soul, this love is pure, and what can claim superiority to love, pure love?"

"Love, so long as tinctured by a thought of self, cannot be absolutely pure; pure love is universal and includes all things, forgetting self. What dost thou love? My soul or body?"

"Thy soul; I have no thought of body."

"Dost thou realize the meaning of those words? If so, there may be hope on higher planes of love."

"I realize the meaning; I love thy soul."

"Canst thou love with all sense of body absent?"

"You speak of higher planes, but if such a love is possible, I can." Was her soul lifting mine to her own exalted height? I felt a spirit power stir in me.

"It is possible; it is a fact. We can love in mind, in soul, in spirit; and the highest love of earthly unions is but a dim foretaste of this grand love. Know you not the meaning of true love?"

"Tell me, my sister; your words uplift me to a higher world of love."

"Then know, what few men know, that every man is complete within himself, and nothing there lacking if he will but search the depths. Love is but the soul's desire for a portion of itself which it has lost, and without which its joy is incomplete. Think not the soul cannot lose a portion of itself; it can. That which we possess yet are not conscious of, is lost, latent as it were, present but unmanifest. Now the perfect being is fully self-conscious of all his parts and attributes, and perfection must be our end and aim. Know that thou art in me and I in thee; and through you I become self-conscious of thyself in me, and through me thou becomest self-conscious of myself in thee. This is the 'Virgin Marriage.' This the meeting of the bride and bridegroom, and the only marriage known in heaven."

She paused; what strange ecstasy her words brought to my soul. How grand and noble! How lofty this conception of divine, eternal love! How debased my hitherto ideals! Now only did I commence to realize the teachings of my parents. How far did my views of the universe expand! How infinite became the field of love!

"My dear sister soul," I answered, all on fire from the inspiration of the moment, "never more will I debase my heart with impure love; even now I feel thy soul within my own, within the invisible essence they throb in unison. From now on I join with thee as a true brother to labor for the same great end."

For several moments we sat gazing at each other in silence, drinking through our eyes each other's souls. She broke the silence with a sigh of joy, and said:

"Long have I waited for this moment, love! Long have I mourned for thee and waited in a robe of black! Now will we go on together, crowned with the virgin purity that entitles us to light?"

"Oh! Sister soul, how kind of thee to wait for me who from sinful dues was yet not free."

She only smiled happily in answer, but her features spoke

volumes.

"Brother," at last she said, and I never heard that word sound so sweet before, "we have tasted of the joy that belongs to the perfectly pure; now we must once more descend to the world and do our present duties. Are you ready for regular instructions?"

"I am ready and attentive, sister." I answered, now having all emotions under control.

"Then the first thing for you to do is to obtain complete mastery over your mind. I know your body, so far as willful acts are concerned, is controlled, otherwise you would not be here. But know that before you can proceed farther you must control your very thoughts, for every thought you think forms corresponding conditions in your mind and body. Thoughts are more powerful and potent than acts. Acts are but the expression of thoughts. Thoughts come first, we are built up of your thoughts; and we are surrounded by invisible powers and potencies created and given strength by the thoughts we think. It behooves you, therefore, to become able to guard the temple of your mind and keep therefrom all things impure. With this control of thoughts you must cultivate the power of thoughts you must be able to set your mind upon a single thing or idea, and hold it there to the exclusion of every other. In this manner your mind becomes identified with the essence of the thing upon which you think, and real knowledge comes. Some secret rules for your assistance in this practice will be given. Now, further, you must control your heart and master all emotions, for here will be your greatest trial, and you must be prepared. Do you love me?"

"With all my heart and soul," I answered, to this abrupt question.

"Then you must be ready to sacrifice that love," she said, with a vehemence that startled me.

"Is that your command?" I asked, not fully under control when such a vital issue was at stake.

"It is necessary and for your good," she answered.

"Then I will; but tell me, what can demand so great a sacrifice as this?"

"Humanity and truth," she answered; "these have nothing before them and everything must be sacrificed upon their altar."

"But what if I love you as an embodiment of these?"

"Then beware; only the less advanced have need of forms to aid them to conceive universals or abstractions, and the personified is often taken for that which it represents. The untrained mind is weak, and no doubt is aided in its upward evolution by forms and symbols upon which to concentrate its thoughts. And you, to night, dressed as Oriental monk, must know that this is the object of the idols of the East; only childlike minds mistake their meaning. Then recall that great man, Jesus, who has been confounded by his followers with the Universal Christ which animated him. For all this, untrained minds can be excused; their worship, if from the heart, is never lost; but from you better things are to be expected. Again our time is up; but before we leave let me give you some final cautions. Heretofore you have had few trials, but from now on your path becomes more rugged; the sacred truths that give all power are only reached through deep, dark and awful passes, for mighty mountains hem them 'round. Through these passes you must proceed alone; no supporting arm can aid you; you must find your inner strength, or you will fail and all is lost. Beware of doubt, and fear, and thoughts of self; these are the snares that trip, the fogs that blind. Wilt thou, O brother, be strong, and brave, and patient?"

"I will, dear sister," I answered, with a determination her strength inspired.

"Then come, let us go; and remember these my final words ? whatever comes to pass, trust in me and kill our doubt."

"I trust, I will not doubt," I answered, as we prepared to leave.

The social features of the evening were over and most of the members had departed; the moments had passed so swiftly that we had consumed the entire time.

"Of course I am your escort home?" I said, questioningly, as we passed the doorkeeper.

"Yes, this time," she answered, as thought to provoke me by the qualification.

Descending the steps we entered her carriage, and were soon rolling rapidly away.

By a tacit understanding we both remained silent the entire

drive, content to feel each other's souls within the depths and communicate in the language of silent thought. We passed through the arch and under the ever-watchful cupid, and were approaching the front steps, when she broke the silence by saying, addressing me for the first time by my ancient name:

"Cleo, for this coming week I give you, as a test of mental strength, to blot me from your mind, and the degree to which you succeed will determine the nature of our next meeting."

"The task is great," I replied, "but for that which follows, and in compliance with your order, I will do my best."

We had now reached the steps and I left her at the front door with a gentle handclasp, no kiss, no caress, only a sweet "good-night."

But Oh! You who mistake a selfish passion and call it love, you know not the divine ecstasy of that mighty love where soul meets soul within the depths unseen. For the first time there seemed no parting, her soul was here in mine; was min with her? And would we thus be forever present, indissolubly united?

CHAPTER X.
TESTS.

ANOTHER week had passed, and I, in accordance with instructions, had striven to the best of my ability to secure mastery over mind. And now for the first time I commenced to realize the power of the human will. Whenever my thoughts recurred to Iole, with relentless severity I cast them away. In order to do this more effectually, I chose deep questions in science, metaphysics and concentrated all the power of my mind upon them. I took the symbols and instructions that had been partially explained or outlined to me, and dwelt upon them separately, and whenever my mind tended to another object I brought it back with firmness and determination.

Likewise, in all the little things of life I practiced concentration; I tried by all possible means to overcome the habitual tendency of the mind to wander, and strove to attain to what he Hindu yogi calls "One-pointed -ness."

On the night for another meeting, I received a note by special messenger telling me to remain at home and continue for another week as I had in that just gone be.

It was signed "Iole," and offered no explanation. Without comment or question I went back to my room, and, in order to stay my thoughts, which now had a tendency to drift more than ever, chose the Ego as a subject for contemplation.

Following certain rules, I locked the door, put out the lamp, and took my position on my heavy cushioned seat. For several moments there was a slight wavering, but, as I persisted, this ceased, and my mind became centered upon my subject. The concentration grew more fixed, a pain commenced to throb within my head. It ceased, and a numbness, commencing in my lower limbs, stole up my body. At the same time an inner suction commenced between my eyes, and burning fire pervaded my upper brain and temples.

At this point a violent agitation commenced in my right side, and a sense of fear came over me. I opened my eyes, which had been closed to facilitate concentration, and ? My God! I was surrounded by a white light, and just beyond it in the darkness, now full of red -colored currents, was a host of horrid creatures, half-human, half-animal, with monstrous shapes and evil features. With a cry I sprang up; the light vanished, the shapes faded away, and with my fame shaking with tremors I was left alone in the darkness. After a time, recovering myself, I lighted the lamp and became more calm.

"I have gone too far," I muttered to myself. "I tempt the demons of the air. If I thus call up elementals, without sufficient strength to master them, I am doomed to madness."

Another week passed by, and I thought I had done my duty well. Evening having come, and having received no orders to the contrary, I took my carriage for the place of meeting. The masked woman motioned me to enter the door at the right as before, and, passing through, I found myself in the presence of the woman before whom I had first appeared, and who was known to me as Madame Petrovna. Without a word she motioned me to a seat, and, fixing her penetrating blue eyes upon me, gazed at me with searching looks for several minutes. I returned her gaze without flinching, and at last she said:

"Brother, your teacher informs that you wish to enter the sixth sub-degree; is this so?

I thought I was already a member of the sixth degree, and, as if she read my very thoughts, she said:

"No, you are not yet in the sixth degree; you are merely a probationer. You can enter only when vouched for by a member who knows you. Your teacher, whom we know as Iole, had vouched for you and affirms that she knows you.

"Now know that by so doing she has assumed an awful responsibility; for if you fail, she must suffer with you the dire results that inevitably ensue. Now be candid, sir, has your teacher asked you to take this step?"

"Only indirectly, by telling me of the grand heights to be attained; I ask of my own free will and without solicitation."

"'Tis well; it is dangerous to proselyte; for, by so doing, we unite ourselves with the results of the failures that may come. You then assume all responsibilities, do you?"

"I do," I answered.

"Do you realize the serious nature of this step? Do you know the responsibilities and duties that it brings?"

"I assume all these, whatever they may be; I am ready and willing," I answered.

"DO you love your teacher?" she answered.

"As strong as man can love," I answered, without hesitation.

"Then do not fail, for, if you do, she too is doomed." Then, as though by a secret sign al, Iole opened the door and entered. She had on her accustomed dress of white, but her beautiful face was unveiled and her long rich hair hung loosely over her shoulder.

"Unmask," commanded the Madame, addressing me, for all this time I had been partly masked.

"Sister," she said, turning to Iole, "Do you know, approve, and recognize him as your brother?"

"I do," she answered, in a clear, certain voice, as she looked at me with a deep and intent gaze.

"Then take him as your full brother; instruct him in the teachings of this degree; we hold you responsible for all failures."

"Brother," she said, turning to me, "our most beloved daughter and sister will teach you the secrets of the sixth degree; and as you love her, as you lover your soul, never, so long as life lasts, divulge them. Let torture seal your lips; let rewards and fame but add muteness to your silence."

"I swear, never will I speak unless permit is given," I answered solemnly.

"Then go on, persevere; surmount all obstacles, and we may meet again;" and at her motion Iole conducted me to a side-room.

Having closed the door and seated ourselves opposite each other at a center-table, she leaned forward on her hands, and, looking me kindly in the face, said:

"Brother, tell me of the experience you had in your room last meeting night."

"Why! How did you find out concerning it? I asked in astonishment.

"By that portion of myself in you," she replied, smiling at my surprise.

"Will you explain more fully what you mean?"

"It is best that you should learn from experience; to explain by talking to you of things perceptible only to senses you have not as yet unfolded, would be but adding mystery to mystery. You can hardly understand what is beyond your experience. When with our aid you have evolved or brought from their latent condition your higher senses, all with be clear. Now proceed."

I then related my experience, just as it was, and when I had finished she said:

"The last three exhortations I gave you, my brother, were to kill out doubt, fear, and love or thoughts of self, the three great enemies of knowledge. You evidently forgot these or failed to do as I told, for fear, and therefore thought of self, brought on this astral vision. But, brother, you should know that so long as you are pure and your thoughts unselfish, you have naught to fear. That white light which shone around you, so long as white, is impenetrable and proof against all evil that may be without. The gods have not left the pure man without protection; he is guarded, even though he knows it not. And further, you are now a member of the Great Brotherhood whose great Protectors, although invisible, are ever present around you." She paused, and I replied:

"Sister, your words recall the teachings of my parents, and fill me with an anxious haste to know more of the Great Brotherhood, its Masters, and my beloved parents who awaits me there."

"Brother, everything must abide its time; the eternal decrees of law cannot be set aside to gratify your haste. You cannot be put into the Great Brotherhood, you must grow into it. Heretofore, little has been told you of your noble parents; now this much I tell you; they live, and are members of the exalted 'Third Degree.' "

"And canst thou tell me of my sister, Esmeralda?"

"She too lives, a virgin sister, and you will meet her in this degree. Now let us to our studies."

As she spoke she drew a rolled parchment from her robe and spread it out between us on the table. It was a kind of vellum, and looked very ancient.

Upon it was a strange combination of numbers, signs, letters, colors, plants and animals; while in the corners were four allegorical scenes.

"This key, my brother, was brought from Thibet, or Tartary, by Paracelsus in the sixteenth century; and, like all the occult works of that great mystic, is incomprehensible to all but the initiated."

Iole had now, indeed, become a teacher; and as she commenced to explain this mystic chart, I became all attention.

"This chart explains, when fully comprehended, all he mysteries of the universe, from the infinitely small to the infinitely great. It makes clear that great, mysterious law? the law of Correspondences ? and, when you understand the workings of this law of laws you will be ready for the great "Third Degree." Here only part is given; this degree. To proceed:

"These signs," pointing to a number of signs, "known to all astrologers, symbolize the seven qualities that make the universe. Now you will notice," she continued, as I bent forward, deeply interested, "these three symbols are separated and there is no sign of correspondence between them. This is a blind; they are really the most closely related of the whole, and symbolized under the words, Sulphur, Mercury and Salt, conceal a great mystery in the constitution of man. Know that the universe came from an all-pervading, primordial, homogeneous substance, every part or portion of which contained in potentiality all the powers that now or ever hereafter shall exist. Now every particle of the present heterogeneous universe, being but a conditioned aspect of the homogeneous from which it came, contains inherent within it all these infinite powers which are ever seeking to express themselves. But the activity of these powers are conditioned by the states of the substance in which they act, and all these conditioned activities, one in reality, make life, will, mind, and all the forces of nature. There is a trinity back of everything that is, and that is ? spirit or will, a self-moving power; substance or other, that inseparable portion of this same spirit which moves; and the third and likewise inseparable fact of motion. Spirit, substance, motion, make a trinity which is a unity."

Passing her fingers to some other peculiar signs, she continued:

"Now there are many different kinds and rates of motion or vibration, and every motion or vibration makes its corresponding substance, color, sound and number. Of the different kinds of motion, this character represents the spiral, this the vortical, this the vibratory, this the undulatory, and this attraction and repulsion. Scientists, by the aid of microscopes, have discovered invisible lives corresponding to all these, and even their form reveals their relation. Let them beware, they are treading on the domains of the occult, and before long may be proclaiming as scientific the much-ridiculed superstitions of the ancients. Under new names ancient occultism is being taught today."

Thus for two hours she continued on this one chart, elaborating with the greatest care each statement.

At the end of her lecture what a wonderful flood of light had been thrown upon my past studies! Many puzzles were explained; but, while many mysteries of the past were now clear to me, the field of knowledge only widened and new mysteries were presented to my view.

"Wonderful, wonderful, wonderful!" I cried. "Is the field of knowledge infinite?"

"Infinite," she answered . "The higher we go, the farther we see, the limits that have bound us ever expanding, ever enlarging, until the vastness of man and the universe give place to a still greater vastness."

"Oh, Iole," I exclaimed, "how much I owe to you ?" Her finger checked me, and she replied:

"Naught but your deserts; in time every man receives the full rewards of his merits, full justice and all her dues, be they good or evil. You delayed yourself, your heart you did not check; and when the past you know, this will all be clear. Now again our lesson time ends," she said, as a musical note vibrated through the room.

"With the key you now possess you must study for some time alone. I simply show the way, you, yourself must do your work. I have now tried to show you the infinity of love and likewise the infinity of knowledge and mind. Man, containing both a heart to love and a mind to think, is the world's great consummation, the end toward which all evolution tends, the object of creation."

"Do you consider man the consummation of all things?" I asked.

"Man, containing all. In him is the universe in miniature. In man is God and demon; heaven, earth and hell; stars, suns and planets; spirits, angels, and all the hosts that be."

"Then, truly, the ancient axiom, 'Know thyself.' Had far wider meaning than most men give."

"Far wider," she answered, "he who knows himself comprehends the universe."

"You just said that all men in time got their deserts; do not men oft en obtain what they do not deserve, and do not many suffer unjustly? Do you believe that justice is certain and that there is no injustice?"

"We cannot say with certainty what a man deserves or what he does not deserve; we don not know his past, which extends through many lives gone by. The innocent do suffer and there is injustice in the world, but this is because man is unjust to man; God and nature are infallibly just and certain. Man has it within his power to go contrary to the laws which should govern his nature, and by so doing can, as it were, pervert nature and establish conditions not in harmony with the divine good. Therefore, in the world of men there is a certain amount of injustice, and men who identify themselves with this world are subject in like proportion to its uncertainties. But they who join themselves with God, and work harmoniously with nature, are never unprotected. Not only are they guarded by higher powers ? the Great Protectors ? but their mode of life unfolds the white-light mystery which you saw the other night. The elemental powers and evil shapes you saw could not penetrate that essence. It is a protection against all things exterior; only that within yourself can bring you harm."

"But," I persisted, "how can you say that God and nature are just when there are so many self-evident inequalities in the world? How explain the inequalities that come from birth? Why is this babe born pure and good, with noble tendencies, when this other child is born diseased, an imbecile, or evil in its tendencies? Shall the sins and errors of the parents be thus visited upon the innocent children, and by nature's God-made law? Conceding that man has the power to pervert nature's laws with regard to results which affect himself, it seems to me that there should be guards to prevent these perversions when the results affect others."

"This is a question the answer to which the world is seeking; but which, for fear of sequences, it seeks blindly. The Church, having no answer, evades it; the pessimist, to substantiate his arguments, proclaims it; and the doubting world, not answered, cries: 'Why should men be just when nature is unjust?' Let us cast an oriental light upon this subject. The character or nature with which every being enters this life is the result which it has built up in many lives gone by. The sins of the parents are not visited upon innocent children, but upon reborn souls of ancient lives whose conserved qualities draw them to the parents through whom they get their new bodies and just deserts."

"Then you accept the teaching of pre-existence and re-birth as an explanation?

"Without these teachings to justify the inequalities among men, duty has no basis and justice is a myth. Without these teachings, the soul's continuance has no logic; conservation has no basis; evolution has no meaning, and the inequalities of life blaspheme the Creator. But, my brother, all this will become clear to you when you have passed through this degree. As she finished speaking we arose and proceeded toward the en trance. Our minds had made time pass almost as rapidly as upon the preceding evenings, and we were among the last to leave.

Iole was most certainly a remarkable woman. Loving me, as I knew she did, with all her heart, she controlled her love with an iron will and gave it no expression. Her conversation throughout the entire evening was in tones of kind and affectionate earnestness, but never once did she show sign of deeper sentiment. As we passed across the portico, I noticed a tall cloaked figure come in off the same and enter the door through which we had just come out; and, as he did so, Iole turned and nodded her head. I said nothing, but could not help but recall the strange adept, Albarez, who always dressed this way.

As the carriage rolled away through the darkness, Iole suddenly broke the quiet by turning at my side and saying:

"Cleo, brother, I see a cloud overhanging you, and I now warn you that you will be tested t o the utmost limits of your strength before long. Be on your guard, and do not fail. Guard well your heart, beware of selfishness, fear and double, and whatever comes, be strong, be brave, be true. Kill out selfishness with universal love; kill out doubt by knowledge; kill out fear with strength; are you now strong?"

She dwelt with peculiar emphasis upon this last question, and I responded:

"If I were always as strong as when in your presence, I never should succumb.

Why, I am always with you, my darling," she said, as she clasped my hand.

"Ah! I forget that glorious truth, my soul," I answered, returning the clasp.

"You must not forget my love of this life and many lives gone by," she replied, as she laid her head on my shoulder.

Oh, the fever of love was coming over my again; the calm tranquility of the higher love commenced to give place to a more restless energy.

I pressed her hand, and as I looked into her face I saw that her beautiful brown eyes were filled with tears.

"Iole," I said, "why are you so sad? Why those pretty eyes thus filled with tears?"

"Cleo," she answered, with a tremor in her voice and form, "my pent-up love would speak."

"My darling, my love," I answered as I embraced her and kissed away her tears, let us be happy in our love."

Now her head nestled on my breast, now her heart beat against my own. Oh, what joy has love! Too full for words we loved in silence. Smoothing back the beautiful brown hair from her broad white forehead, I kissed her brow with fervent kiss. And now her loving arms are around my neck and fond caress she whispers:

"Cleo, my darling, I love you, I love you."

And now the carriage stops and we are home.

"Ah! Must we part so soon?" she sighed.

"'Tis only for a little while, my love," I answered; "but, my darling, why did you repulse my love so long?"

"That was but a test to try it. Cleo," she answered, as I lifted her from the carriage.

"Then from now on our love shall know no barriers," I said,

as I kissed her goodnight, "you are to be mind ? my own true loving wife, will you not, Iole?"

"My own darling husband," she answered, and with a lingering caress we parted.

Back to my home I returned; now all my thoughts made one continuous dream of love. Iole my wife ? my darling wife.

Thus a week went by, and I appeared before the inner guards. The patriarch and woman in black bother looked at me sharply; when they had their scrutiny in silence, a hitherto unknown door opened, and at their command I passed through. Looking aroun d, I found myself in a room finished in a combination of green and indigo. Around the walls were a number of isolated glass compartments, each containing a large cushioned seat, a shelf of books and a small table, while upon the glass doors of each was a hieroglyphic character. In the center of the room, almost surrounded by a table hung with indigo-colored trimmings, covered with mystical characters, sat a man of undeterminable age. His curly chestnut hair, thin brown beard and light mustache, gave him an appearance of youth, which contrasted strangely with the lines of thought and experience which marked his white forehead and face. No one else was in the room, and as I entered he motioned me to a seat near him at his table.

"My brother," he said, in a kin d, low voice, "I am from now on to be your teacher; and that you may know the reason for the transfer from Iole to my charge, I will say that you failed to pass certain tests necessary to entitle you to the privilege."

"I failed!" I gasped, with a vague apprehension of fear.

"Yes, you failed; but only because she sought to take you by extraordinary means to the seventh sub-degree, of which she a member. You failed because you had not sufficiently developed your will to control your heart. Before you can pass into the seventh sub, where she now is, your will must be made supreme king."

A suspicion commenced to steal across my mind, and I asked:

"What have I done? When did I fail?"

"When you yielded to her love and your heart's desires last meeting-night," he answered.

Now all became clear, her love had been a test; she had

warned me of a trial, I had declared my strength to meet it; she then tried me and I failed. Those tears had been caused by mingled love and misery; loving me, she was condemned to try me, and those tears had been caused, nor only by her suppressed love, but by the thought that I might fail. Then, I having failed, and knowing the results could not be worse, she had for the time let loose the floodgates of her heart and nestled in fond love upon my bosom

O God! What trials were these for human beings: could any mortal man overcome them? Turning to my new teacher, I asked, with lips trembling with emotion:

"Could any human being pass such tests and not yield to such supreme affection?"

"My brother," he answered solemnly, "the degree to which she sought to take you is super-human. When you reach it you will be more than man as he is now known."

For a moment I sat in thought, my teacher looking silently on.

"And does this mean separation?" I asked, steadying myself.

"Until you have the strength to meet her in her proper sphere, you must remain apart. No more will it be permitted her to descend and suffer again for you; you must from now on fight your own battles and unfold and rely upon your own strength."

As he ceased speaking a fierce determination arose within me, and I said:

"My teacher, oft before have I said 'It shall be done,' and failed; but now for the last time I say, 'Nothing shall bar my progress.' What course shall I pursue?"

"Your course must now be regular; and, while slower, it is sure and certain if persevered in First, you must labor for complete mastery over mind, and when this is accomplished your will, developed by the process, will be sufficiently strong to master your heart. Both heart and mind must be mastered your and controlled before you can pass into the next degree."

"Then I am ready, and without delay put myself under your direction," I answered, with firmness. "What is our course? What shall I do? Let me proceed at once."

My teacher, with an indulging smile, replied:

"Aspirant, your fierce impetuosity speaks well, but remember that enduring growths come slowly. Learn all patience and strive to realize the eternity of time. Your fist duty will consist of solitary meditation and study. In addition to the instructions you have already received, you will be give more; and in a private room. Devoted to no other purpose, you must ponder faithfully upon their meaning. Every meeting-night a lecture will be given here, and when it is finished you are to retire to one of these compartments, which shall be yours exclusively, and meditate upon the instructions given. If, at the end of six months you have acquired sufficient control over your mind to restrain its wanderings in the midst of the greatest confusion and diversity of surroundings, you will be permitted to stand trial for entrance into higher degrees. In the mean time it is hardly necessary for me to tell you that you cannot possibly succeed unless you regulate your habits of living. The animal nature cannot be subdued when it is constantly being stimulated by animal food; neither can the life energies find expression in the highest mental activity unless the strictest continence is preserved. But to you these orders are unnecessary, for if there had been the slightest exception here you would never have had the privilege of associating with one so pure as Iole."

At this point a number of students who had evidently left the room for the time being, reentered, and the teacher commenced a lecture, saying by way of introduction:

"Brothers and sisters, a new member has joined us in our search for truth, and for his instruction I will call your attention again to the three professional requirements necessary for entrance into this degree. We do not seek knowledge to store it away unused within the chambers of our brains. We seek knowledge that we may be useful in the world and beneficial agents for it. With this end in view, we make as indispensable requirements a knowledge of art, medicine and law.

"Art, that under the forms, colors and symbols which only give it meaning, we may scatter far and wide throughout the world our noble teachings. Under the cloak of art, through which the blind will never see, we present our truths to all who seek the light, and impress unconsciously even those who love the night.

"By music, subtle language of the soul and inseparable from art, we calm the outer nature and soothe the soul that lies buried in the man of sense. By the secret power of sound we reach the souls of the most debased, and stir them, even though it be ever so little, to a higher life.

"We learn and know medicine that we may relieve the suffering and mitigate the world's great pain. Here vast are the opportunities for good; for, in this charnel-house of life, pain and misery contend with death to keep the world in woe. Great is the happiness that comes to him who relieves the miseries of another; therefore, both for duty and for happiness, we seek to be physicians.

"We master law that we may protect the helpless, defend the innocent, and secure justice in the world of men. We must excel in law; not law as perverted for cruel and selfish ends, but law, the rule of right, in whose courts the weak with equity can meet the strong, and purity and poverty contend with crime, greed and gold.

"But know that we do not confine ourselves within the narrow limits that the outside world puts around these fields. To comprehend these grand professions, man must make the universe his study and understand himself. Know that science cannot be without philosophy, the science of the essence, the science of that great unity whose trinity we know as color, form and sound."

He paused, and assuming a low, conversational tone, commenced a secret lecture on the great triune mystery of color, form and sound, as made clear by numbers.

Having finished his discourse thereon, he handed each member a chart, giving me one also, as well as a key to one of the compartments. Going to the one designated I unlocked the door and entered. Unrolling the chart upon the table I found it to be a cipher-key; and taking the books from the shelves I found they were in similar characters and treated on spiritual magic. This was the commencement of a course of study which continued for six months. All through the study hours of this period the chief teacher sat in the middle of the room and kept a careful watch upon each student; while at the end of each session he took all charts and keys. During these six months I had, with a determination that was almost cruel, banished Iole from my mind. I determined, if need be, to tear out my very heart; an irresistible impetuosity to master all came over me, and I made my assault upon the Kingdom of Heaven with violence, as it were. On the twenty - seventh night my teacher told me that, if I so desired, I could try the necessary test of strength preparatory to entrance into the next higher degree.

"I desire the test," I answered, with confidence; at the same time, recalling my past failures, I shut my teeth together with a grim determination to succeed.

"Then follow me," he answered coldly.

I now had an idea of what the test would be, and was therefore better prepared. I knew it would be a test of mental concentration. They would give me a subject for thought, and then try, by means of noise, confusion and other devices, to divert my attention from my subject. I recalled Socrates, who stood for an entire day lost in deep thought, even while the army was moving in confusion around him. I remembered the Hindu yogi who, during the Indian mutiny, sat for hours silent and immovable while the cannons thundered over him and the bullets hissed around. With mind on the alert I accompanied my companion to the test. With a mask on my face, he led me to the center of the crowded ballroom. The lively strains of a quickstep filled the hall and dancing figures were gliding around me. Keeping my eyes upon the polished floor, but ready at any instant to turn them within, I was led to a cushioned seat and my teacher whispered the one word ? "Within!"

Instantly, I threw all the power of my will and mind into the deep. Music, forms, time, space and all things vanished; a confused roar arose within my ears, a clanking throb pulsated in my sub-cranial organs, and then all was nothingness. All sense of self died out; I was no more. Three hours later I found myself alone with my teacher in his study. When the change was made I knew not, but a wonderful light filled my soul.

"The mysteries of the universe are not to be revealed," he said significantly; and then added:

"You passed; not even Iole or your parents aroused you. Let your next tests be met as successfully and all is well."

Ordinarily his remark about my parents and Iole would have disturbed me, but now a serious calm and immovable indifference was upon me.

"Are there any more tests?" I asked, with a feeling of power.

"None from me," he answered, "If you wish to proceed write out your application and I will give it to the proper parties; but remember, I do not advise you so to do; you must apply of your own free will."

A fearless recklessness now possessed me, and I answered:

"I go of my own free will; I choose with deliberation; give me a blank."

Without a word he handed me an application-blank, and in a firm, bold hand I filled it out.

"Brother," he said, as he took the application, "this act of yours shall be kept with the most inviolable secrecy by me; see that you do not expose yourself to unnecessary dangers by revealing it. You need come here no more. If the seventh degree council see proper to consider your application, you will hear from them direct; if not, assume your duties in the world and do all the good you can for your fellow-man. The seventh degree council is not bound to receive any one; by this application our relations are severed and you pass outside of our jurisdiction. Forever maintain silence concerning the instructions you have received, and perhaps we may meet again. Now you may go. Good thoughts and pure aspirations protect you."

With a coolness that was surprising, I left my teacher and returned to my rooms at the Durant mansion, little dreaming of what was so soon to follow.

CHAPTER XI.
THE BLACK BROTHERHOOD.

A CALMNESS and self-possession I had never before experienced now settled over me; I determined to take everything with a stoical indifference, and be surprised at nothing that might come to pass. This state of mind met its first test upon the following morning, for who should I meet at the breakfast-table but my old friend Garcia. After an absence of two and a half years, during which time I had heard nothing from him, he had suddenly reappeared. He met me with a cordial handshake, and in answer to my question as to where he had seen so long, said, with a knowing look, that he had been in the East. As it was a rule never to talk upon any subject connected with the Brotherhood at the table, I questioned him no further. After breakfast he accompanied me to the hall; and when we were alone, said:

"Brother Alphonso, I have something very important to tell you."

"Very well, Garcia," I answered, "we will go to my room."

When we had entered the room and I had closed the door, he took a seat beside me and said:

"Alphonso, I have come all the way from Abyssinia to see you. The great Master who is Protector of yourself and parents, seeing that you are surrounded by a great and deadly peril, has forthwith sent me here to warn and prepare you. You must know, Alphonso, that your parents would not have entrusted you to my care unless I had the highest recommendations and was worthy of that trust."

"I have not the slightest doubt of your honesty and integrity, my brother; what is your communication? Of what would you warn me?" I asked.

"In Paris," he answered in a low voice, "there is a branch of the Red Dugpas of Nepaul, a band of black sorcerers, and they, having learned that you seek initiation into the White Brotherhood, have laid a plot to lead you from the true path into their red association."

"How could they find this out if it were so ?" I asked guardedly, remembering my teacher's warning of secrecy, and wondering if Garcia really knew of my application.

"My brother," he replied, "while all the secrets of the school are well guarded, and every one is pledged to silence, the knowledge that you have already acquired must make you aware of the fact that there are other means of securing this knowledge. These men are sorcerers and necromancers, and most skilled in the black arts. By their nefarious practices they evoke the astral embodied dead, call up elemental spirits, and make the invisible messengers do their bidding. In this manner they obtain knowledge of the most carefully-guarded secrets and use them for evil ends."

"But," I persisted, "why should they choose me for a subject? I work not for evil ends."

"So much more the reason they should seek you. They love evil and mark all aspirants for the Great Brotherhood; they are the enemies of all that is good and pure, and they would have you identified with them in their evil work."

"Strange they should choose me who love only the pure and good," I answered, veiling my secret suspicion of another test.

"True, my brother, it may appear at first sight strange, but once they have you in their power they will cause your entire nature to become perverted; and the divine knowledge you have already received will only make you a more powerful instrument for evil. Many aspirants for the White Brotherhood have thus been lost, and are now identified with this Red Band, where they use their divine powers for hellish purposes. Recall the kabalistic axiom: 'Demon est Deus inversus' ? the devil is God inverted."

"Well, my brother," I answered, with an inward being that I was strong enough to meet the evil one himself, "I am very thankful for your warning, but I am ready to meet the devil himself and all his demoniacal hosts." Then with a feeling of spiritual power I exclaimed:

"Do you know, brother, that I am divine? Yes, I am God; in this temple which you now see is God Himself; and what power has Satan over God?"

The inspiration had come upon me in a moment, and I felt the full power my words implied.

"'Tis well, my brother, I am glad to hear you speak so confidently, but be on your guard; I have warned you, there my duty ends. And know this, an infallible sign, no branch or section of the true occult school, the White Brother hood of the East, will ever ask a penny for occult instructions or demand a price in money for initiation."

"This I well know, my brother, for over two years I have been receiving instructions, and not a cent has been asked from me."

"So far, Alphonso," he replied, "you have been in an outer section of the true White Brotherhood; but my Master would not have sent me here to warn you unless danger threatened. Recall the words of your father when he told you that, so long as you were pure and unselfish, the Great Protectors would guard you; and I now state that it is at the orders of one of These that I am here to warn you. I must now go; I can do no more, but again I warn you."

With these words, and before I could further question him, he arose and departed. Scarcely had the door closed behind him, when the hall-boy announced that a gentleman was waiting for me in a carriage at the gate.

"Do things commence to move so soon?" I asked myself, as I proceeded to the gate.

As I approached the carriage the door opened and a masked man motioned me to enter. As I did so he whispered the password of the sixth degree, and made he salutation sign. Having entered, he pulled down the blinds and closed the door and the carriage rolled rapidly away. For half an hour we rode on in silence, the carriage, judging from its motion, making several turns. At the end of this time it paused for a moment and I heard a gate click; then we again moved on. In five minutes we came to another stop, and my companion, speaking for the first time, said:

"Be kind enough to put on this hood."

As he spoke he handed me a black silk sack, and without and ascended a flight of steps. Along a bare, hard floor, which echoed our footsteps we proceeded, until, passing over a threshold, my hood was removed and I found myself in a room with no apparent openings, even the entrance through which we had come being concealed. In shape the chamber was an exact cube, and its bare, blank walls were painted black as night, while four red lights filled the room with a lurid glare. Even the carpet was black, and, to make the scene still more somber, twelve masked forms, completely enveloped in robes of black, sat around a table of the same ebony hue. My conductor seated me at one end of the table and took a chair at my side, thus making six forms on each side with the thirteenth at the end directly opposite me. Not a word had thus far been spoken, but, instead of timidity, this strange and unusual proceeding favorably influenced my mind and I became possessed with a courageous strength. Then speaking in a low, penetrating voice, that sounded cold and harsh, he said:

"Man of earth, what rash folly impels you to seek admission into this Brotherhood?"

Not the least perturbed by his severe manner and my somber surroundings, I answered:

"The folly of knowledge and the desire for power."

"Knowledge to take advantage of the ignorant" power to exalt thyself on earth?"

"No," I answered with vehemence, "knowledge to aid and help my fellow-man; power to do so with effect."

"Dost thou not already know enough for this? What is there for thee to learn?"

"The known to me is but an atom to the unknown; but a sand grain on the seashore; but a drop within the ocean. There is the knowledge of the nether world, the soul, the spirit, and all the infinitudes that lie within their depths."

"And thinkest thou that the mind of man can know these things? Dost thou not think this vast knowledge reserved for God alone?"

"What belongs to God belongs to God-like man; the mind conjoined with spirit has no limits set beyond which it cannot go, even the deepest mysteries of God it comprehends."

"Mind conjoined with spirit? How think you this can be done?"

"By establishing the conditions necessary for that union, by evolving the instruments responsive to those powers."

"You think, then, it is possible for man to evolve and bring forth higher faculties, more perfect instruments for the manifestation of knowledge, and possibly unknown and la tent senses?"

"All these," I answered.

"Dost thou think that this can be done while man remains on earth?"

"Even while on the earth, if he is from earthly things set free and master of the flesh."

"Knowest thou the dangers that surround all who seek to unfold these faculties and higher powers without being properly prepared?"

"Many dangers threaten them," I answered.

"Ah! And few are those who are prepared. Rash man, return before it is too late. Once thou hast crossed the threshold there is no return. Forbear! Death, madness, life-long disease and misery mark those who fail. Return to thy duties in the world; enter not the dangerous and rugged path, where failure means despair."

"Sir," I answered firmly, "you have my application, it is not withdrawn; I have considered and am ready for all ordeals."

Truly there is no strength like that which comes from realizing the presence of God within. An inner power urged me on, and I determined to follow its promptings.

All through this dialogue the twelve robed figures had remained silent and almost immovable, but their gleaming eyes, peering through their hoods, never left my face. Now with one voice, deep and sepulchral, they spoke:

"Rash man! Forbear! Forbear!"

But no; listening to my inner voice, I answered, "I persist."

Each form immediately clasped his hands in a peculiar manner upon the table, and the leader spoke.

"Hast thou parent, wife, child, ward or relative in the world depending upon thee for protection or support? Are you by duty bound to any one on earth?"

"I am duty bound to none except the duty owe to all; my parents and all relatives have passed on."

"Art thou willing renounce thyself and all the world for truth?"

"All for truth," I replied.

"Art thou willing to become a beggar on the earth, despised , tortured, slandered and forsaken for truth?"

"All for truth," for the third time I answered.

Taking up the black cube before him on the table, the leader again addressed me:

"Candidate for sacred knowledge, do you know the meaning of this cube?"

"The black cube is the symbol of the lower man and the four elements and principles which make his earthly nature."

"'Tis well," he answered, as he commenced to pass the cube around the table. Now I noticed that there was a small opening in the cube, and as it passed around the table each figure put something in it; evidently they were balloting upon my admission. When the cube had returned to the leader he appeared to weigh it in his hand and then addressed me:

"Man, we take no one upon his own declarations of strength; you must, like Christ, descend into hell, endure and overcome its torments and prove if you can that you are worthy of this knowledge and the privileges you seek." Then drawing a black and a white card from his robe he handed them across to me and said:

"We give you seven days for final decision; consider well your course. If, on the seventh day, you renounce your candidacy and conclude to return to the world, burn the white card; if you are still determined to persist, burn the black." As he finished speaking he removed the covering which lay upon the table, and a human skull resting between a pair of cross-bones was exposed to view. It shone with a phosphorescent light and a sickening odor emanated from it. At a motion all arose, and, with black-gloved hands pointed at me, commenced in weird chant:

"Dead! Dead! Buried deep in a tomb,
Thy spirit is lost in the world's night and gloom.
But the sun is now rising, and the day draweth nigh;
Yet before the ascension the body must die,
Yet before the ascension the body must die!"

As the chant ended my former conductor again covered my head with the hood, and I was hurried away to the carriage and driven rapidly back to the Durant mansion.

My thoughts now returned to Iole, but this time, when mind was well controlled, they were a source of strength. My training in the sixth degree had not been for naught, and I could now check the restless agitation which had formerly carried away my heart and been my weakness.

"How grand and noble she must be," I murmured. "What majesty of mind, what wondrous will, and yet what a loving and sympathetic heart. Ah! She is the embodiment of human perfection; strength combined with gentleness; mind conjoined with heart. Yes, I too will attain to her exalted plane, and be a humble brother laboring with her for the good of man."

On the following day Garcia again came with me to my room and reiterated his warning.

"Alphonso," he said, "remember that the Great Brotherhood require no tests except those which are mental and moral in their nature."

"I will remember, my brother," I replied, but made no mention of the incidents of the last few days. As the week passed by I entered upon a partial fast and confined myself as much as possible to my rooms, spending much time in thought and interior communion. On the seventh day I took a light breakfast and repaired to my room. All the morning I meditated upon the divinity in man, and strove hard to fully realize my own divine nature and the fact of the Universal Christ being in all men. At the noon hour, when the sun was in the mid-heaven, I drew the cards from my pocket and prepared to make my choice. Now I noticed that the white card was a triangle while the black was a square.

"Ah!" I exclaimed, "if I burn the white I destroy the divine man, the God-trinity; if I burn the black I destroy the lower man, the black square or cube. God-self forbid that I should destroy thee, immortal soul, far from it. The black shall be consumed." As I uttered the words I kissed the white triangle and tossed the black square upon the glowing coals of the hearth. A bright red flame sprang up; a sickening odor filled the room, and before I could help myself I sank back in my chair, facing the hearth, from which I could not remove my eyes. And, my God! As I looked a hideous face formed in the flames; it grew to twice the natural size, and as I gazed with a strange fascination I recognized my features. But, O God! How wicked and malignant! A sinister, leering, look, a cruel, gleaming eye, and deep wrinkles of debauchery! The horrid face seemed to draw me to it, and I was fast sinking into a lethargic state when, by a mighty effort of will, I aroused myself and cried:

"Away! Away!" A violent tremor shook my frame, and with a groan ? yes, it was an actual groan, the monster faded away in the flames. Springing from my chair I threw up the window and leaned out to escape the noxious vapors which now filled the room. Then, going to my desk I took out a chemical preparation I had discovered and compounded in my studies and threw it on the flames. Immediately a more peasant odor filled the room and my strength came back.

"Heavens! I must beware," I said; "this is probably but a foretaste of what is coming."

Evening came, and while I was now myself again, I had taken no food; I had no desire to eat and so abstained. Darkness had come one, and I was pacing up and down my room buried in thought and surrounded by the gloom, when a light knock was heard upon my door. I had o desire to be disturbed and at first did not answer, when a peculiar rap of the sixth degree was heard. I now opened the door, and before I could speak a black-robed figure entered and whispered:

"Close and lock the door."

It was the voice of Iole, and without a moment's hesitation I obeyed.

"Cleo," she said, in a suppressed whisper, "I come here at the risk of my life. If I am found, or it is learned that I was here, tomorrow my floating corpse will be taken from the Seine. Are there two doors to this room?"

"There is an exit through the toilet-room adjoining," I answered; "what is wrong? Why this unseemly visit?"

"First," she answered, "if any one comes while I am here I must leave unseen, and you must, under no considerations, reveal my visit."

"Very well," I answered, wondering if this was to be another test and putting myself immediately upon my guard.

"Cleo, I have, unknown to my Brothers, come to tell you that you have fallen into the hands of the Black Brotherhood, the Western branch of the Red Dugpas of the East. My Brothers said they had warned you through the proper channels, and would do no more, that you must meet the Black Band and fail or triumph. This is terrible and I fear that you will fail, because these monsters stupefy the mind with noxious drugs and you would not be yourself. Therefore, contrary to the usual rules, but not in violation of my oath, I have come to warn you in addition to the warning they have already given. By so doing I have made myself an attractive center for the malignant influences of the entire Black Brotherhood, and the currents of hate which circulate through the astral world are even now being hurled against me. But by the power of my eternal self I will withstand them, and my love for you would not permit non-action."

"My darling sister," I said, moved but still under restraint, "I thank you from the bottom of my heart for your kindness and self-sacrifice; but if it is indeed as you say, and I am about to become a subject of the Black Brotherhood, so let it be. With the strength and determination which now possesses me, I will even become a brother of this infernal order that I may by so doing carry the powers of God even into the depths of hell. If they want me, let them beware; they may not know their subject."

"Oh, my brother! Do not be thus deceived. Once bound by their infernal charms and surrounded by their demon spirits, you never can be free. Wait, and the Great Brotherhood will in time give you an opportunity to enter into their sacred temples. Indeed, I will make myself your advocate. In a few minutes a member of the Black Order may be here; do not go with him ? wait."

"No, my sister, the die is cast; and, life or death, failure of triumph, I go. You in the past asked me to trust you; now I ask you to trust me. You fear I have not the strength; be not alarmed, I have all strength; and whatever comes, I can no more than die. With the motive that now possesses me, I feel that death would be but the entrance into a new and higher life ?"

A light knock upon the door interrupted our conversation.

"'Tis he now," she whispered, as she stole toward the adjoining room. "Wait, my brother, wait! Do not go, do not go!"

But a devilish determination now possessed me, and I opened the door with my mind fully made to proceed without advice. Unlocking the door a black-robed and hooded figure entered and closed the door behind him.

"Are we alone?" he asked.

"We are," I answered.

"I thought I heard voices," he replied, eying me through the darkness.

"I am always talking to myself when alone," I answered, fully determined to protect Iole.

"Ah! A habit which means insanity or genius. Have you destroyed or made secure provision for all secret documents you may have?"

The masked man had given the secret grip and password, and I answered:

"I have no secret documents; when I left the sixth degree all papers were returned."

"Well and good; have you made your will and left no clue as to where you are going?"

My God! I thought, this sounds deathlike; but without show of uneasiness replied:

"My will needs no attention now; I am not going to die just yet. As to where I am going, I do not know myself."

Without answering my visitor arose, and at his motion I followed. As we went through the door he whispered to me to lock it, then we passed swiftly along the carpeted hallway without word or sound. When we reached the intersection of the cross hall my conductor, who was a little in advance and who seemed to know the hall perfectly, saw Monsieur Durant crossing the end and drew me back into a doorway until he had disappeared.

Then taking my arm, he lad the way to the side entrance and across the lawn to a side gate where a carriage was in waiting. He opened the seat beside me, at the same time closing the door and pulling down all the blinds. I heard the driver lash the horses and then we rolled rapidly away into the night. Relying upon the protection of a few signs and passwords, I was going with an entire stranger I knew not where.

CHAPTER XII.
DEATH ? LIFE

THE carriage was driven rapidly for about five minutes when it came to a temporary stop, and I heard some one climbing up in front as though to the seat beside the driver. Then we continued on again for at least three hours without a single stop. During all this time my companion was as silent as the grave, and the only idea I could form of the route taken was from the turns which the swift motion of the carriage made plainly perceptible and the sound once made from crossing a bridge. At last we came to a stop and I heard a low whistle, shortly followed by another; then the carriage moved slowly forward and in a few moments came to a stand. As on the preceding drive my conductor handed me a hood, and without saying a word motioned me to put it on. Silently I obeyed, and together we got out. Pulling down my hood to see that it was actually on, my companion took my arm and we ascended a flight of steps. During a moment's stop at the top I heard a whispered conversation, but could not understand. We now crossed what I took to mark the door. Then my conductor's hand left me, and each arm was firmly grasped by a pair of strong hands, and I was hurried in a half run over a noiseless floor. In a few minutes we came to an abrupt stop and my hood was removed. Looking around I found myself again in a large, cubical-shaped room with no apparent openings; but instead of being finished in black, as was the room of my former experience, everything was blood-red in color. Four lights, surrounded by red globes and burning with a red flame, filled the chamber with a dim and sickly light. Around a red center-table, as on the former occasion, were twelve figures, but his time all robed in crimson gowns corresponding with the color of the room. The first object to attract my attention was a gigantic black vulture standing by and eating from a large red howl resting in the center of the table and filled with decaying flesh. As the bird ate his horrid mess a sickening stench arose.

"My God!" I thought, "This is black magic sure." The noxious smell gagged me and I staggered back. As I did so a most diabolical laugh arose from the figures around.

"Ha! Ha! Ha! Ha!"

Then one of the figures lifted his hand ? which was not a hand, but a gigantic, blood-besmeared paw ? and pointing it at me said in a voice cold and heartless:

"To-morrow your body will be his food." Then all around in chorus chanted as though in diabolical glee:

"Ha! Ha! Ha! Ha! Be his food, be his food, to-morrow!"

"Poor man," said the first speaker in the same icy tone, "you have yet one chance to return. Take it and go back."

Now came Garcia's warning; now did I think of Iole; the foul odors sickened me, but with a determination which bordered on desperation, I answered:

"No! Go on!"

Quick as thought the hood was again thrown over my head, and two strong hands seized me on each arm and forced me in a run for some forty steps, when I was again brought to a sudden stop and the hood removed. I was in a room like the one just left, but finished throughout in green; and, as though by instantaneous change, my conductors were dressed in like-colored garments, as also eleven figures who sat around a center-table as before. My conductors seated me at one end of this table and each took a seat beside me. The robed figure at the end opposite now drew forth some papers, and addressing me said:

"Are you ready for the oath?"

"I am," I answered firmly.

Passing me the papers in his hand to the figure at his right, the latter took them and in deep solemn tones commenced to read:

"THE OATH. "I believe in the eternal, immutable, relentless and universal reign and rule of law.

"I positively do not believe in the forgiveness of sins, or the possibility of escaping or expiating them by or through any means of substitution or penitence. I believe that every evil thought, every evil wish, every evil word and deed brings to man a corresponding and not to be evaded pain.

"I do not believe that even God, angels, death, or all the powers that be, of heaven, earth or hell, can avert the sufferings that follow as the effects of evil thoughts, desires, or acts.

"I believe that from the humblest molecule of the most degraded and noxious matter to the highest and most exalted essence that pervades the minds of God-illuminated geniuses, all is life.

"I believe that every atom in my form is filled with life; I believe that every atom in my form is a life; but that all are bound by the power of my unconscious will to work together for the good or my organism as a whole.

I believe that, even as my body is filled with a vast multitude of lives, even so is the circumambient air, the all-pervading ether and all-material and immaterial things, visible and invisible; through and in all are warming,

innumerable hosts of beings, beneficent and maleficent.

"I have considered all this; I understand; I believe; yea, I affirm.

"And now, in the presence of all these and my superior, I do most solemnly swear a nd affirm; in the presence of my immortal soul, in the presence of God and angels, in the presence of all eternity, to reveal, without permit, the teachings, persons, symbols or proceedings of this lodge, either by word, act, sign or intimation.

"I further swear never to reveal the signs, pass-words, grips, symbols, times or places of this lodge and its members.

And I further swear, that not even death, torture, cell, flaying, rack or flame can force me to violate this, my most sacred and solemn oath; neith er will fame or ill-fame, power, misrepresentation or ignominy lead me to break this my most sacred pledge.

"Hear and register ye this my most sacred oath, pledge and affirmation, Gods, angels, demons, hear! Now have I sworn, and now do I, in calm, sound mind add this never-to-be-recalled invocation:

"O, swarming lives that fill my form, if I should ever, now or in eternity, violate this solemn oath, consume me! Gnaw in slow agony my vital parts! In awful cancer eat me!

"And thou, O, demons of destruction, who dwell in air around, when I seek relief in death seize my surviving soul and force it back to earth again! There at thy pleasure give it pain, and thus may my eternal life be filled with awful misery! Thus do I swear, and thus do I evoke."

The reader ceased, and for a moment all was silent; then the leader spoke:

"Man, you have heard the oath; do you understand, accept and sign?"

"I understand, accept and sign," I answered.

The leader handed the paper across the table, and, having again carefully re-read, I signed.

Having taken the signed oath, the leader handed another paper across the table and said:

"Write as I dictate."

I took the paper and pen and he commenced, as follows:

"Be it known to all whom it may concern, that I, Alphonso Colono, am tired of this life, and after due thought and consideration have concluded to drown myself in the Seine ?"

"Hold on!" I interrupted, as I dropped my pen, "that is untrue, and will bring dishonor on my name."

"Ah!" said the leader, "you still care for the opinions of the world, do you? We thought you had killed out all thoughts of elf; did you not burn the black square?"

I made no answer, but thought to myself this is risky business. Then, concluding to view it as a test, I took up my pen and wrote as dictated.

"Now sign it," said the leader; and, with some hesitation, I signed.

"Now sign this," he commanded, as he handed another paper across the table.

Taking it up I found it to be a check upon the Bank of France, and reading as follows:

Pay to the order of Count Alexander Nichol Five Hundred Thousand Francs.

frs. 500,000?

Now the force of Garcia's warning came to me.

"My God!" I said to myself; "what he said must be true ? the White Masters never ask for money. They spurn all material recompenses or rewards. Are these the Black Brothers with stolen livery and symbols? Well, I have gone too far to turn back now, and, by the eternal I will proceed, let come what may. Yes, I will continue, even to the death. Count Nicholsky! Why, he is the famous Russian mystic who is supposed to be the famous Russian mystic who is supposed to be the richest man in Europe. Could it be possible that he had secured his wealth through this nefarious order? The leader noticed my hesitancy and said sternly:

"Well, will you sign?"

"Yes, I sign," I answered, as with a bold hand I signed away my entire fortune to an unknown man.

"'Tis well," said the leader. "If you pass you will need no wealth; if you fail, your last letter will identify your floating body in the Seine."

With this cold-blooded speech he put both papers carefully away in his robe and drew forth a deck of peculiarly colored cards. These he shuffled and passed around the table, each figure shuffling in turn. Having passed entirely around, he cut the returned deck and laid it in the center of the table. Each man now drew a card in regular order around the table, the leader making the last draw. At a signal each one turned his card and an instantly checked murmur of surprise arose.

"Man," said the leader, with savage sternness, "do you belong to any other occult Brotherhood?"

"Not that I know of." I answered.

"Well, Brother hood or no brotherhood, you are surrounded by invisible powers, and this being the case, contrary to all precedent, we, even at this late hour, give you an opportunity to withdraw. We do not wish to assume the responsibility of what threatens. Woe to you if you fail; and woe to her! Man!" he exclaimed abruptly, and his tone was fierce, "we care naught for your poor, miserable life, but the fates here say that if you fail our virgin sister, Iole, is doomed."

"I will not fail; go on;" I cried, between my set teeth.

"Man! The elemental powers you evoke will shatter life and mind and make a raving maniac of your sister ? forbear!"

"I will not fail; her blood be on my head. Go on!"

The words had scarcely left my lips when all was black as night, and the room was filled with strange and awful sounds. Strong hands seized me and a terrifying voice whispered in my ear? "Run!" Forced as I was, I obeyed. I soon found that we were in a narrow, vaulted passage. On, on, we ran, the stone floor echoing our footsteps. All was dark, but no longer having on my hood I could dimly discern the vault above, while my footsteps told that we were going down an incline. On, on! My companions were panting for breath and I was almost exhausted. Still on and on; would we never stop? Suddenly I was tripped and fell to the floor, the hands of my conductors left me, and I heard the one word in a hollow, mocking voice ?

"Die!" Immediately I felt the floor sinking beneath me ? down, down, down, into the very bowels of the earth; and all was inky blackness. At last it stopped with a jar, and looking around I beheld a phosphorescent skeleton standing at the opening of a dark passage. It had the power of motion, and in its left hand it carried a human skull which emitted a red light, while with its right it motioned me to follow.

At the same instant, and while I hesitated to follow this uncanny guide, a voice which seemed to speak from my stomach said clearly and distinctly:

"Follow, and never turn back; behind you lies destruction, your only hope is on. Follow!"

Having regained my breath during my ride downward, I arose and prepared to follow. As I did so the skeleton turned around, and as though floating proceeded along the passage, I following. The air commenced to become damp, cold and musty, but I continued in the wake of my grim guide. Suddenly, like vapor, it vanished, and I was again alone in an impenetrable gloom. Hardly knowing which way to turn or what to do I stood still, when the same interior voice again spoke and said:

"Advance; go on."

Reaching my hand out to the side I felt the wall; it was cold and slimy. Feeling my way I proceeded cautiously to advance, when the wall abruptly came to an end and I almost fell upon the floor which had suddenly become rough. Stooping down I felt a rock and concluded I would rest awhile; but as I sat down on its cold, slimy surface, a hissing sound arose, and my hand came in contact with the cold body of a snake. Hurriedly rising, a huge bat flew past my head and a swarm of others commenced to around me. Somewhat nervous, but still possessing a wonderfully cool head, I made another forward step. The air had now become full of flying bats and all around was the hissing and noise of serpents.

"My God!" I exclaimed, "am I in truth deserted?" And again the mysterious voice within spoke and said:

"We never desert those who call with sincerity of heart and are worthy of our care."

This strengthened me, and I again thought of my divine self. But now a snake commenced to coil around my feet, and with a momentary terror I rushed forward, only to strike a rock and fall into a viscid pool. A suction drew me down; I could not rise, and commenced to sink. Vainly I battled; now to my breast, now to my neck it rises until it reaches my mouth.

"My God! My God! Have all indeed forsaken me?" I cried, as the viscid, tar-like mass reached my mouth. As though in answer to my last despairing cry I ceased to sink ? my feet had reached the bottom. Now my mind again became quiet, and I felt for a place less deep. "Ah! Thank God, I have found it!" I cried, as I again rose in the glue-like mass until it only reached my breast. Laboriously I made my way along, each step making the pool less deep, when ? oh horror! I am in another whirlpool and down I go! Vainly I strive, while the fluid is thick and viscous, the bottom seems to slide and I sink slowly to my mouth again. For the second time I stop sinking, and slowly and with toil reach a more shallow place, only to again be drawn into another pool. Now the truth dawns upon me. I am crossing a series of pools, and as fast as I get out of one I sink into another. Oh, merciful power! How wide is it? How long must I thus labor? Will I never reach the other side?

Again the inner voice speaks: "Have strength; persevere." How long I struggled thus I knew not. I could not go back, for all would then be lost; my only hope bay before me, so I continued to struggle. I had sunk into the fourth pool, which was denser than any before, and whose surface was covered with a putrid corruption which almost smothered with its sickening odor, when, almost exhausted, and resting for a moment in the depths, a red light appeared in the darkness. Looking around I saw a boat approaching. It contained but a single occupant, and was drawn forward by a black rope which hung as if suspended in the air, and upon which were numerous bats. The red light shone from a skull fastened on the prow, and by its rays I saw that I was in a large cavern. As the boat drew near, I saw that the solitary occupant was a man dressed in red; his face was also red and had an evil look, while a red skull-cap with a bat's wing on each side gave him a still more sinister appearance.

"Lost man," he said, in a voice intended to be smooth, but which grated harshly on my ears, "pledge me your soul to do as I may bid and I will lift you from this mire and make you King of Earth!"

Raising my head sufficiently to speak, I asked:

"And who are you who would thus require a pledge before you give assistance?"

"I am King of Night, the ruler of the earth; matter is my element, all material things are mine."

"Then go," I answered, "I seek you not. Spirit is my element and I prefer to die, for death is but entrance into spirit life. Away!"

Without a word he tapped the rope, the boat was drawn rapidly away and I was left again in darkness. I had now concluded to die and end it all, for I was completely exhausted; but no sooner had I surrendered when a new strength arose, and the inner voice, louder than ever before, spoke and said:

"I, thy God, the Christ within thy soul, am with thee. Fight on! Work! Work! Work!"

With renewed vigor I returned to my labor, determined at least to die fighting. Six pools had now been crossed and I was in the seventh. Whether it was from growing strength or less viscous pools, I knew not, but each pool since the fourth had been less difficult to cross. And now I had crossed the seventh pool and again reached land. A cry of thankfulness escaped my lips and I was about to pause for rest, when the inner voice again spoke and said:

"Go on! Go on! Never tarry; delays are dangerous."

Now relying solely on my inner guide, I started forward, and as I did so I saw a light reflected against the cavern walls from some place in front. The distance I had descended must have been deep down in the earth. Hurrying forward I turned around a projecting rock and came upon a smoldering campfire. Beside it sat a horrid looking hag affectionately caressing a huge serpent coiled around her body. The fire was evidently a center of attraction, for around it swarmed numerous other snakes and lizards, while the bats were constantly darting over it. When the woman caught sight of me she laid down her snake, and, advancing, greeted me with a blood-curdling laugh.

"Ha! Ha!" she screeched, as she extended her long bony fingers and curved them like claws, "Ha! Ha! Another victim." Then as she looked more closely at me, her manner changed and her frame commenced to shake, while she wrung her hands and broke into a mournful lamentation.

"Man! Man!" she cried, "go back! Go back! See this old hag! Ten years ago she was young and beautiful, a princess of a royal house! Now behold her, cursed victim of a gang of monstrous murderers!"

Then looking around as though she feared some one would hear her, she huskily continued:

"Like you, I gave up all for knowledge and sought admission into the Sacred Brotherhood, but was deceived and fell into the hands of this Black Order. Like you, I crossed the tarry pools; but I would not kill. No! No! I would not kill. Man, ten years ago my heart was turned to stone. Stone! Ay, more than stone; to adamantine flint. But thy face recalls what I once was. Ah! If they find out my life will be to pay; but I must warn you, for you have touched my long-lost heart. Heart! Ah! It is better to have a heart and die than to fester here among these vampires." Without giving me a chance to speak, she leaned forward, and peering at me with her sunken eyes said, hardly above a whisper:

"Man, down that passage they will meet you and command you to take a human life. No one can join their Brotherhood who has not killed a man; their compact is one of blood." As she spoke she pointed down a narrow passage to the right. "But," she continued, still speaking with suppressed voice, "one chance is left you. They demanded this of me; I refused, and they threw me back here in this dismal cavern to live a death amid the slime of earth. Ah! Who would think that I would thus speak ? I, a monstrous hag! But you have touched my heart. Many souls have I sent along that dark passage, but you I cannot. Listen: For long years I was buried in this dismal gloom without one ray of sunlight; but one day I found a passage which leads out of this awful hole. It is not guarded, and it is your last chance. I risk my life in telling you. But, ah! How many lives have I, since my first refusal, helped to destroy? Some hellish power of theirs has made me a criminal with them. Blood! Blood! How many lives have I now taken? Then cannot I take my own? You have touched my long-dead heart. What! Has this hag a heart? Ha! Ha!" For the first time she paused and glared wildly around.

But I had determined to be guided solely by my inner voice, and this mysterious speaker within had, all through the woman's wild and desultory talk, kept saying: "Go to the right! Go to the right!" It spoke so loud that I thought the woman must have also heard it, but, as she continued to glare around in silence, I spike:

"My poor sister, give me a firebrand to light my way; I will continue to the right, join the Brotherhood, and see that you are relieved from this dismal place."

"Lost! Lost! Lost!" she cried; then regaining her first appearance, clawed at the air and laughed that same witch laugh. "Ha! Ha! Ha! Ha! Yes, I will give you a torch; go on to your death ? go on." She carefully brushed aside her slimy pets and got a flaming piece of wood. Handing it to me, she pointed her long bony finger down the passage, and with a leering laugh urged me on.

"Go on," said my inner voice; and with dripping clothes I hurried onward.

The passage was rough and had many devious windings; swinging my torch, I must have proceeded along this way for about three-quarters of an hour, when I entered a narrow, vaulted passage leading upward. Along this I continued for about fifteen minutes, when it came to an abrupt end. A blank wall blocked the passage. Swinging my torch over my head I could see no opening. But stooping down I discovered a small hole near the floor on the right side. It was scarcely as large as a man's body, but, with torch in front, I crawled through, to find myself in a large, black room surrounded by a number of black-robed figures. A number of torches lit up the chamber, and looking around I saw a coffin beside a newly -dug grave in the center of the dirt floor of the chamber. In front of the open grave and coffin sat a man, bound in a chair like a captive. Now I recalled with a feeling of horror and doubt brings fear, and as these thoughts found place in my mind a tremor ran over me; but with an earnest invocation to my inner self for guidance and strength I gave no outward sign of weakness.

"Give him his robes," said a figure, who, from his dress, I took to be the leader; and as a masked figure with a suit of black clothes and a gown in his hands advanced, he addressed me and said: "Candidate, you have passed the first ordeal, but many more await you. Put on new garments."

Then turning to the man with the garments, he said: "To the bath."

Gladly I followed to a bath at the end of the chamber, thinking they at last were beginning to show some consideration for myself, but all the time wondering if they would try to make me take the life of another. Having changed my garments, all the time under the eyes of my silent conductor, I was led back to the chamber, and two figures advanced and took my arms and led me in front of the bound man, while the black-robed assembly gathered in a circle around. As I stood in front of the bound man, whose face was only partly masked, the leader advanced with a long, ugly-looking dagger, while another figure, robed in red, came forward with a bloodstained bowl.

"Candidate," said the leader, "it is your glorious privilege to secure initiation by meting justice to a traitor. This man, in violation of his most sacred oath, has revealed our secrets to the outside world. All to whom he gave these secrets must now die, but he must first expiate his crime; and it is your grand privilege to do the work and thus bind yourself to us by ties of blood. Carve out his traitorous heart and put it in this bowl." As he finished speaking he offered me the knife. I had now fully determined upon my course of action, and, raising myself to my full height, I answered with power and dignity:

"I will not take human life; by no man shall man's blood be shed; all life is sacred and vengeance belongs to God."

A hiss arose from the assembly and the leader, grasping the knife, advanced in front of me and said:

"Do you refuse? Do you defy our laws and orders?"

"Yes, when contrary to the laws of God and eternal law."

"Then you, yourself, shall die," he hissed, and raised his arm as though to strike, when a cry arose from those around:

"Stay! The coward, bury him alive; the worse than traitor ? bury him!"

A dozen strong hands seized me. "Better truth than self," I cried, as they bound me hand and foot.

A storm of hisses greeted my remark, and, bound until I was rigid, I was thrown into the open coffin. All is over now, I thought; I have indeed fallen into the hands of those sworn to evil. Had my search for truth been but a chimera of my imagination? Had my deluding fancy led me to my ruin? Well, so be it; if the God-powers cannot protect me in my purity of heart and purpose, I at least can die in search of truth. As these thoughts passed through my mind, a calm and restful peace settled over me. How glad I was to die! How sweet is death! In their hurry they broke the glass of the coffin -lid as they fastened it over me.

Then I was lifted up and felt myself being lowered into the grave.

"So end all cowards!" greeted my ears, and then the dirt commenced to fall upon the coffin. But how peaceful I was; a great joy filled my heart. "All for truth! All for truth!" I kept repeating. Suddenly the fall of dirt ceased, and I heard excited voices; then a loud report and an awful roar filled the room and I felt my coffin rising. It was lifted from the grave, the cover taken off, my bonds cut, and I was removed. As I stood erect once more, with mind calm and clear, I saw that not a black figure was in sight: all were dressed in indigo.

"We have bought you with a ransom," said the new leader; "one of our members has agreed to do your duty to the Blacks, and you are saved."

"I want no man to do my duty; every man should do his own," I answered.

"We will attend to that," replied the leader, then turning to one of his men, said:

"We have saved him from the Blacks; he seems a worthy candidate, and if he will pass our tests, we will accept him as a brother. Take him to our chambers, make his brand and get his number."

Instantly a hood was thrown over my head and I was led forward between two conductors. In a few minutes we came to a halt and, the hood being removed, I found we were in another large chamber with a glowing furnace at one end.

"Disrobe," said my conductor, as we came to a table near the wall. I had thus far obeyed and was yet alive; I therefore concluded to still obey and take all chances, and so without a word of dissent commenced to disrobe.

"Now let me take your measure," he said, as he motioned me to stand in front of a peculiar chart upon the wall. This chart was covered with small squares made by intersecting white and black lines upon a yellow background. In the squares were letters, symbols, signs and numbers, painted in various colors. Against this chart I took my stand with heels together and arms outstretched, while a man who had just approached, and who wore a white cube hat, marked my outline on the chart.

"What does he measure?" asked the leader, as I stepped aside.

"By the black lines, the four lengths which make his height are equal to the four which make his width, and he is therefore a perfect square. By the white lines, the seven which make his height are in exact proportion and equal to those which show his width, and he is therefore the square of seven of number of forty-nine."

"'Tis well; put on your garments," said the leader.

The white-capped calculator had now gone toward the furnace, and the leader continued:

"Bring on your iron," I answered, fully confident of my will power.

The brander now advanced with a glowing iron and I laid my bare arm upon the table.

"Brand the figure seven," ordered the leader, and in obedience to his command the red-hot iron was placed upon my arm. A darting pain shot through me, but with clenched fist I held my arm unmoved. Before he could complete the figure the word "Hold!" rang through the chamber. The brander drew back and the leader arose.

"Who thus commands?" he asked. "A herald from the king," replied a white-robed figure who now advanced and handed a letter to the leader.

"Who informed him before the hour?" he asked, turning to the messenger.

"The secret wires which communicate all thoughts," replied the herald.

"Candidate," said the leader, turning to me, "you are summoned to appear before the king. His herald will conduct you; follow where he leads."

At a motion from the herald I arise and followed. Straight toward a black wall we proceeded, but when we reached it a hidden door flew open and we passed through into a small vestibule-like room finished in pure white.

"Take off the black and don the white," said my conductor, as he opened a cabinet filled with white silk garments fragrant with perfume; "nothing that wears the black can cross the river and appear before the king."

Ah! I thought, the day begins to dawn. As I removed my black garments and put on the white, soft and pleasant to the touch, a feeling of indescribable happiness came over me. My heart seemed to be burning with a consuming love, and, although I had had no food for many hours, a new strength arose within me. An airy lightness filled my body, and looking at my form I saw it had become a pearly white. Having robed myself, my conductor led me from the vestibule into a large, white-walled cavern filled with a radiant light. It was of immense size, and the floor at our feet was of golden sand; thickly strewn with shells, while in front flowed a rippling river of crystal water. The distant shore was hidden from view by a white mist or vapor, and listening I heard the roar of a cataract below.

"Candidate,' said the herald, "this is the last river; this stream you must cross in a boat without oars. If your faith is strong in truth and justice, if you doubt not that the pure and good are protected, you will cross in safety; for the Brothers of White never desert those who in purity of heart rely on the good for protection. But if you doubt, if your love for truth and purity is not strong enough to draw the powers of truth and purity, then must you drift over the falls and into the cataract whose roar you hear. Have you strong faith in justice, truth and right? Have you strong and pure love? Will you undertake the passage?"

As he finished speaking we reached a white boat drawn up on the sand by the river, and I answered:

"Yes, I will cross the river; I believe the purity of my motives will draw to me the protection of the masters.' My faith, indeed, was strong, and a great love filled my entire being.

"Noble brother of to-morrow," said my companion, as he pushed the boat into the river and I got in, "may the power of your heart and mind reach the protectors of the good." With these words he gave a powerful push and sent the boat far out into the stream.

No sooner was the herald out of sight than the thought came to me, how am I to cross this swift stream without a single oar? But immediately the counter-thought came, the Gods and Masters will protect their children if found worthy. With this thought I became calmly indifferent, while the boat drifted down the stream. Quietly I lay in the boat, enjoying the rapture of the love that filled me. Louder and louder became the noise from the cataract; swifter and swifter grew the current, and the boat shot on; but, lost in the happiness of the interior light, I gave no heed. And now the boat darts forward like a thing of life, shaking in swift motion; but still I was lost in a subjective reverie and stirred not. Suddenly a strain of celestial music filled the air around and rose above the roar of water. My eyes had been closed, but I now looked up and ? behold! The radiant light around me was full of angel-faces. I arose on my arm, and as I looked around I saw a white boat rapidly approaching. It was drawn by golden ropes, festooned with flowers, in the hands of angel cupids. Swiftly it drew near, and the floating throng struck up in chorus ? "Love Brotherhood and Truth."

And lo! As I gaze a queenly form leans forward in the prow of the boat and ? joy of heaven! It is my darling Iole. She reaches my boat, checks it with a golden anchor, and then extends her arms to greet me. Once more I was saved on the brink of the abyss. I was now no longer blind; the spirit had unfolded; and, conscious of my right to love her as brother of her sphere, I stepped in beside her and locked her in my arms. Tenderly our lips met to seal this purest union of two souls, purged, as it were, by fire. The cataract grew fainter; the boat, pulled by unseen hands, moved swiftly over the water.

"My noble brother, victorious over all things earthly," she said tenderly.

"My darling sister, queen of love and goodness," I answered, with all the fervor of my heart.

"We love as God intended all should love," she whispered.

"Yes, my darling, that pure and holy love of soul for soul within the depths of spirit and where no thought of earth is present. All hail the divinity of love, pure love!"

CHAPTER XIII.
THE WHITE BROTHERHOOD.

TIME, in itself, is an illusion; it depends upon states of consciousness. When struggling in the black pool each moment seemed an hour, each hour a day. The same holds good for the man whose mind dwells on the things of earth alone and whose thoughts are sensuous in their nature.

The secret of happiness lies in forgetting self, and any slight diversion, business or amusement, which brings this end, brings a proportioned happiness; but the happiness which comes from a willful and conscious forgetfulness of self exceeds all others, and brings a state of consciousness in which all sense of time is lost.

As the boat was drawn swiftly through the water we became lost in each other's love. My heart, like hers, had now become responsive to the divine vibrations in the celestial soul, and the happiness that comes from this state cannot be told. Our thoughts were again brought back to earth by our coming to a stop on the sandy shore. At the same instant the clairvoyant vision and clairaudient hearing, which had revealed to me the celestial presences in the ether, departed, and I beheld the mysteries of the invisible world no longer. But Iole was still with me, and looking up I beheld a white-robed assembly on the strand around the boat.

"Arise, brother, your trials are over, and you have only won," said Iole.

Hand in hand we stepped out upon the sand. The white-robed assembly stood around with heads uncovered in reverence to the sacredness of our love, when a beautiful woman advanced to meet me.

A cry of joy escaped my lips.

"Triumph of love," I cried, "it is my long-lost sister, Esmeralda!" Beautiful in youth, divinely beautiful now! Like all those gathered around, her face revealed her spiritual power and love.

"My noble brother," she said, as I embraced her fondly, "I told you we would meet again, but neither you nor I ever dreamed of such a meeting."

"They live," she replied, with a glad smile, "but still farther on, members of the Third Degree; and we shall meet them there. But, my brother, we have met more recently than you think."

"When and where?" I asked in surprise.

"As the simple gipsy girl, known as Rahula, who met you at the ball."

"Ah, that explains your silence and timidity as you stood beside the stately Turk; but why did thus conceal you identity?"

"I was forbidden to make myself known; you had trials to meet, and the occasion was also a test for me." At this point a noble-looking old man with a long gray beard and large golden girdle around his waist, advanced, and, bowing low, said in kind and gentle voice:

"Brother, let your sisters lead you to the royal chamber."

As he spoke he made a motion to the assembly and all formed in lines to make a triangle, he, as leader, forming the apex, while I, with Iole and Esmeralda at my arms, marched in the center.

What a contrast since I had donned the robes of white! Now all was beautiful and my trials seemed all passed. We crossed the cavern and entered a broad vaulted passage walled with marble and trimmed in gold and silver. Everything was lighted by a diffused light from no apparent source, and I could not help but marvel at the beauty of my brothers and sisters as their faces shone under its radiance. Fully half of those who formed my escort were women, and as we marched along the passage Iole said:

"You now see man as the noblest work of God, where perfect form responds to mind and spirit."

"Yes," said Esmeralda, "and you can now more fully realize the grandeur of that philosophy which teaches that it is for the evolution of perfect man that the universe came into being."

"Yes," answered Iole, "the chief end of God is to glorify man, and the chief end of man should be to glorify God."

"And the latter can only be done through the former," said Esmeralda, "for it is only through man that God can be glorified."

"Then," I replied, "if man but does his full duty to man, he performs his full duty to God."

"That is the sum of all duties; man's duty is to man," they

both replied together.

We no reached a gilded gate which opened before us, and we entered a large, white chamber, hexagonal in shape and with a pyramidal roof. Around at the top of the walls was a golden finished frieze containing the twelve signs of the zodiac in relief, while at the side of the chamber, opposite the gate through which we had come, was a white throne, in the center of which, in a golden chair, sat a man of apparently middle age. His remarkably handsome face was beardless and gave him a youthful appearance, while his features looked like those of a man of age and thought. His uncovered head was crowned with thick and long golden curls, while his blue eyes shone with a luster even more wonderful than that of my companions. Dressed in the loose and flowing costume of the ancient Greeks, his manly form revealed the perfections of human development.

At the left of the enthroned king sat a man who looked like an Apollo; his form was also only partly clad by flowing garments, and his figure thus revealed was indeed a symbol of strength and power. He evidently represented or symbolized the sun, for his hands rested upon a disk -like shield with a central dot and an encircling margin in gold. At the left of the king sat a woman whose brunette beauty was marvelous to behold, her black eyes and hair contrasting with wondrous effect with the pearly form which showed all its lines of beauty through he light and flowing drapery. Her white and shapely hands rested upon a large silver crescent and she evidently symbolized the moon.

Dare any one brand this scene as immodest?

None but the pure were here. He who cannot view, without a blush of shame, the human form when a perfect temple of divinity, stands self-confessed; his mind is poisoned with impure thoughts; his imagination corrupted by the taint of lust. Crossing the white floor of polished marble, we approached a long white table in front of the throne. I took the seat facing the king, while Iole and Esmeralda took seats by me on each side. Then all the sisters of the escort took seats upon the left, while the brothers took those upon the right.

And now I noticed that the constellation Leo marked the zodiac above the throne, and in it were the sun and moon in close conjunction.

All had thus far been silent, but now the gray-bearded leader arose, and, with a bow to the king, commenced to speak:

"Most high and noble king, another star has risen, another child been born into our kingdom; and we have brought him here to receive you blessing and adoption."

The Master-king bowed with a smile, and in kind and gentle tones addressed me:

"Dear brother, gladly do I welcome thee in the kingdom of true brotherhood. It adds to our joy to see one more joined with the small minority. All greet you as our brother."

As though in answer to his words, all the assembly around looked at me and cried in chorus:

"Our brother, we greet you as our brother."

How different this king from the kings of earth. I thought; he greets me as a brother, and does not deem a gentle smile and words of tenderness as inconsistent with severity and power.

And now, without noisy cry or spreading gesture, he leaned forward in his chair, and in a calm, earnest, and soul-stirring voice spoke:

"Brother, our special explanations and instructions will be given to you by the proper teacher; but I will now lay out the square upon which we build our temple.

"There is one God, one man, one Brotherhood, one truth; these are our corner-stones, upon these we erect our structure.

"God is the Infinite and all-pervading Spirit, formless, immutable, eternal and incomprehensible to all save itself.

"Man is an individualized manifestation of God in self-imposed conditions; a center in the Infinite Essence around which the spirit vibrates and through which it flows forth and reveals itself in the world of forms and things. "The one Brotherhood is humanity, the sum total of all the individualized centers of the divine activity, which, while apparently separate, are one in life and essence.

"Truth is the full, self-conscious realization of God within its individualized manifestations and the illumination that comes to each therewith.

"God comprehends all truth; and man, as God individualized, can comprehend all truth through God in him."

He ceased speaking; but the wonderful magnetism which accompanied his words remained, and for some moments a profound stillness reigned. The meaning of words uttered with a spirit-impress cannot be expressed in type; sound has a power unknown to writing.

Now the gray-bearded leader arose, and again bowing in respectful reverence to the king, drew forth a white box from his robe. Shaking it in his hand, he threw four dice upon the table. Three times he shook and threw, then turned to the king and said:

"The throws sum fifty-one, and each time seventeen; the invisible powers who rule these throws decree that our sister Iole shall deliver the instructions." He turned to Iole with a bow. Pressing my hand upon the table, she arose and, with a graceful and reverential bow to the king and leader, addressed me: "Is my brother's number forty-nine?" I looked to the leader, and as he bowed I answered, "It is."

"Then," she said, addressing the leader and king with bold unflinching eyes, "the meaning of this choice becomes revealed; fifty -one plus forty-nine makes the square of ten, whose meaning you all know."

The gray-bearded leader gave an inquiring look at the king, who again leaned forward and addressed me:

"Brother, the invisible powers say that you aspire to still higher degrees; is this true?

"I aspire to reach the highest summit, yea, even to God-hood does my soul aspire," I answered, with a wonderful lightness of heart and consciousness of strength.

Without reply the king made a sign to the leader, and he and Iole took their seats.

The lightly draped Apollo at the right of the king now spoke:

"I represent the sun, symbol of life, center of vitality and heart of the solar essence that throbs through all within the boundaries of our solar sphere. I am the spirit as it acts, and manifest in matter; but my sign conceals a mystery and has two meanings; learn thou this secret and thou shalt never die."

He ceased, and the woman on the left, in a clear, musical voice, spoke:

"I represent the moon, symbol of subtle matter, the essential substance necessary to form and growth. I am the vehicle of spirit and the base without which it could not act; my sign, too, conceals a mystery, and has two meanings; learn thou its secret and thy form, made perfect, will not dissolve."

She ceased, and the king again spoke:

"Ever since the time when we met in the columned hails of Thebes and Memphis, Osiris and Isis have been with us; and their perfect and harmonious union in you will make you Horus."

As he spoke all eyes turned toward the zodiac mist cover it. As the substance enveloped the sign, it seemed alive with golden atoms which moved and vibrated rapidly therein. The cloud continued but a moment, when it disappeared, and the sign was visible once more; but instead of the sun and moon as before, there was a golden disk with a white cross therein. As I wondered by what strange mechanism this phenomena was accomplished, the leader arose and gave the order: "To the hall of learning!"

The assembly immediately arose, and, with united bow to the king, marched in double column from the hall.

We proceeded along a passage not unlike the one through which we had entered, until we came to another vaulted chamber.

The frieze of this chamber was also a zodiac with movable planets in the different signs, while the great stars also had their places. The walls around were covered with mystic symbols, circles, triangles, crosses, squares, lines, spots, letters, allegorical scenes and numbers. On the four sides of the chamber were four remarkable pieces of statuary: a golden lion, an ivory man, a gigantic eagle and a bull. In the center of the hall was a long, low table, made of a solid block of marble, and upon it were cubes, miters, spheres, and like symbols. But there were two pieces of art above all others the most remarkable. Near one end of the table was a solid cube of the blackest marble, above this, supported by four lotus-capital Egyptian columns, which rested upon the four corners of the cube, was a pyramid with square base of transparent whiteness. In the center of the space between the base of the pyramid and the top of the cube were two marvelous figures close by a greenish-colored thread which connected the pyramid with the cube. One was a demoniacal-looking dwarf, made of some blood-red material, who with leering and malignant features, was trying to cut the thread with a blood-smeared sword. The other figure was a noble-looking man made of ivory. With features, every line of which expressed an agonizing pain, he fought back the monstrous dwarf with his bare and bloodstained hands and arms. This piece of art held me with an irresistible fascination, until I was drawn by Iole to an equally remarkable symbol at the other end of the table.

Here, in full life-size, was a man of pearl nailed upon a black cross, while encircled around him and over the cross was a huge serpent which, with its body emitting a red phosphorescent light, drank the blood which actually dripped from the nail wounds of the tortured man. The veins of the man were distended and every line of his body expressed torture; but while his face showed pain, it expressed wondrous fortitude.

A shiver ran through me, and turning my eyes away I saw across the table a meditating Buddha sitting upon a gigantic lotus with petals of pearls. The calm look upon that meditating face was in marked contrast with the tortured look of the figure upon the cross.

All these had been viewed in a few minutes. We now stopped on the vacant side of the table, and, at a motion from our leader, a middle-aged man with light curly whiskers and long brown hair stepped from the ranks beside him and addressed me:

"Brother, the trials through which you have passed are not without their meaning, and when explained they will, no doubt, be impressed indelibly upon your mind."

As he spoke he pointed to a large vulture carved from black material, which rested near him upon the table.

"Ever since the day when we left the now lost Atlantis for a new home in the land of the Pyramids, the vulture, as a destroyer of all corruption and things foul, has been the symbol of a sacred power. The initiated hierophants of Egypt did not use the vulture symbol without reason; and, like Prometheus among the Greeks, every one who enters here must let this power consume his liver. But, unlike Prometheus, he must kill its growth or, like him, be bound to the rocks in pain and misery."

He paused a moment, as though to let the words impress me,

and then continued:

"Next, no man can enter here who has not killed all thoughts of self, and extinguished every selfish aspiration and all desires for life, unless that life has an unselfish purpose. The tests to try your pride and love of life, determined how you stood. When we asked you for your wealth, you doubted; those were there who could read your colors, and your thoughts were not concealed. Know that here no evil thought can be concealed, your mind is an open book. Know also that doubt is a canker-worm which ever breedeth fear and paralyzes strength; not doubt of forms, and creeds, and dogmas, but doubt of the eternal excellence and superiority of truth and justice. He who doubts not these eternal principles ever adheres to the right, confident that, no matter what appearances may indicate, he will in the end succeed and triumph over all.

"Know, also, that we have no need of your money; what wealth we need, our knowledge of nature's powers enables us to get. Now hear the explanation and meaning of your further trials. When you had passed the tests of selfishness and cast aside the world's ambitions, we considered you as man before the time of Adam.

"Man was then a celestial being, pure and innocent, but without knowledge. Prompted by an inner intuition which dimly told him of his inherent but latent possibilities, he aspired for wisdom and experience. This aspiration brought a momentary light, and, gazing out into the radiant depths of space, he beheld a vision of what he might be. Across a black and murky pool, enveloped in dense clouds of smoke and noxious odors, he saw a radiant sphere where men, once being like himself, had evolved to the heights of perfection and become as gods, knowing good and evil, and masters of all the powers of mind and will. The almost latent light whispering to him said: 'Being, it is within thy power to be like them, knowing all things, and conscious of the knowledge; but to reach that height thou must cross that pool of black and murky matter, descend into its depths and conquer all its horrid creatures. It is only by passing through a world of evil that thou canst know what evil is; and it is only by this knowledge that thou canst know and realize the good.' 'I have no knowledge and know not the meaning of your words,' answered the celestial being to the urging spirit within 'but something within tells me to listen to you and if you prompt me on this journey I will trust your guidance.'

"Then did the inner light reply:

" 'O being! I would share myself with thee and make thee wise and God-like; I not only urge thee to the journey, but give thee this my promise: Through this awful pool of matter I will go with thee, and if thou wilt but rely on me will ever guard and lead thee to the free upon the other side. But before thou dost this journey undertake, listen to my warning: Two paths lie through this awful whirlpool; one straight and certain and not over-dangerous in its nature, the other devious and with many pitfalls which make it most dangerous and productive of much pain. The first is trod by those who take me for their guide and learn the nature of suffering by sympathetic identification with those who suffer, but who do not themselves bring suffering because they keep free from the causes which produce it. Many who start with me lose sight of me when the vapors gather around them; then, not hearing or listening to my guiding voice, but deceived by the perfidious beauties which ever tempt them, they take the second path. Great is their misery! Long and painful is their path! Thus deceived, they may descend so lo w and stray so far that I can no longer reach them; then they die; absorbed in matter their substance returns into the All, and I return to help across another being. For know you, celestial being, that it is my nature to seek to be a being with individuality; but it is only by union with one like you that I can realize my aspiration and reach the other side. You give yourself to me, and I will give myself to thee; and together we will make the journey. Separate, thou art devoid of mind, and I am formless essence; together, you will bring to me individuality, and I will bring to thee a mind with knowledge.' "

The speaker paused; his deep and earnest words had stirred my soul and roused my intuition, and it told me the hidden meaning of his dialogue.

Iole, evidently anticipating what he next would say, now clasped my hand and held it as the speaker continued:

"As in the universal evolution two paths lead to Nirvana, so here below two paths lead to this chamber. Your loving sister sought to lead you here through the path of love and light, but, like most, you wandered and had to take the dark and downward path into the depths of earth. A skeleton, which symbolized the death of spirit in the tomb of matter, led you on until you reached the very slime of earth and fell into the pool. But thou hadst not entirely lost sight of thy inner self, and listening to its promptings thou hast won.

Hadst thou been blinded by thy fears and doubts and not heard thy inner self, thy soul would have been lost. When the king of matter tempted thee, thou gavest up thy life and all the world's ambitions. This surrender was thy victory; for with this last renunciation thou commenced the ascent, and the spirit brought thee strength. Know, O aspirant, that ambition and the love of life are the king passions which bind the soul to earth. Men laud ambition and in her name try to justify their selfish fight for power and fame; but what is selfish ambition compared to that more noble aspiration which, forgetting self, labors for mankind? Your death brought life and strength; you crossed the pool and met the witch. Most truly did she tell you that you must kill a man; no one can enter here who has not accomplished this, but that man is the lower self of him who seeks to enter. When, listening to your inner spirit, you refused to take a human life, you killed your lower self; into the grave you put it, and the burial brought you peace. Peace brought you resurrection; you ascended to a higher plane and your spirit was enthroned within the form which was a tomb, but which now is a willing instrument of the higher self.

"As the path you entered led downward, the one by which you returned led upward; the farther you descended, the darker things became; the higher you ascended the brighter grew the light. And now do we all welcome the brother of the great degree."

He finished, and those around repeated in chorus:

"All hail our new-born brother! All hail our new-born brother!"

The orator took his position in the ranks, and the gray-bearded leader, with a bow to Iole, made a motion, and the assembly immediately formed into couples and departed.

"I will leave you to your other sister," said Esmeralda, as she took the arm of a tall blonde brother.

"What is the course?" asked the leader, as he passed Iole.

"The law shall rule," answered Iole, as he departed, leaving us alone in the room.

"Now, my dear brother, I will explain some of the symbols; but remember that some symbols have more meaning than can be given in the largest book, and these symbols have many keys and therefore many meanings."

As she spoke, she led me the white pyramid connected with the black cube by the slender thread of tree.

"Recall the words of the orator, and the meaning of this symbol will be plain," she said, as I gazed in silence at this truly marvelous work. "The white pyramid symbolizes the higher self, the spirit of the pilgrimage; the black cube symbolizes the lower man or the celestial being after it is lost in matter. The being has sunk so low that nothing but a thread connects it with the higher self, and the passions and desires that arise from matter, and which are symbolized by the red demon, would sever even this frail connection and destroy the soul. The white figure symbolizes the spirit in the form which it takes when in matter, and it is fighting and striving to preserve the connection, although by so doing it perpetuates its pain. But rather than again return and commence a new pilgrimage, the spirit hangs on to its degraded vehicle until the last hour, hoping that by so doing it may at last bring it back to the path from which it has wandered. For know you, that the being once conjoined with spirit on this pilgrimage has a will of its own, a will which the spirit cannot overcome unless the will permits. The spirit is all-powerful on its own plane, but becomes conditioned, as it were, when in matter. The contest seems unequal; the white man has no weapons except the power of persuasion, to which passion will not listen, and the cruel sword of the dwarf falls relentlessly upon his bleeding arm, which would soon give way, but that the pain heals it as fast as it is cut away. See the agony written on his countenance! Many men thus allow passion and desire to torture their higher natures until at last the demon conquers, the threa d is severed, and the soul is lost."

As she paused for a moment I questioned.

"But, Iole, can anything be destroyed?"

"Not in its essence," she answered, "both matter and spirit, as such, are eternal and indestructible; but their individualized or special combinations are not unless the will that rules them so wills. At this separation of the lower from the higher, or spirit from matter, spirit returns into the Universal Spirit and matter into the universal matter; but the individuality that came from their union is lost. Know that the occult teaching that man can lose his soul is most scientific when correctly understood. All souls either attain to spiritual individuality and pass on to God-like perfection, or are dissipated and dissolved. Many men now live on the earth whose higher souls have left them; such are the monsters who sometimes appear in the forms of men and startle the world with their wickedness. But this is a vast and deep study? this study of the soul; let us proceed to the other symbols."

Near by rested a large black cube, and as we came to it she said:

"This you no doubt understand, but it has many meanings; let me explain:

"This black cube symbolizes the four elements or principles which make the lower man; that is, earth, water, fire and air, or the essences which these words symbolize."

She pressed a spring, and the ends and sides of the cube unfolded on the floor and formed a cross, four squares high and three squares broad.

"You see," she said, "that by counting the center twice there are seven squares, which symbolize the seven principles which make the complete man. As a black body is an instrument of torture for the spirit which inhabits it, so here we have the cross likewise an instrument of torture; and as man with arms extended makes a cross, so also does the cube enfolded. Likewise man with arms extended makes a square of four equal measures; the four which make his width, and four times four equal sixteen, a perfect square, and the fourth power of the dead, two. Such is mystic mathematics."

We closed the cross into its cubic shape and approached the other wondrous symbol. For a moment she stood by in silence; then in a deep, solemn and soul-stirring voice, said:

"This explains the mystery of Christ, the meaning of the crucifixion and the mystery of pain. The black cross, as just explained, represents man's lower nature, this body, a tomb for the spirit and an instrument for its torture. Nailed upon or fastened to this cross, or form of flesh, is the Divine Man, Christos, the Son of God. The serpent encircled around is the serpent of desire and passion, lust, avarice and hate, and its life depends upon the blood which issues from those bleeding wounds. How truly does this symbolize the life of all men of earth; it is a universal symbol, and applicable to all men, for every man who feeds his lusts and passions or yields to the lower nature, crucifies the Christ within him. Every evil act we do, every impure thought we think, every evil aspiration or desire, tortures the divine man within ourselves, and feeds this horrid monster of desire with fresh blood, which represents the life of Christ, drawn with acutest pain."

She paused, and I thought ? how beautiful, yet how pathetic, this interpretation of the story of Christ; how much misunderstood this wonderful allegory, teaching a universal truth.

"Iole," I said, "I see that you give an allegorical interpretation to the story of Christ; do you believe that a historical Christ existed?"

"That a character existed around whose life the Christ-story was built, I have no doubt; but the Universal Christ, the divine in man, has always existed and has never died. All ancient Scriptures have an esoteric meaning, and under the form s of allegories and symbols the great truths of the universe and man, the macrocosm and the microcosm, are veiled; but veiled so lightly that all who seek can find their meanings. Paradoxically, the most deeply hidden is the most open; but the blind pass by and will not see. The universe is built upon simplicity, but superficial and selfish minds know not the meaning of this word. Men seeking for a mystery overlook this truth; relying solely o the intellect, they scorn to see philosophy in the simple parables of every -day events. But Jesus thus taught, for parables were his constant method, and his philosophy of human life, thus dimly veiled, was told to his disciples. St. Paul, his eminent successor, taught in like manner, and, still later, Origen and Clement of Alexandria. All the Gnostics and Neoplatonic Christians taught the same, and down to the time of

Constantine the esoteric meaning of the Scriptures was acknowledged."

Again she paused, and as I stood looking at this solemn symbol of the mystic Christians a wonderful compassion arose within me.

"Come," she said, "these wondrous symbols must be explained at length some other time; we will now pass to the others."

Then she explained the meanings of the man, the ox, the lion and the eagle, dwelling with great care upon each; suffice it to say that the mystic language of the Hebrew prophets was for the first time made clear. Having thus received a brief synopsis of the many symbols in the hall of learning, we left the chamber of that name and proceeded along another corridor. If I had ever doubted that knowledge came from the unfolding of an inner faculty, I now doubted it no longer. I was beginning to realize this inner light, but Iole seemed to already possess universal knowledge. No question could I ask but what I got an answer; and thus continuing our conversation, with active minds and hearts attuned to the same key, we proceeded along the corridor on our way to the hall of choice.

CHAPTER XIV.
"VIRGIN LOVER."

WHEN the mind absorbs all our energies we forget the body; there are those who can become so lost in mind that they can have their limbs amputated and hardly be conscious of the pain. Likewise men under intense mental strain can labor far beyond their ordinary endurance.

As we walked along the corridor, I learned from Iole that eighteen hours had passed since she, after tempting me, had got on the cab with the driver during the first short stop. It was now the middle of the day, and for twenty-four hours I had not tasted food; yet, strange to say, I felt no hunger. Had the consuming lives ceased to work since my initiation? Iole answered my silent question by saying:

"Before proceeding to your next ordeal in the all of choice it is but proper that you should have some food."

"Then you are still subject to the necessity of food?" I asked, with a smile.

"Yes," she answered: "while our mode of life reduces the amount of food we use to a very small amount, still we are not so high as to dispense with it altogether; it is said that the members of the 'Third Degree' are above this necessity to us, or at least almost so, repairing what little waste takes place in their physical bodies by a concentrated elixir, the secret of which they alone know. But we, my brother, have much to accomplish before we are so far along; and I will join you in a light repast."

Up to this time all the rooms and corridors had been lighted by the same diffused light, which seemed to be an incandescence in the air; but now, passing through a door and up a stairway, we were in a hall with windows on either side open to the light of day. This hall was richly carpeted and hung with paintings, and as we passed along several robed brothers and sisters met us with kindly greeting.

Wherever this building was, it was of immense size. The hall was fully a hundred feet long, and, looking out the windows as we passed, I saw that a large open court was on each side. Both courts were immense conservatories, containing large trees of many varieties and flowers and plants in abundance. Reaching the end of the hall, a robed figure confronted us. In answer to his challenge Iole whispered something in his ear; he bowed and we passed on.

"That was a guard," said Iole; "and as it is my privilege I will now communicate the passwords.

"The one to be used in coming out is the Sanskrit word, 'Janana,' meaning knowledge; the one to use when entering is 'Naga,' the Sanskrit word for serpent; and when you give them never speak above a whisper."

We had now passed into an interior hall and come to a door at the right. Pushing a concealed button in a rosette near the floor, Iole opened the door and we entered.

I saw immediately that we were in a private room, and looking to one side I beheld a life-size painting of my beloved companion. Noticing my admiring glances, for it was indeed a work of art, Iole modestly remarked:

"Do not think this a display of vanity, my brother; Zerol insisted upon making me a subject, and, like a good sister, I had to humor him; but to keep from making an exhibit of myself I hang it in my private room."

"What ill-chosen modesty," I replied, "to deny people the enjoyment of such a picture and the elevating influence that must come from such a work of art, and such a perfect subject."

"Hush! My brother; recall the words of Socrates when he said, 'Flattery is worse than a vulture, for the later consumes only the dead while the former eats up the living!'

"You will probably be my guest for some time," she continued, as we took seats at a small table near the side of the room, "and you must consider yourself perfectly at home; every one in this degree is proved pure, and we therefore indulge in no forms or ceremonies with one another; such are necessary only in the world of shams."

"It does one good to get among people where such freedom reigns," I answered; "in a world where all are hedged around by forms and ceremonies how many sympathetic souls are kept asunder. I take you at your word and all my actions shall be free."

"Be free," she answered with a smile, as she extended her hand across the table and we clasped in true good-fellowship.

A young man, evidently a Hindu, now entered with a tray containing our repast.

"You see," said Iole, as she poured our cups of chocolate, "the members of this degree eat in private; it is one of our rules; but you being so intimately related" ? and she smiled with a bewitching smile _ "we can eat at least once together."

"And only once! No oftener?" I asked, eying her affectionately across the table.

"Well, that depends," she answered; "from now on I am your obedient servant, and whatever you say will be done."

"Now see here, my pretty coquette, are you trying to tempt me again?" I asked. "If you are you will fail; for I have sworn to be a monk."

She looked into my eyes searchingly and replied:

"No, you will be tried with no more temptations of deception through me; my duty has been performed to you and yours to me. The deceptions I had to simulate were trials to me as well as you; loving you, I had to deceive you and try and lead you to your ruin. Could any trials be more severe? But I did my duty, and, thanks to thy inner self, you did yours; and now we meet upon the plane of equal brothers a deception will nevermore come through me. This is a solemn affirmation and you can rely upon it in the future."

Without giving me a chance to reply, she continued:

"As to your being a monk, I would say that the noblest men of earth have been such; and it seems that to be a monk is an indispensable requisite to the highest perfection."

Checking as exclamation of admiration, I asked:

"And did you all this time implicitly obey, without question or doubt, the commands of your brothers?"

"I did," she answered. "I had been with them for many years and during all, that time they had taught me nothing but what was good and pure, and their lives were filled with beautiful simplicity and self-denial, they had always acted most nobly, and I could not doubt them. Then they had taught me that there are protecting powers overshadowing every being, and that these powers are proportionately strong as the divinity in man is strong. They taught me that those whose aspirations were pure would in time succeed, no matter how great the temptations. I believed these teachings, not simply because they told me so, but because my reason was convinced and my heart accepted the conclusion. This belief in protecting powers brought great peace to my soul and became a source of strength, for I did not believe in Providence as taught in the world, and my ideas of God were too far off, too exalted. I needed some intermediate link, and this teaching of protecting powers ? Masters, Protectors, supplied the need."

She spoke with deep earnestness, and I remained silent as she continued:

"Before this, how cruel the world seemed; how heartless, how unjust! I could not conceive of the Infinite setting aside the laws that rule the universe; I could not conceive of God as some gigantic knight going from place to place in the twinkle of an eye and protecting the innocent and guarding the helpless. Even when a child I wondered how such a God could be every where at once; but when they told me of the Masters and Protectors, perfected men of long-lost races, who had evolved far beyond all men how known in the world, and who worked for truth and justice, I deemed the teaching reasonable. For if man evolves, who can mark the limits of his evolution? As we are above the savage, so there are those who are even farther above us. Some of these exalted men still live on earth, but in undecaying bodies; and, unknown, they go from place to place throughout the world, working ever for the right, protecting the innocent, guarding the helpless and alleviating suffering. Still higher ones have evolved beyond the power of death; and, renouncing the privileges of Nirvana, exist in the invisible. They forfeit the bliss of heaven and hover o'er the earth, laboring in the world of mind for the uplifting of mankind. Unknown, unhonored, they live a living death for man, for infinite is their compassion."

She paused, her large, brown eyes filled with a wondrous light, her face illuminated with divine love. What speech has the power of that which comes from a pure and earnest heart? Her words were fast throwing me into an enchanted spell, and it was well, perhaps, she ceased, to let me ask:

"And you believed that these great powers, Protectors and Masters, would guard me so long as my heart was pure and my aspirations noble?"

"I had not the least doubt of it," she answered.

"Well, my love, I will remember your smile, and avoid further comparisons with vultures; but tell me ? do they allow love here? Do they permit marriage? Or are they all monks and nuns?"

It was well I had mastered myself and learned the power of will, for with a look which formerly would have undone me, she answered:

"Love, as divine man would give meaning to that word, we teach; the love of soul for soul. We have talked upon this great theme before, and what held there holds here. But beware of that love which gives a single thought of self."

As she said this she looked at me with a deep, significant look; and then continued:

"Marriage, as the world gives meaning to that word, we know not. Marriages are not made by man -enacted laws, churches, or any human institutions. Marriage is the harmonious union of two similarly attuned souls for a pure and holy purpose ? soul-development, and the providing of tabernacles for subjective conditioned souls seeking re-embodiment. Marriage, as a means of gratifying sensuous desires and lusts, or to satisfy uncurbed appetites and passions, we abhor. As a true brother I can speak to you with candor upon a subject which ignorance has branded as improper. We hold that the generative organs are most holy and directly related to the divine creative power; and any misuse of them is the most unpardonable of sins. The ancient phallic symbols have been much misunderstood, and superficial minds have been unable to see their sacred meaning. Blinded by a modesty which is only on the surface, the world mistakes ignorance for virtue. Oh, how civilized our savagery which degrades and pollutes these sacred functions!"

For the first time her words ad a tinge of scorn as she continued:

"What is the world to-day but a vast whirlpool of savage lust?

may the savage forgive me for that slander," she added quickly, as though she had used the wrong word. "It is only civilized man with his glossy exterior who perverts these sacred functions ? not even the cattle stoop so low as he. Then what a code of morals governs these relations!" she exclaimed with flashing eyes, which showed that, notwithstanding her usual calmness, she had a heart of fire. "Do you know," she said leaning forward, "that if I was man I would hide my face in shame to demand of woman what he makes no pretense of having ? purity. For shame! For lasting shame that any man should sanction such a code of morals! But woman, heaven pity her blind ignorance! She permits this evil, for she overlooks in man what she never overlooks is woman."

She straightened up in her chair and her hitherto animated face became overspread with an expression of wonderful sadness as she said:

"But passion is blind, deaf and dumb, and heedeth no persuasion; only pain can kill the monster. Blessed be pain!"

"My dear Iole," I said, as she again paused, "if I ever loved you before you can multiply it by infinity now. I concur with you in every word you have said, and I would that all the world would do the same. Now you said that you would obey and be my humble servant; will you?"

She looked at me searchingly and replied:

"Will you be a good master?"

She spoke in a serious tone I did not exactly understand, but I seized the opportunity and said:

"No, but a good husband, my darling Iole."

"You are to be a monk," she answered quickly, with neither a yes nor a no; "and this reminds me that I have not answered that part of your question. We are not all monks and nuns, although many are; but monks and nuns of a peculiar kind as you will learn as you proceed."

She had evaded an answer, but I now asked doggedly:

"And do you really think I ought to be a monk?"

"That is for you alone to decide ? but not here," she added quickly, as I was about to speak; "there is one rule in this degree which I might as well announce to you at once, and that is that every man must choose of his own free will and without advice.

This is one of the most important rules of occultism."

"Well, then, I will have to trust to my own inner voice," I said, at the same time wondering which she would prefer me to be.

"You can find no better guide," she answered, and as though she read my thoughts, continued:

"Never do anything just to please somebody; do it because you think it is right, and remember that the less self there is in any decision, the nearer right it will be."

"But," I answered, "would you make conscience the sole guide in life? Is not conscience relative and very uncertain?" "In all ordinary men conscience must be conjoined with reason; with the initiated conscience and reason are one. Truly, in most men, conscience and reason are relative; but not because of the instruments through or in which they work. Conscience and reason, *per se*, are attributes of the Infinite, and as such are perfect; but they are qualified by the conditions in which they manifest, and therefore appear to be imperfect. A perfect musician can make only imperfect music upon a defective instrument, and likewise God, as conscience and reason, can make only imperfect expressions in imperfect men. The more perfect you are, the more perfect the expressions of your God-like attributes. Most truly did Jesus say, 'Lead the life and you will know the doctrine.' He who leads a pure, unselfish life has a sense peculiarly his own, and the information or knowledge which it brings is incomprehensible to those who do not possess it. Be free from self, for self continually perverts the truth. It is now one o'clock," she added, as she looked at her watch, "and I must leave you for a while. Make yourself at home and I will return for you before long."

As she spoke she arose and left the room, and I with all the authority of a would-be brother or husband, I knew not which, commenced to make myself familiar with my surroundings. In addition to her reception-room, there was a suite of bedchambers and bath and toilet-rooms. These are indeed peculiar monks and nuns, I thought, as I surveyed her elegantly furnished apartments. How can she indulge in such luxury when there is so much poverty and misery in the world? Surely here is an inconsistency.

I now noticed the picture of a remarkably handsome man hanging on the wall near her bed, and instantly the thought came to me, have I sufficiently overcome my lower nature to be above the pangs of jealousy? What if she had another lover, could I surrender or give up to him? Straightening up, I answered my own question with a determined yes. If need be I will give her to another. I turned, and as I did so I beheld myself in a large mirror opposite. I started back; I hardly knew myself. How white my face, possibly made still whiter by the spotless robe I wore. My eyes hone with a brilliant luster, and I remarked ? truly interior improvements bring corresponding results without; a perfect form is a symbol of the God-manifesting attributes within it. Is this not the secret of Grecian art? I returned to the reception-room and was standing before a hitherto-unnoticed picture with Iole's signature in the corner, when she entered. Like all the works of these brothers and sisters, it was a work of art. It was a night scene upon a dismal swamp, and over the dark waters three evil-looking men were rowing in a boat. Between them was a beautiful woman in white, bound like a captive. The dripping trees, murky clouds and flying bats caused me to shiver, and thought of my recent experiences.

"Iole," I said, "where did you get the idea of such a dismal picture?"

"There is a legend connected with that pictures," she answered, as she stopped beside me.

"What is it?" I asked.

"Your recent experiences ought to tell you," she replied, "but I will repeat.

Those three dark and evil-looking men are named passion, Desire, and Avarice; the white-robed woman is the virgin nature in man. The black boat trimmed in red represents the lower nature, which is controlled by the three oarsmen. The swamp represents perdition or the pool of matter. Now the legend says that these three men have time and again drowned this beautiful virgin in the swamp; but, by some miraculous means, she always escapes when they go away. Again and again do they capture her and take her back. Now there are two conclusions to the legend, and people differ as to which is true: Some say that despairing of ever destroying her they put her in a black sack, and tying a large stone to it sunk her in the pool to rise no more. Others say that one night she succeeded in persuading her captors to listen to a song; and while she was singing the full moon came up, and the oarsmen were transformed into angels of Love, Virtue and Mercy, and elected her their queen, and that she took them away to a far-off land where only gods can dwell."

"I see," I said, with admiration, "that all your art has a purpose."

"All true art has," she answered. "Never was there a more powerful and universal teacher than art; and great is the influence we exert in the world through its mysterious language, the meaning of which, while often incomprehensible to the intellect, seldom fails to reach the soul. But, my brother, I have come to conduct you to the hall of choice, the council there awaits you."

As she spoke she opened the door, and having passed through she led the way along the hall.

"Iole," I said, as we walked along the corridor, "how do you reconcile all this palatial magnificence with your claims of humanity, when there is so much poverty and misery in the world?"

"My brother," she replied, "do not be deceived by appearances; the world cannot be saved by money or wealth, however much good it may do in isolated cases. The wealth we have here does not in the least diminish that which we have to use elsewhere." With this remark she smiled significantly, and continued:

"Wealth and luxuries are not to be discarded except by those who cannot master them; while surrounded by wealth, we do not allow it to consume our souls like the avaricious men of earth. We believe n art, in music, in sweet perfumes and beautiful homes; but we do not allow the possession of such to blind us to the fact that everything here on earth is temporary and fleeting. We do not allow any magnificence to separate us from the poor; but we wish and long for the time when they can enjoy with us. Whether wealth is good or evil is determined by the influence it exerts upon the heart and mind. We who have learned to control and keep pure these God-attributes do not allow them to become smothered by a lust after material things, no matter how beautiful they may be. Remember that everything on earth is good in itself, and only its perverse use evil."

"You say, sister, that money and wealth cannot save the

world; what can?"

"A reformation of man, an upbuilding of character, a purification and elevation of mind and heart; no external remedies or superficial palliations will do it. Everything objective is the outcome of that which is subjective. To change the visible you must change the invisible; and this can be done only through mind and heart."

"But," I interjected, "cannot the invisible be changed by the visible? Will not the proper environment bring about this much - desired internal state?"

"To a certain extent, yes:" she answered. "The objective and subjective mutually interact upon each other; but the great power is in the subjective, for the mind and will have power superior to environment, and it is a pernicious teaching to say that they have not. There can be no changes in environment without changes first occurring in the minds and hearts of the people; they both go together. Man, if he only will, can, even in the most antagonistical environment, rise above al external influences; and this is one of the greatest and most important teachings of occultism. All occultists believe in the omnipotence of that God-power, will."

"Do you believe in free-will?" I asked.

"That is a word much misunderstood," she answered. "Man is influenced both internally and externally in every at he dose, and, therefore, he is not absolutely free, but nevertheless, he has the power to choose, and this power is superior to all influences."

"But are there no exceptions to this? Have not some people sunk so low that they have lost this power?"

"There are," she said sadly; "the lost soul has no will of his own, but only the will of his demon self which feeds on desire and passion; to this monster he has surrendered his will, and he must obey its orders. But," she added as though to brighten this last sad statement, "as long as that small green thread connects the pyramid and the cube, so long has he the power to rise."

With these words we turned down a cross-hall and stopped before a robed brother seated in front of a door.

"The cock crows," said Iole.

"The dawn approaches," answered the brother, and he opened the door and we passed through. We entered a room finished in white and gold, and found ourselves in the presence of seven white-robed figures seated around a large table of the same pure color. The features of all were unconcealed, and at the head of the table I recognized the king of the morning. The three at his right were men, the one next him being he who had represented the sun. The three at his left were women, and she who had represented Luna likewise sat next the king. Two vacant seats were at the end of the table opposite the king, and at his motion we took them side by side.

"What does the sister say?" asked the king, and all eyes immediately became fastened upon me, "the unseen intelligences, who rule the apparent accidents of life, have spoken through the mystic language of numbers and say that you are worthy to become a candidate for the exalted 'Third Degree.' Few men are so found in the world; of all her fifteen hundred millions not a thousand such exist. This does not mean that you are exalted above all others, but that you have the possibilities that will make you great, and that these can be unfolded in one life. In other words, though you know it now, you were a student of occultism in lives gone by. Now, brother, do you earnestly wish to enter the path that leas to this higher degree?"

"I do," I answered, in a clear, firm voice.

"Remember, brother, we do not advise you to take this step, neither do we urge you not to as has been done before. All who reach this degree are considered as having enough wisdom to decide for themselves. You understand?" "I do," I answered.

"Then let there be no secrets here. We know from the colors visible to clairvoyant sight that you and our sister Iole are of the same vibratory key; your auras blend without discordant measure; she is perfectly attuned to you, and you likewise to her. This shows that you are sympathetic souls and explains your love for one another."

Iole pressed my hand under the table, and I returned the clasp as the king continued:

"Your love has been perfectly evident to us, for we have likewise loved; and love is no mystery those who have truly loved.

"Now two paths lie before you, and this is the hall of choice; do not choose hastily; if desired we give you time for due consideration.

"The first route is known as 'virgin husband.' By this route you take our beloved sister in the holy bonds of marriage." I clasped Iole's hand, but received no clasp in answer. "Your souls attuned to one harmonious chord give nature's parental joys. Pure parents, with minds informed, have children like themselves, and a boy and girl will bless your home, teach you the beauties of parental love, spiritualize your souls and take your places in the world when you pass on. When they are thus prepared to take your places, when you have reared them in a life of love and done all within your power to help unfold their inner strength and fit them for a life of duty, you will both be called and admitted into the exalted ranks to which you now aspire." For a moment he paused, and then in the same low but earnest voice continued:

"The second route is that called 'Virgin Lover.'" Again I clasped Iole's hand, but still received no answer. "On this route there is no marriage except that pure and most exalted union of soul with soul without a single thought of body ? a marriage the meaning of which the impure world know not.

"On this route you pass through quick and awful trials of seven years' duration, when, if you both have persevered, it will be thy privilege to pass on. Seven years will consummate an entire change within thy body, and all the atomic particles that make it will be replaced by purer ones impressed with the aspirations which characterize your higher life. Now if you take this second route, this council is your master and its orders are your laws; for we but represent a higher council, and during your seven years' probation our commands must be obeyed. Consider well. The first route gives you a loving wife, a happy home and sweet-faced children playing on your knees or romping with you and your darling Iole in fields of flowers. Picture to yourself this home of sunshine, heart and joy, where life is an almost constant caress of your loving wife, and where beautiful children kiss your smiles and nestle in your arms. Listen to the music of their laughter as it mingles with the songs of birds; listen to the prattle of their infant speech. In fancy garland yourself and those you love with fragrant flowers, inhale their sweet perfumes and enjoy all that nature's spirit power has made beautiful and good."

Again he paused as though to give me time to dwell in rapture on the scene, for his words had a magic power; and as he spoke a mirage-like panorama filled my mind. Then, when my heart had reached the highest pitch of parental love, he continued in a voice intensely serious:

"But remember that all this must end, for everything on earth is limited by time. Recall the words of Jesus, our Great Brother, when he said, he that forsaketh not cannot be my disciple. If you would pass beyond time's limitations you must sacrifice all these. Mistake not, this is not a rule to be given to the world; we speak to you alone as one who would elect himself a member of the 'Third Degree.' Men of the world can have no higher aspiration than a home. A pure and beautiful home is the most sacred thing on earth, highest ideal upon which the noblest of the world can set their hears, the greatest power to purify men's souls and bring them to God, the grandest temple in which the human heart can offer up its aspirations to an infinite and all-pervading Love. And we, as an organized body, are working with all our power and might to make this world a world of homes and fill it with love, happiness and peace. But there must be a few great souls to labor in a higher sphere; and these, the Great Elect, must renounce even the purest happiness of earth, until through the influence they exert on men they have brought the universal consummation, perfection on earth. Brothers of the 'Third Degree' make this great renunciation. Humanity becomes their family, all men their children, and no earthly joys will they accept until all men can share them. But let not our speech determine your choice; both sides you now know. While more effective and mighty work can be accomplished in the path of renunciation, much and great work can be done in the path of parental love." Again he paused as though to emphasize his words, and then continued:

"You can choose now or after seven days; do naught in haste. If you choose the path of 'virgin husband' you take your sister Iole as your loving life; if you choose the path of virgin lover you must love each other through the Universal, and an hour may see you severed in the world of forms. In the first path you are both bound together in this world, in the second, apparently separated, but united in the Universal Soul. And that you may know the nature of possible orders if you choose the second path, know that the end of a great cycle draweth nigh. A ferment which has long been gathering in the world of mind will soon break forth; even now it has broken forth in the East, and war is threatening in the West. Before this century ends, kings and rulers, principalities and powers will rise and in violence fall. Ah! A dark cloud impends; the invisible is threatening and awful! War, pestilence, famine and conflagration will ere long expiate the accumulated Karma of the ages. When these times come we will guide and work unseen, and bring to the appointed end the decrees of retribution. In these labors we need men and women who have no fears, to whom life is eternal and indestructible, and self is not. Such must be free from all personal ties and such are the brothers of the 'Third Degree,' and their disciples on the second path."

He paused and, as a moment's death-like stillness reigned all eyes were turned on me; then in a slow -measured voice he asked: "Aspirant for the 'Third Degree' calmly now, do you wish time? Or do you choose now? If now, which path?"

Ah! Which? I asked myself. I clasped Iole's hand, but she gave no sign; her hand was cold and motionless, and with impassive face she sat with a far-away look in her large brown eyes. The king had dwelt long and dispassionately upon each side; it seemed that he had endeavored to make the influences of each equal in power. On the first path I pictured my childhood home with Iole as wife, and I as father.

On the second path was immediate and ceaseless labor on the fields of war and carnage; on the first was a life of love; on the second a life of labor; on the first was Iole my darling wife; on the second, separation!

Ah! It was again a conflict between self and duty. I recalled Iole's words, "Forget self," and casting doubt to the winds and looking Iole in the face, I turned to the king, and in a clear ringing voice replied:

"I choose path the second."

Immediately a single chord of wondrous sound, as from some gigantic instrument, vibrated through the room; a violent tremor seized me; my eyes grew dim; every molecule in my body seemed to be striving to fly away from every other; and with a feeling as though I was being consumed by an internal fire, I lost consciousness and sank into oblivion.

CHAPTER XV.
A HONEYMOON

WHEN I returned to consciousness I was lying in a dimly lighted-room; I felt a pair of warm lips press my forehead and heard the loving voice of my beloved Iole say: "My darling brother, how grand and noble! You did not fail this time ? spirit bless you ? bless us both." She had not discovered my return to consciousness; should I simulate and enjoy her caress? No, now I could enjoy it when awake. "Iole," I said, "I am better now. What is the matter? Was it a weakness for me thus to be overcome?" "Far from it, brother," she replied; "the fact that you only fainted proves that your organism is highly developed and perfected; had it not been so, that key-note which unloosed the terrible powers of sound would have been your death. The next time it will have even less effect, until by and by your form will be pure sound substance. Do you know, brother, that but for the wills which checked it, that note would have shattered the walls of the room? To ordinary men it would have been instant death, not unlike paralysis; it kills and not a drop of blood is shed. When you made your choice you took your life in your hands, for no one can enter on the path you chose unless he can pas this test, and he who presumes must die. But you must now rest," she said, as I was about to speak; "go to sleep, and in the morning I will tell you more." Willing to be obedient to her orders I dropped back in my bed, and turning off the light she left the room. When I awoke in the morning the sun was streaming through a large window across the room. Much refreshed I arose, and found myself in a luxuriously furnished private apartment. On a chair at my bedside was a suit of dark blue, broadcloth clothes, and lying upon them a note, which read as follows:

"When ready for breakfast push the button twice; dress like a gentleman of the world. ? Iole."

"Whoever furnished these clothes knows my tastes, and that I am a crank on colors," I remarked, as I put on the elegant silk underwear, azure blue in color, and the immaculate white shirt with black and white interlaced triangles for studs and Chaldean swastika crosses for cuff-buttons. "They have even furnished my little black tie," I exclaimed, as my favorite bow came to view, "and this coat fits as though made to order." Not even the shoes had been neglected, which, finely polished, were near the chair. Having adjusted my toilet to my satisfaction before the glass, I rang the bell. "Even a watch and chain," I remarked as I read the time of the day.

In a few moments a side-door opened and Iole appeared with a smile and pleasant "Good morning, brother." Stepping through the door with her I found I was in her reception-room of the day before.

"Have they intruded me into your apartments?" I asked.

"Not without my solicitation," she answered. "Unless you object and think it unbecoming of true modesty, we will, in a certain manner, live together from now on."

"As brother and sister?" I asked.

"As brother and sister," she replied.

"And can I kiss you as a brother?" I ventured, as I viewed her bewitching beauty in her morning wrapper.

"You can," she answered with an affectionate smile.

"How good and kind true brothers and sisters are, and how very, very good are you, my loving sister," I said, as I kissed her.

We now took seats at the table, and she removed the cover which had been thrown over our repast.

"I well teach you some dietetic rules," she said smilingly, as she poured out a glass of crystal water. "The first thing in the morning is a deep inhalation of pure morning air and a drink of God's greatest beverage ? pure water."

"Blessed be the gods of crystal water," I answered, as we took our drinks.

"Next is some genuine nutrition in the substance of a bowl of oatmeal or cracked wheat."

"Why, even our dietetic tastes are the same," I exclaimed, as she poured out the rich cream.

"Which may explain our other similarities," she replied; "the food we eat determines to a wonderful extent the thoughts we think and our habits in general; eat foods which stimulate passions and your life will be one of passion; eat pure foods and you will think pure thoughts and lead a pure life."

"But where is your strength-giving meat?" I asked, feigning surprise at the absence of an article I never used.

"It is in the human slaughter-house called the world, in particular that part called Christendom; it has no place here. Meat gives strength as oil makes a fire ? very hot, but of short duration. If you take enough of it, and your digestive organs can stand the strain of almost constant use, it will keep you going; but never expect to accomplish anything in the line of thought so long as your stomach requires all your life energies. So long as nature grows grains, vegetables, fruits and nuts, there is no need for us to establish a red vibration in our bodies, or to kill a single evolving creature."

"And do you believe, Iole, that animals are evolving men?" I asked, seizing this opportunity to hear her ideas of evolution.

"No, it would be erroneous to so state it. There is an entity in the animal which in time evolves into a human form; an intelligence which has been deeply hidden within that entity then unfolds, and a human form with a mind functioning therein is the result ? in a word, man. But that which in time evolves into man cannot be said to be man until it has so evolved. There is that in man which has been through all the lower kingdoms, even to the mineral; but man, as such, never was in any of them. This is one of the great secrets of occult knowledge; through that, in them, which has been through all kingdoms, men can know all kingdoms; and not only know, but control great portions thereof, and herein is the secret of magic."

"Well, do you believe that mind evolves from forms?" I asked.

"It seems to me," she answered, "that I have already expressed myself upon this subject, but to be clear I will repeat: Mind in itself, as a universal, is altogether separate and distinct from form; but it needs a form or instrument through which to manifest itself to itself; that is, to become self-conscious it had to become an individual, which required a form. Now mark, this does not limit the existence of an individual to a physical body; there may be other forms or bodies, as astral or akasic, even though their shape is different and they are invisible to ordinary eyes. Bear in memory that the brain and all forms and organisms are but instrument was perfected, mistakenly concluded that the instrument caused the mind, when it is really the reverse; mind, working from within, causing the perfection of the instrument. If this were not so of what use would be thought, study or meditation? Realizing this fact, the true student does not study to accumulate a vast store of information, but because by so doing he develops his brain organism and makes it a more perfect instrument for his mind. The progress made him who thinks exceeds beyond all comparison that made him who merely memorizes."

I was about to question again, when she checked me by saying: "Our digestion will be bad if we put all our vital energies in our heads while eating, just as the reverse is true. Everything at its proper time; let us now do our duty to our bodies, we need them for the present in our labors."

The remainder of the meal was spent in more shallow water, and having finished she insisted on a walk among the flowers in the court. I readily consented, and for the next hour we enjoyed the beauties of nature in the court and garden adjoining. Although the natural tendency of our minds was to philosophy, for the time being she would talk only upon less serious topics; and as I wished some general information I took advantage of this opportunity to ask her of my surroundings by saying:

"Iole, may I ask you where I am?"

"Certainly," she answered, "you can ask any questions, and if they are of such a nature that I cannot answer them, I will tell you so. You are at the country chateau of Count Eugene Du Bois, about three hours' rapid drive from Paris."

"And do you know, Iole, that as well as I know you I do not even know your name of nationality?"

"Oh, Iole is good enough," she answered with a smile. "I have had many names in my time, but none suit me better than those of ancient Greece."

"But what is your nationality?" I persisted. "You speak about a dozen languages with equal fluency and I cannot even detect any peculiarity of accent."

"Well, I have tried as much as possible to get over this idea of nationality, and probably I have to some extent succeeded. I believe in but one nation, and that is the whole earth; I believe in but one race, and that is all mankind. When I am in France, I am French; when in England, English; and likewise wherever I am. If you desire something more definite, consider me an Aryan from ancient Aryavarta. Now let that suffice; it is time for us to go to the parlor and get better acquainted with our brothers and sisters. At ten o'clock we must again appear before the king."

As we proceeded along the hall toward the parlor, I asked:

"And who is she to whom you first took me, known as Mme. Petrovna?"

"None but the 'Third Degree' members know; she is a mysterious woman and is here, there and everywhere. She left a few days ago for England, but where she now is no one knows; she is always on hand when wanted."

"And whose place was that which I was ever after unable to locate because of the glamour you threw around me?"

"It is the residence of Count Alexander Nichol sky to which you refer," she answered, with a smile.

"And do you stay there when in Paris?" I asked.

"No, not since Madame left," she answered.

We now entered the parlor where all were gathered together in social converse. Esmeralda was there and greeted me in her old affectionate way, and made me acquainted with her handsome partner, Henric Ulson from Stockholm. Time passed and I was unconscious of its rapid flight, until Iole came and told me it was ten o'clock and the hour for appearing before the king. Two guards were passed before we reached the hall where his room was located, and it was evident he received only those who had reason for seeing him. At last we reached a door before which another guard was sitting. Iole gave the password, but he answered that the master was engaged at present. She then took out her watch, and I saw that it was exactly ten o'clock. Stooping down she whispered something in the guard's ear; he bowed and entered the room, leaving us without. I was about to question, when she pressed her finger to her lips in token of silence. The guard soon returned and we were both admitted to an outer room, the guard telling us to wait until we were called. Taking seats by the window we waited several minutes, when an inner door opened; and as the king appeared and invited us into an inner room, Albarez, the mysterious adept, passed out. I could not be wrong; it was the same tall, cloaked figure I had seen in Mexico, London and the Grand Opera House; but without show of recognition I entered the inner room with Iole. The brother and sister who had represented the sun and moon were seated at the usual table in the center of the room; and, as was the custom, we took seats opposite the king, thus all facing one another.

"Brother and sister," said the king, "you are now both full members of the seventh sub-degree of the fourth degree, and probationary candidates for the exalted 'Third.' Our great degrees approach unity as they go up, and you therefore pass through the Fourth before you enter the 'Third.' Now for at least a year we have no special duty for you to perform, but during that time you must prepare yourselves for the labors which will then fall to your lot. This preparation requires a special course, and must be as follows: You must live together, and attune your beings to such a degree of responsiveness that you can communicate with one another even though thousands of miles apart. With two natures already as responsive as your now are, this should not be difficult to accomplish. The sole secret consists in throwing your minds into the same state of vibration, or condition of ether, at the same time. You must, therefore, be almost constantly together for this period; you must try to think the same thoughts, eat the same kind of food, have the same hours for rising, retiring and meditation; must have no secrets from one another, must love and cherish and never allow a discordant note o come between you ? in a word, you must strive to live as one being. We will need your services at the end of the year; we have looked into the future as so far determined, and know what is coming. Now, to better accomplish the desired end and prepare you for your labor, the council has voted that you live together as man and wife. As such you are entitled to all the privileges of true married life, subject only to the restrictions which your souls impose. During this year of preparation you may also be doing a certain labor. We desire that you form a personal and intimate acquaintance with our most prominent and advanced members of the different European as soon as possible. Call it a honeymoon tour if you so desire," he interpolated with a smile. "When can you start?"

As he asked this question I looked at Iole, and she answered: "To-morrow, Master."

"Very well; you must first proceed to Berlin, then to St. Petersburg, Moscow, Vienna, Constantinople and Rome; and I will prepare you letters for these places. You will communicate the secret password, Iole?"

"I will, Master," she replied.

"Then you may go and prepare for your departure; you are now man and wife by the sacred ties of our Brotherhood."

"We witness," said the man and woman, who had heretofore been silent; then at a motion of dismissal from the king, we left the room and proceeded to our apartments.

"My darling wife," I said, as I caressed Iole after we had entered.

"I am your wife, and your slightest wish shall be granted," she answered affectionately; "but do you know the rules of the Brotherhood upon this relation?"

"Not all. What are they, dear?"

"That I am your wife only as your equal, have equal rights with you in every matter, and am sole owner an possessor of my body."

"I would have received you under no other considerations, and should spurn to marry a woman who would not claim equal rights with me in everything pertaining to that relation," I answered, with conviction of the justness of my answer.

"I know that, my dear," she replied, "but shall we be husband and wife, or 'virgin lovers?' "

"It shall be 'virgin lovers,' " I answered without hesitation, and she clasped her arms around my neck as I sealed the compact with a kiss. The next morning we were ready for our wedding tour.

"I never go encumbered by unnecessary baggage," said Iole, as she pointed to her small leather trunk; "if necessary a grip will answer."

"Evidently no part of your education has been neglected," I answered in admiration, recalling the luggage of the ordinary bride.

"The Master wishes to see you," said the Hindu waiter, after he had served our breakfast.

"Then we will go immediately," answered Iole, leading the way to his part of the building. This time the guard admitted us without question, and we passed into the room of the king. He was alone, and as we entered he drew forth from his robe a packet of letters.

"These," he said, "will introduce you to the imperators of the different capital groups; they are written in hieroglyphs which Iole will teach you the meaning of, and which only the initiated can understand. But even though this is the case, under no circumstances allow them to be taken from you, as anything written in this manner now will excite suspicion and lead to trouble. The first letter is to the imperial physician at the court of Berlin, the second to the body surgeon of the Czar, the third to Nicholas Penousky, Governor of Moscow; then there are letters to the minister of war at Vienna, the physician of the king of Italy, and a high official at the Vatican. You see that while we are comparatively small with regard to numbers we make up in quality, and have powerful members scattered far and wide throughout the world; but back of these, unseen, there is a force against which no majority can prevail, and the next cataclysm of Europe will not be a thing of chance."

As he spoke these deeply significant words he handed me a peculiarly torn card covered with signatures, only about half of which remained, saying:

"Should any one, at any time, present to you the missing portion of this card, obey him as a member of the higher council and give him your full confidence." Then handing me another paper he said:

"Here is a check on the Bank of France for frs.500, 000, signed by Alphonso Colono. You can get him to endorse it and the full amount will be at your disposal," he said, smiling. "We are much obliged for your kind contribution to our cause, but we have no urgent need. Some even say that, if we chose, we could pay the national debts of the world in a fortnight. However true this may be, we have no need for your money at present. The other paper we destroyed; you are now at liberty to depart. Adhere strictly to the rules given, observe well all localities, and learn all information and things which may be helpful in the future. There are certain rules in regard to correspondence from time to time with me, but Iole will inform you concerning them. You may now start on your journey—the Protection powers of the Brotherhood go with you." He bowed and we departed.

A half hour later a carriage was announced, and with my satchel and Iole's small trunk on top, we were soon rolling rapidly away toward Paris. Thus commenced our peculiar wedding tour.

Nearly a year passed by, a year of happiness and study. Iole and I had become as one being; our tastes were similar, our desires and aspirations all alike, or tending to the same end, and a more harmonious union could not be pictured.

We had visited nearly all the important capitals of Europe, and had become acquainted with the members of the different lodges who, like those of Paris, represented the most refined and intellectual people of their respective countries. The political condition of the Continent was anything but quiet; there was an almost universal uprising of a revolutionary nature among the discontented masses, and governmental circles were in a ferment. Upon all these subjects we had to keep informed, but nothing interfered with our prescribed course of training. All this time we lived as "virgin lovers"; and while married before the law and so considered by society, were as brother and sister. The king and his council had given full sanction to the sex relation, neither the laws of nature nor man forbade, and I knew that my slightest wish would not be refused by Iole; yet, notwithstanding all this, I refrained. This was one of my most triumphant victories over the King of Evil; for, in the words of Buddha, "Nothing is more difficult than to refrain when nothing hinders." Temptation has no power upon the moral man when he knows that by yielding to it he will violate a moral law. But here, without pride or vanity, I say naught restrained except the ideal of and aspiration for a purer love, higher life and knowledge; but these are powers the potency of which few realize. He who has a pure ideal constantly before him, or in his mind, will not be led astray by things debasing; and a mind absorbed in an earnest quest for truth and knowledge will not find time for impure thoughts.

We had left Rome and were spending the beautiful month of May near Florence, at the suburban villa of Seg. Parodi, the head of the Florentine group. One beautiful day Iole and I had been visiting the places of interest in the city; we had been through the great cathedral, spent several hours at the Loggia, and studied with delight the many wonderful paintings of the Pitti Palace.

About three o'clock in the afternoon we started on our return to the villa; having reached the top the ridge near the suburbs of the city, we stopped our carriage and gazed back upon the grand panorama spread out before us. It was such a day as only Italy can boast of, and I shall always recall it with pleasure. Above, the blue Italian sky with here and there a fleecy cloud painted in rainbow hues; below a vast sea of roofs, and far above them the tower of the Palazzo, Giotto's campanile, and Brunelleschi's dome.

"And this is where Dante walked the streets and with meditating mind muttered the words of hi 'Inferno,' " I said, as my mind recurred to that little understood writer.

"Yes," replied Iole, "and do you know that his 'Inferno' is one of the most masterful allegorical descriptions of hell that was ever written?"

"Yes, when correctly understood," I replied, "but what is your idea of hell, Iole?"

"Hell," she replied, "is a state of conscience mind, or body; or a condition of consciousness caused by these states, either separately or together."

"Then you do not consider it to be a place?"

"Not in the ordinary sense of the word," she replied; "hell cannot be geographically located either on earth or in the starry depths of space. To explain further, hell is suffered on two planes, the material and the astral. The earth represents the material plane, and on it we suffer for evil physical acts and the mental acts which are indissolubly linked thereto; therefore, in one sense, earth is hell. But after earth life we enter the astral plane and suffer from the disintegration of an astral body, built up by passions and desires during the life just passed. All punishments are suffered on the planes in which the causes that produced them operated. Punishments are the effects of evil or wrong acts, and not the imposed penalties of an extraneous God."

"But may I ask where this astral plane you speak of is?"

"Astral matter in its pristine purity is everywhere; but that particular condition to which I refer pervades and surrounds the earth. As on earth there are great vortices of suffering and pain, so, likewise, are there vortices of misery in the astral substance; and in this sense only can the word place be applied to hell. When you die your astral self will be attracted to some vortex where the conditions exist which are most similar to its nature, just as on earth we are drawn to particular communities; but with this difference: On earth we can, if we will, leave any community, no matter how strong the attraction; but in the astral world man's will has left him for the time being, and he gravitates to where his passions and desires take him."

"And what is your idea of heaven?" I asked.

"Heaven," sh e replied, "is also a state or condition of consciousness, but its invisible plane is more properly called akasa than astral."

"When a man dies, then, he does not fly off to some remote star like Alcyone or Arcturus?"

"He does not; his spirit simply sinks into the akasic essence which fills all space. Verily 'the kingdom of heaven is within you,' and in more senses than one."

As she spoke we both turned, as by a common impulse, and saw a closed carriage rapidly approaching. Its occupant could not be seen, but as it went rapidly by Iole turned to me and asked: "Did you hear anything?"

"Yes;" she checked me as I was about to speak, and said, "Write it out."

As she spoke, she wrote on a piece of paper, and doing likewise we exchanged. Both and written the same words —"Report at once."

Not a vocal sound had been heard, but both had heard the same command coming as from the inner throat.

"A high degree brother is in that cab, and we must report at once," said Iole, as we followed in its wake.

We were but a short distance behind when it drew up at Seg. Parodi's villa, and saw a tall man with a long indigo-colored cape get out and proceed quickly up the path as the carriage turned and passed us on its way back to the city.

"That was certainly Albarez," I said to Iole, "and I expect our honeymoon is over and he is here to call us to our labors."

"Well, this life is duty and we must not neglect it," she replied quietly.

"Duty is our law," I replied firmly, as we turned into the lawn.

"And the doing of our duty brings us the highest happiness," she answered; "no matter how far apart we may be in the body, we are from now on always together in the great Soul."

We had hardly entered the front hall when the stranger, who was indeed Albarez, and who observed no ceremonies, met us and without a word motioned us to follow him into the parlor. Having closed the door with the usual caution of all members, he said:

"It is hardly necessary for me to produce the duplicate half of your cards or proceed to the formalities of passwords, as you both know me by sight. You are both to report immediately at Paris. Europe will be in a conflagration in a week. A train leaves Florence at nine o'clock to-night; you have four hours in which to meet it. You know your duty. Now find Seg. Parodi and tell him Albarez awaits him in his parlor." Knowing that Albarez would never talk except when necessary, we proceeded without a word to our respective duties, Iole going to our apartments to pack her trunk, and I in search of Seg. Parodi.

Two hours later we saw the adept and Seg. Parodi mount two of the latter's swiftest horses and ride away towards the hills. Not another word of instruction had been given, but nine o'clock found us boarding the cars for Paris, and in a few minutes we were thundering away toward the French metropolis. Looking out the car-window, while stopping at Milan, I saw a man dressed almost exactly like Albarez board the train. He stepped on the platform of our car, and as I turned he entered and approached us. There was vacant seat just in front, and as he took it he very furtively made the sign of the seventh degree. We answered and he gave the password; then as we whispered the challenge and he answered, we knew he had important business with us. Looking cautiously, but with apparent carelessness around, he drew a small package from his coat, and handing it to me whispered: "Give that to King Eral, and under no circumstances let any one gain possession of it. If cornered, pull the discharge cord." Then without another word he walked through the coach and left the train. We saw him pass through the crowd outside and disappear around the depot just as the train commenced to move. All went well and we were approaching the French line, when a number of men dressed as soldiers entered the car. Scarcely had they entered the door when Iole whispered:

"Give me that package —quick!"

Without a word I obeyed. "Don't know me," she whispered, and immediately got up and went to the far end of the car. Wondering what could be the meaning of her action, I kept my seat and looked out the car-window. The men approached, carefully scrutinizing every one they passed, and strange to say, while no such word was spoken, I could hear from within in constant repetition the word —spy! Spy! Spy!

Reaching my seat a satisfied look came over the face of the leader and he ordered, "Stand up!"

"By whose orders?" I asked with dignity.

"By orders of His Majesty, the King of Italy," he answered, loftily.

"And what for?" I persisted.

"For a spy with secret documents," he answered, as his men commenced to feel and search my clothes. Iole by some strange power had divined their intentions, by clairvoyant sight had seen their thoughts, as it were. Would they search her also? Would I escape but to see her suffer? "Strange," said the leader, when they were unable to find what they expected: "where is the woman?" "There is his companion," said a passenger, pointing to Iole. "Search her," commanded the leader. A feeling of fear stole over me, but recalling the rules to never fear I became calmly indifferent, and accompanied them to where Iole was seated.

"You have been misinformed or made a mistake," I said, as we reached her.

"We will soon see," he answered grimly.

Iole was as calm as any one could be. "Oh," she said pleasantly, "you take us for spies, do you? Well, you are wrong; search me if you please."

"We must have been misinformed," said the leader, but with a suspicious look as the search was completed and nothing found. Our grips and seats were ransacked but no discoveries made; even Iole's checked trunk was searched, but nothing to awaken suspicion found; indeed, our baggage was of such a nature that it would allay suspicion. "Well, we have been misinformed," repeated the leader, as he and his men left the car at the frontier and we continued on our journey.

"Where is the package, Iole?" I asked, when they had gone and were safe in France.

"It is safe," she answered briefly, and I questioned no further; but at her solicitation we seated ourselves in the rear of he coach.

No other incidents happened. Arriving in Paris she arose, and in a manner that would not attract attention, reached down into the coal in the fuel box and drew forth the entrusted package. Putting it in the inner folds of her garments, she said:

"We must ever be on the alert from now on, and never, not even under the most trying circumstances, loss our self-possession. Now let me hear you pledge that you will never by sign or action, reveal a secret through rear or pain that may be brought to me."

"I pledge," I answered, as we got off at the station.

As though our arrival was known in advance a special carriage met us, and we were driven immediately to the residence of Count Nicholsky.

I had not passed beneath the little Cupid and his chained tiger for some time, and as we now saw him again, still standing on his golden egg, I recalled to Iole our first meeting.

"Yes," she said, "that time our victorious Cupid was a sign of meeting; this time, no doubt, he is a sign of parting. Are you ready and prepared to face any emergency?" she asked, in serious tones, as though she read a dark future.

"Never fear or have a single doubt of me; let come what may, I am ready," I answered, as the carriage drew up in front of the great Corinthian portico. As we got out a tall, cloaked figure, with long golden hair, passed through the entrance.

CHAPTER XVI.
ST. GERMAIN—WAR.

WE entered the parlor and Iole immediately sent the brother who served as usher to notify Count Nicholsky of our arrival. He soon returned with orders for us to report at the council chamber at once. Being familiar with the place, Iole led the way along the same rich hall described before, to a room upon the second floor. A woman dressed in black, not unlike Iole when I first met her, challenged us at the door before which she stopped. Passwords were exchanged and we entered. Around a table in the center of a room finished throughout in azure-blur, sat seven persons whom I soon learned were seven of the most remarkable persons of any age. At the right sat the king whom we knew as Eral, and opposite him the mysterious Madame Petrovna, but with features wonderfully different from those she possessed when I first saw her. Her face was now remarkably white and beautiful, all the harsh lines and wrinkles had disappeared, but her blue eyes still shone with that wonderful light. Beside the king sat two men whom I afterwards learned were Count Nicholsky and Eugene Du Bois. Beside the Madame sat the man whom we had seen enter when we got out of the carriage; he was tall and sparely built, with long golden hair and a light, curly, chestnut beard. This man, whom I knew from his position at the table was the superior of all, had no certain age; his pale, serious face was not marked by a single wrinkle, yet I knew he was not young. His eyes were blue and shone with a fiery luster, and I noticed that his hands throbbed as they rested upon the table. That this personage may be no mystery, I will say that he was the celebrated Count de St. Germain who was a high initiate, and possessed the power of separating his eternal body from the form which dissolves. We took the two vacant seats opposite this great adept, who then motioned for King Eral to speak. "You have a package for me?" said the king. Without a word Iole drew forth the package and handed it across the table. Unwrapping the silk cloth around it, a platinum case came to view, and as the king pressed a concealed spring a lid flew open and a closely-folded paper fell upon the table. The Madame now passed him a bowl which sat near her, and the king immersed the paper in a fluid therein. Taking it from the liquid he spread it out upon the table, moving his hands back and forth over it without touching, all the time breathing upon its surface. In a few seconds a closely-written message commenced to appear upon the heretofore blank paper, and the king read the following message, which gave us the first intimation of the intelligence we carried: "The German-Russian alliance is perfected and all has been signed and sealed. The German forces under Von Kral march at once on Paris by way of Brussels, and the Russians under Neouli strike Vienna. The royal powers of Italy are not yet certain, but the people are with us, and Austria and the German democrats join with France and England. Vivani, commander-in-chief of the Italian army, notwithstanding the King, is with us and will join Maximilian, commander of the Austrians, and check the Russians at Cracow. Let the French meet the Germans near the historic fields of Waterloo and avenge the past. I leave for Berlin this hour.

"SAROY."

Not a sigh of surprise or emotion was discernible on the faces of those around the table as this startling news was read, but all looked intensely serious as Count St. Germain spoke and said:

"Has Careau answered our order to put Napoleon Marleon at the head of the French army?"

"He has. Napoleon takes command to-day and both await our further orders," answered Nicholsky.

"Then tell him to proceed with not less than two hundred thousand men to Waterloo at once. It is again the Latin against the Slav, but this time our cause is right and Rome will win. Russia will destroy the imperial Germans because of this unholy alliance, but not one foot of ground will she gain in Europe. Napoleon II. , Far greater than Napoleon I., will make all Europe outside of Russia one great republic, and Paris shall be its capital."

"Do you speak as Master?" asked the Madame, "is England certain?"

"We will receive a messenger to-day who will bring the news that Albert has abdicated because of wide-spread and dangerous insurrection, and that our man, Oliver G. Harkley, the Radical leader, has been declared protector. The fates decree the triumph of the people, and I speak as one who knows."

The count suddenly stopped, motioned silence, and assumed a fixed and trance-like posture. All remained quiet while he, with rigid features and staring eyes, sat motionless. For fully ten minutes he sat thus, all around the table breathing with suppressed breath in unison. Suddenly be regained his normal state and said:

"A Frenchman, a spy in the employ of the Germans, just arrived at the central station. He is a young man of twenty-seven years, about five feet ten inches in height, sparely built, and with an almost unnoticeable mole under his right eyebrow, a dark, waxed mustache, a smooth chin, and a light-brown suit of clothes. Notify Careau to seize him at once, before he enters No.— on the Rue de Rivoli, whither he is now bound; to be sure and send a man to intercept him, and do not let him destroy certain messages he has in his inner vest pocket. Also tell Careau to watch Gen. Moron and give him plenty of rope; he is a traitor and in league with our enemies, but he must not be arrested yet."

As he finished speaking Count Nicholsky bowed and left the room.

"Now," continued St. Germain, "we need four responsive pairs at once; I have other fields to attend to; can you furnish them from among your western members, or must I go East for them?" Thus speaking he looked at us penetratingly, and turning to Eral asked:

"Cannot this pair make one?"

"We think they can," replied the king.

"Sister, have you severed all the ties which bind you to your royal relatives?" he asked Iole, to my great surprise.

"I have," she answered briefly. Now like a flash the knowledge came to me. Iole and the Princess Louise whom I had seen saved so miraculously in London were one and the same. This explained the striking familiarity of her face when I first met her; the momentary glance I obtained of her, as she sat behind the flying steeds, had impressed her features upon my memory. All these years I had been the brother and companion of a royal princess, but she, in true simplicity, had not made a single show of station or exhibited any signs of pride. While these feelings of admiration were active within me, the count, addressing Iole, continued:

"Then, sister, you must enter the cap of Napoleon Marleon and communicate to him all in formation transmitted by your brother, who must immediately enlist with Von Kral. Not a movement of the enemy must be concealed from him; and we, as the secret powers that make such men great, will see that he lacks no information. Through the communicating power of responsive minds your brother can keep you informed of every movement of the Germans, and this without the delays which traveling spies couriers cannot help but meet."

Then turning to King Eral he said:

"There must be pairs to communicate between the other armies, and, if necessary, one must be at every throne in Europe. Mind will be superior to powder and cannon and all material inventions in this contest. The thrones have laughed at the claims of occultism; before long they will wish they had not. Give the brother and sister the necessary instructions; I have a call from the East."

As he finished speaking he arose and left the room, and Eral addressed us: "Brother and sister, your year has been well spent; your colors show that your minds are one and your souls responsive. You understand the science of mental communication, for you have practiced it for a year: but some additional instructions will be useful to you in the field of labor into which you now enter. Whenever written messages are to be sent, soak the paper upon which they are written in a certain liquor of nitrogen and put them in a platinum case which will be given you; then place therewith a small percussion-cap operated by connection with a cord extending from the box. When captured, as a last resort, destroy the message by pulling the string. But written messages must never be carried or sent when mental messages will answer the purpose, for the latter leave no clue, neither do they excite suspicion. If either of you should wish to communicate with us other than through each other. Or either should be killed, you can use an exceptional method, but only as a last resort. This method is most dangerous and must be used with greatest caution. We will give each of you certain powders, which, if you can find an hour when no one will disturb you,

you can take, and they will enable you to reach some of us, no matter where we are. But never take them when there is the least chance of being disturbed, for death would be the result. One hour will suffice, and this can frequently be obtained in the night. When you separate; you must also set your watches with each other, and never change them as you move from place to place. In this manner you will always be able to concentrate your minds in communication, at the same time little variations can be overcome. Further, as a precaution, you must never know one another — not even in death or torture. By power of will control yourselves. Now, until this evening, you are at liberty; at five o'clock you both leave for Berlin. Go unencumbered by baggage and take separate seats, but in the same coach; and whatever happens do not know each other."

With a wave of the hand he dismissed us, and the council adjourned. Three of the members had not uttered a word, and the mysterious Madame Petrovna had made only one remark; but it was evident from their attention that not a word or act had escaped them. When we left the council-chamber Iole, who was perfectly familiar with the house, led the way to the dinning-room, and with all the authority of a mistress ordered our breakfast. As we ate our meal she said: "My brother, are you fully equal to any emergency?"

"I am," I answered, full confident.

"Then remember that not even imprisonment, death or torture is to lead us to betray our cause or forget our duty." She spoke as though she had a premonition of evil, and I answered with reassurance:

"Nothing that the minds of men can conjure will lead me to betray or neglect my cause or duty." Then by a kind of tacit consent we finished our meal in silence. Having but a short time until my start for Berlin, I took an hour to go to the city. The streets and thoroughfares were thronged with excited multitudes.

Flaming bulletins announced the declarations of war, and in large letters I read that Napoleon Marleon, a captain of artillery, had suddenly and almost without precedent been appointed to the command of the army by Gen.

Careau, minister of war. A Napoleonic fever had seized the

populace, and the city was full of volunteers of every nationality. "Napoleon! Napoleon! Vive le Napoleon! Vive le Napoleon!" rang through the streets. As my carriage was passing through the Place de la Concorde, the crowd became so dense I had to stop. The National Guards, with their new commander at their head, were marching down the boulevard. The stirring strains of the new war-song, "Liberty," full of fire and passion, rose from a hundred bands. Looking at the new Napoleon I saw he was a young man of not over twenty -seven years; he was mounted upon a magnificent white charger and rode with stately carriage. He was slightly taller than his eminent predecessor, his face white and almost bloodless, his thin lips pressed closely together making his mouth look firm, while his deep -set, steel-gray eyes flashed coolly here and there as he viewed the multitude as one born to command. As a gigantic silk banner bearing the white lily of France waved near him, a smile overspread his stern and determined features, and he lifted his plumed hat and bowed. Instantly a great cry arose from many thousand throats and the words, "Vive le Napoleon! Vive la Republique de l'Europe!" echoed and reechoed through the place. The belief in re-incarnation, scattered far and wide by the theosophists and oriental teachers, had now become almost universally accepted throughout the West, and especially in France. Many thought their great Napoleon of Austerlitz had been born once more to avenge the fate of Waterloo, and accomplish that which he had undertaken a century too soon.

The papers were full of startling headings. England had joined with France and was landing two hundred thousand men at Hare under Gen. Nelson. The cry was, "On to Brussels! On to Berlin!" As I drove on I thought, how few saw or were aware of the silent power behind all this tumult and action. The great Powers work unknown, but they do not interfere with the actions of men, but when the time of Karmic retribution comes they help to guide its action.

Thus thinking I returned to the residence of Count Nicholsky. As I entered the front hall the Count de St. Germain met me; no one else was in the hall, and coming up to me he said: "Alphonso Colono, for the next five years all Europe will be bathed in blood and all life will apparently be uncertain; you will have to be in the midst of the conflict, but let me tell you, as one who knows, that neither you nor your sister Iole will suffer injury. Have confidence in what I say; no matter how near death you both may come, you will both be protected and escaped. You both have great duties when this war is over, great heights lie just beyond, and you both shall reach them." As he thus spoke his wonderful eyes looked into min and seemed to read my very soul; without thinking of answering stood in silence as he turned away and was gone. Proceeding to Iole's room we laid out our program, and that evening at five o'clock, with nothing but hand-satchels, we left on the train for the German frontier. Iole was to accompany me to Berlin and return with certain messages from Dr. Rankel, imperial physician, whom I had met a year before and to whom I had letters of confidence. It was through him that King Eral had said I would get my position as body surgeon of Gen. Von Kral. Here I would be right at the center of action and miss no information. The train on which we were passengers was loaded down with troops, proceeding toward the contemplated field of battle; but they did not continue our way long, as they turned off toward Brussels. Thinking all was safe while we were in France, we rode together until we approached the German frontier, when we both adopted the German tongue and took separate seats in a coach for Berlin. Everywhere excitement reigned and everybody was under military surveillance. Notwithstanding my boasted indifference, I felt a little uneasy about Iole as we crossed the line, for she had been instructed with one of the platinum cases containing messages for the Berlin lodge. Feeling sure she would be searched before we crossed the Rhine, I took a stroll to the far end of the car, stopping as I passed her seat and speaking to her in German. She turned away and looked out of the window as though to avoid my advances, but at the same time furtively slipped me a note: Returning to my seat, I read in the cipher-writing of the order the following note:

"I shall be arrested before we cross the Rhine, but there seems to be a purpose in it and things must take their course. According to orders, I will not destroy my messages until the very last; and whatever comes you must make no sign. Remember!

"Iole"

The means by which she had obtained this information in advance was not an entire mystery, for I knew that she had clairvoyant sight. Strange to relate, while not possessing this faculty, I had clairaudient hearing, and could hear, as it were, the unspoken thoughts of those upon whom I concentrated my mind. At the next station a young German entered the coach and seated himself beside me. "I thought you had a companion," was the strange remark with which he familiarly addressed me. Suspicious at once I gripped my thumb, the challenge sign of the seventh degree; but as he did not answer I concluded he was a spy and replied:

"No, I have no companion; what made you think I had?" As I answered, I concentrated my mind upon him to read his thoughts, but found it of no avail. Somewhat puzzled at this failure, and wondering if he had obtained a clue to my membership, I remained silent until he should reply. After some moments' waiting he gave the sign of the sixth degree. I had been informed by Eral that no members lower that the seventh degree were in the secret movement, but I answered his challenge. Now the reason of my inability to read his mind was made clear—sixth degree members all know how to control and guard their thoughts. Having exchanged passwords, he handed me a passport, and we entered into conversation which continued until we reached the Rhine. Here a military detachment entered and demanded passports. What will Iole do? I thought; if she only had my passport she could pass unsearched.

With this idea in mind I started toward her end of the car, but the officers were there first. Knowing better than to make myself known, I took a seat near by.

"Your passport," said the officer in charge, addressing her.

"I have none," she replied.

"Then you cannot cross the Rhine," he answered.

"I must go to Berlin," she responded.

"What is your business there?" he asked, eying her veiled closely.

"That I will report to the proper authorities," she answered, to my surprise.

"Ah! You will? Men, search her," he said, turning to his assistants.

"I request lady searchers," she said, arising with dignity.

"Ah!" said the officer in charge, "you are a spy."

"I am not spy, but I have business in Berlin."

"What is your business?"

She made a sign, and a startled look came over the face of the officer as he leaned toward her, and she whispered something in his ear.

Her communication seemed to turn him wild with glee, and at the same time transform him; tearing her veil from her face he seized her with rough hands, and with a mocking laugh cried: "A spy of the Black Art Brotherhood! Search her! Ha! Ha! One of your insane members turned traitor this morning and gave your Order away. If the idiot had not been suddenly struck by a fit and gone raving mad, we would now know all your nefarious plots." Biting his tongue he suddenly checked himself, as if he had said too much, while at his orders his men seized her roughly. By an almost superhuman effort of my will I restrained myself, as they roughly searched her.

"Look under the seat," commanded the leader, when they found nothing. Her satchel, with its contents, lay upon the floor, and the upholstered seat was taken up in their search, while Iole stood by calmly watching every movement.

"Ah! Here it is," cried one of the men, as he took the platinum box from a small hole cut in the bottom of the seat. Quick as flash, and before they could divine her intention, Iole seized his hand and pulled the cord attached to the box. There was a muffled explosion, the sides of the box bulged out and the lid flew open; but a mass of charred paper and ashes was all that remained.

"The devil!" shouted the leader; "handcuff her and take her in charge." As he spoke another squad of men approached from the other end of the car.

"A dangerous spy," said the new leader, "what kind of a devilish mechanism was that she had to destroy her dispatches?"

"The devil alone knows," replied the first leader; "these French always were in league with sorcerers and those who deal in black art work. Where is your passport?" he suddenly asked, turning to me.

"Here it is," I answered, handing him my pass.

"You talk German, but you don't look it. What is your nationality?" he asked, eying me suspiciously.

"By birth an American, by Sympathies German," I answered boldly.

"Well, you know a winner," he answered gruffly, as he moved on. Iole, with manacled hands, having been led into another coach, I was left alone to my thoughts. Colono, I said to myself, remember the words of St. Germain and be calm and confident. Then I questioned, how did the German who gave me my passport know me? Ah! Now I know, a society sign was on my large seal ring and he had seen it. Should I take it off? No, it had served to my advantage so far, and I would leave it on. But how was I to communicate with the French commander since Iole was in the hands of the Germans? What had Iole said when she whispered to the officer? Had some one betrayed his trust? Had the Masters for protection to their cause struck him with madness? Or had his oath, sealed by a solemn invocation, indeed drawn upon him the destroying spirits he had evoked? Thus thinking, I remained quiet until the train reached Berlin. Acquainted with the city from the year before, I lost no time; and without even waiting to see what was done with Iole, hurried t other residence of Dr. Rankel, determined to tell him at once of the circumstances. The doctor immediately responded to my note by appearing in person and inviting me to his private study. Being a high-degree member I had no hesitancy in telling him everything; and in answer to the questions I put with my account, he said:

"Albarez and Saroy are both in the city, and I will notify them at once, if they have not already learned of her capture. They will do all that can be done, and, under the present circumstances, you know that will be much. As for you, you will proceed without delay to the headquarters of Von Kral; I will provide you with all necessary recommendations and papers from the imperial court.

That night I stayed with Dr. Rankel, and early the next morning he handed me the confidential prison report to the imperial court, with a significant smile, and I read:

TREACHERY OR SORCERY. Yesterday a woman who gave her name as Louise Gray, and who is an English spy in the employ of the French, was captured on the train *en route* for Berlin, with important secret messages to French emissaries here; but when caught she destroyed her messages by some explosive apparatus in the package in which they were carried. She is a bold and daring woman, and the officers brought her, under heavy guard, immediately to the imperial prison, where she was confined in one of the inner and most secure cells with strict order given to place a double guard around her. These precautions were well taken, but proved futile; for last night, in some mysterious manner, she escaped, and no traces can be found of her whereabouts. The only explanation that the prison general can vouchsafe is very weak, and he has been removed

and confined until it can be investigated. He says that about ten o'clock last night, while he, himself, was at the outer entrance, two strangers approached him. One, in a voice which had a strange and irresistible power, ordered him to lead the way to cell No. 93, the one in which the woman was confined. Unable to disobey, he did so, and the other stranger remained at the outer entrance. He has but a dim idea of what followed, but he faintly remembers leading the way to the cell door and opening it, and then accompanying the man and woman back through the corridor, giving some explanations to the hall-guards, he know not what. He was found at the outer entrance an hour before he revived. In the mean time the birds had flown. He swears that he was hypnotized or made a victim of black-art sorcerers, and the guards seem to verify his claims; for three of them were found lying in a room near the outer entrance in the same death -like stupor. All they remember near the entrance; further than this they have nothing to say. Additional weight is lent to their statements and claims. By the revelations of the German occultist, Kroez, who was struck by madness before he could complete his disclosures. This dabbler in the black art said that the Franco-English alliance is backed by an organized band of sorcerers and magicians, who are in league with the devil, and possess supernatural powers. We have never believed much in these claims than our cold reason knows of; anyway, the people are hearing of these things, and lacking information, are becoming fearful and superstitious. Still another link in this chain of evidence is the fact that the woman gave the officers the secret passwords of the German spies, and would have passed through without question but for the revelations of Kroez. All passwords have been changed, and orders issued to seize all who use the old. In the mean time every effort will be made to get at the bottom of this organization; but because of the people, all public information concerning it must be prohibited.

When I had finished reading, Dr. Rankel smiled and said:

"Iole, with Albarez, is now well on her way to the French army, and Saroy has left for Vienna. Poor Kroez as a raving maniac can do no more harm; fearful is the penalty to him who violates his oath when he has invoked the demons of destruction.

Kroez, after twenty -five years of almost constant study without any thing or altruistic motives, had stumbled, as it were, upon one of the great secrets of occultism. The discovery was of course immediately known at the eastern headquarters of the great adepts, but what could they do? Kroez was not pledged, and if left alone without the higher light, so necessary to the right use of his knowledge, would use it for unlawful or evil purposes and become identified with the Black Brotherhood, which really does exist, and thus become a power for evil.

Three courses were open: Death, perpetual guardianship, or adoption. But not even the Masters have a right to take life, while perpetual guardianship would require the constant overshadowing of Kroez to prevent revelations or wrong use of his powers. This would keep the overshadowing Master from his other labors; therefore, only the third course lay open, he would have to be adopted into one of the outer branches of the Great Brotherhood. Some of the most celebrated occultists had thus by their own labor discovered some of the great secrets, had been adopted, and had become tireless and useful workers in the great cause. Then, the chances were that when Kroez became associated with the Masters, and knew that they really existed, he would become a devoted disciple; anyhow, he would be pledged and bound by his invocation, and if under his invocation he violated his pledge, death or madness would follow swiftly upon him. Therefore he was adopted; but his adoption could not wash away the unexhausted Karma in his nature. Instead of controlling his nature, and through pain and suffering allowing the evil to exhaust itself, as one of the most celebrated occultists of the nineteenth century had done, he allowed it to master him and violated his pledge. The result was swift and inevitable; he was not struck by Masters, but by the elemental powers he had evoked when he violated his pledge. He lost his soul; while, if he had adhered to the Masters, he would have been united with his God.

"You will join the division which leaves the city this morning on its way to join Von Kral; when you arrive go immediately to his headquarters and present these papers."

He handed me a package of papers and continued:

"When he sees these he will give you his full confidence, and signed as they are, you will be his most intimate companion. I also give you a clairvoyant analysis of the constitution of Von Kral, and the number of his organism, so that you can, if necessary, read or even influence all his thoughts. Further, since the treachery of Kroez, all the passwords of our order have been changed; I will give these to you as communicated to me by Albarez and Saroy. In the future answer no signs of the sixth degree, as they are not in our movement other than as individuals; member s there follow their own inclinations, but we are bound together as a unit. Now you can go. Report at division headquarters, and when you have joined Von Kral, keep Iole informed of his every movement."

When the doctor had finished I shook his hand, and having carefully placed away my papers, proceeded to division headquarters. With the letters in my possession I found a ready admittance to the immediate company of the general, and was soon *en route* towards the field of action. That night we camped in a village not far from Berlin, and I determined to try and have a mental communication with Iole. Ten and five o'clock at night were the two fixed hours we had agreed upon for lengthy communications, but every hour throughout the day we were to call each other, so that no demand for special communications as yet, I retired between my blankets and patiently waited for the hour of ten. At last it came, and assuming a restful position I concentrated all my mental energies upon my sister, at the same time sounding our keynote. My efforts were not without result; she answered. An astral current commenced to throb through my temples and pervade my brain, then came the words:

"All is well; Saroy has left for Vienna, and Albarez and I are hastening on toward Brussels. I am a peasant girl on a crowded train and the conditions are not the best; therefore, if you have no special information, be content with the knowledge that all is well and we will communicate tomorrow."

"Very well, my dear sister, all is well; good spirits overshadow thee. Good-night."

"We will meet in dreamland within the hour; goodnight," she answered. As the current ceased to flow through my temples, I sank back to sleep.

CHAPTER XVII.
NAPOLEON THE GREAT.

TWO weeks passed; two weeks of rapid marching and concentrating forces, and we were upon the historic field of Waterloo. I was body surgeon to the German commander-in-chief, Gen. Von Kral, who now commanded four hundred thousand men. All was discipline and the most expert training present everywhere. For a week Iole had communicated with me regularly every night, from the secret council tents of the new Napoleon. The hostile armies now lay facing each other, and the next day would, without doubt, witness such carnage and destruction of life as the world had never seen. Ten o'clock was approaching, and having read the German general's thoughts throughout the day, I had important information to communicate. To my great satisfaction I had suddenly developed, or become possessed of the faculty of clairvoyant sight, and could see the mental images of the general as he thought.

Ten o'clock struck and I assumed a passive and restful position between my covers. Hardly had I became silent when a voice as though from my inner throat said, "All is well."

"All is well," spoke my mind in answer. "Then communicate first," came back the response. Feeling the current flowing from me, and knowing, therefore, she was passive, I became the active end and spoke mentally as follows: "Von Kral will strike tomorrow unless the totally unexpected happens—here is his plan:

"He will repeat the field of Marathon; advancing with a weak center, cloaked by apparent strength, he will mass his men upon the flanks. He will let Napoleon pierce him but to let him fall into a deep ditch, not unlike the sunken road of Waterloo, now dug across his rear. Behind this ditch he has a jaggy fence, and this he calls his trap. As the French pass through the center, he will close upon them on the sides and rear and annihilate the whole; no quarter will be given; he means extermination. All told, his force is four hundred thousand strong, and he will himself command the right while Frensterine leads the left. If not prepared to meet this strategy, but give the word, and an eastern potion will be more powerful than all the guns of war."

Finishing thus I became passive, the current reversed and the following answer came:

"We employ no such means; these men are but the instruments of Karma, and we as agents of the Masters cannot annul the dues men and nations have by their evil acts brought upon themselves. We can but control, guide and keep within its proper limits, and bring to its appointed end this awful whirlpool of Karmic retribution. What men and nations sow, that they are bound to reap; and neither Gods nor Masters can annul or set aside the law. When the hour arrives that marks the limits of this retribution, then if these men persist and defy our order, we may act, because the ends then justify the means. But no such methods must be pursued until permit is given by those who know the limits, so say Eral and St. Germain. Now I report to Napoleon at once; be ready to receive an answering report at twelve."

The circuit broke and I sank off to sleep with will set to awake at twelve. At the appointed time I awoke and felt a current as before.

"All is well," came the call.

"All is well," I answered.

"Napoleon is a peculiar man; he seems passionless and impenetrable; but he cannot escape the inner eye which can see and interpret his very thoughts. He received my communication in rapt attention; his white cheeks flushed a faint re; his lips became more firmly set; his eyes filled with a burning flame, but he said nothing. He then looked at me with admiration in his eyes, and questioned me of my powers; but I refused to speak of them, and he knew better than to insist. Strange as it may seem, he is no brother, but he knows of the Brotherhood's existence and realizes that its members possess great and abnormal powers. He says little, but I know he realizes that his strength is not all his own, and we, his human instruments, are not his only aids. His intuition does not deceive him, for he is overshadowed by the invisible Masters and is dimly conscious of it. Now I give you his plan as I saw it form in the mental substance agitated by his mind. He will form a powerful center, and of it himself take charge. Likewise two powerful flanks, with a thin veil between them and the center, through which the enemy may rush. The flanks will not advance, but the veils and center will, but only so far, when the two sides of the enter will face about, and back to back, meet the enemy on right and left. When the Germans have pierced the veils, our center will wheel with one accord and present a solid front; the flanks will close in upon their sides and in a U they will perish; no quarter will be given. Your safety rests with the higher powers, but they will see to it or tell you what to do. Rest calmly now, good-night; we will communicate again at five."

"Good-night," I answered, and again the link was broken.

For some time I lay lost in thought, thinking of the weeping widows, orphan children and desolated homes this war would cause; thinking of the maimed, crippled and misborn children who always follow this cruel and wholesale butchery called war. Oh! Why will men persist in the evil and injustice which brings this slaughter?

Why will men be led by selfish leaders to thus, without reason, kill their fellow man? Why cannot brotherhood reign throughout the world and fill it with peace and love/ why cannot homes and holidays replace forts and battlefields? Then my thoughts turned to religion, and I queried, —how can men who believe in a great, omnipotent God-King justify his silent permission of this bloody carnage? A hundred thousand widows protest again it; four hundred thousand orphan children add their cries. Then I turned to philosophy. No, said I to myself, whatsoever men or nations sow, that they must also reap. The law of cause and effect is eternal and immutable, and not even God Himself can set aside or destroy his law without his self-destruction. As long as men sow seeds which sprout in war, so long must wars continue. The consequences which follow evil thoughts and acts cannot be forgiven, and it is only through suffering that they can be expiated and exhausted. O, may this awful massacre consume all the germs of evil! O, may the cloud of evil vapors which now o'erhangs the world be dispersed, and a spiritual light fill the hearts of men with peace and love! Then I thought of Jesus, the meek and lowly Nazarene, and muttered: where is war? Not amid the teeming millions of the East unless stirred up by western intrigues. Not among the heathens of the Orient. No; but among the so-called Christian nations who blaspheme by their acts the name they steal. At last I fell asleep and dreamed of the coming battle. Spread out before me were all the armed hosts, but what attracted my attention most was not the moving masses of men who trod the earth. No; over the field of battle was a host more fierce and awful. The air was filled with malignant faces on forms half-human, half-monster; their mouths and hands were covered with blood, while their features were frightful to behold. Every form that fell upon the field of conflict was seized upon by a dozen of these blood-sucking vampires, who drank his ebbing blood. The more they drank, the more insatiable became their thirst; until, bathed in human gore, they laughed with demoniacal laughter and fought among themselves. Above this bloody swarm I saw a lesser host of white-robed spirits, who in cal tranquility watched the conflict raging in the red vapors beneath.

Suddenly I was aroused from my sleep, and looking up, to my surprise, found Gen. Von Kral leaning over me. "Colono," he said, "come to my tent at once." Wondering what this midnight visit could mean, I looked at my watch and hurriedly followed. It was half-past four and almost time for another communication with Iole. Reaching his tent, just adjoining mine, he said: "Doctor, I have reasons to believe that my camp is full of spies; I don't know whom to trust, and I have a very important message which must be delivered to the king without delay. In you I have confidence, and you must take it. Go with it as fast as horse can take you to Berlin; or, better, proceed to the nearest station and take a special engine. A horse is without; go at once and lose not a moment's time." As he spoke he handed me a package, and not daring to disobey I hastened to the horse in waiting. Soon I was beyond the pickets and flying along the highway. Knowing it must be near five o'clock I drew up for a moment near a narrow strip of woods, and striking a match saw by my watch that it was just five minutes to five. I could not fail at this critical moment to communicate with Iole, so I turned into the woods and came to a stop. Jumping from my horse I assumed a restful position against a tree, and centered all my thoughts upon my sister. Almost immediately

I felt the current and the signal cam—"All is well."

"All is well," I answered in mental speech.

"Communicate first," she replied.

"By a sudden and unexpected call, I am on the way to Berlin with a message from Von Kral to the king. I shall not be able to return and cannot keep you informed; have you any advice to give?"

"I will consult Germain, he has just arrived," came back the answer, and the circuit became weak, the current feeble, but did not altogether cease. A few minutes passed when the current commenced to pulsate, and she spoke:

"Is your message sealed?"

"It is," I answered.

"Then hold it to your forehead and I will read," came back her answer.

Doing as she commanded she commenced to read:

"Napoleon will be overthrown to-morrow. Another sun will sink upon subjugated France. Victory is assured and royalty is triumphant. No more will the cry of 'Liberty' ring on Europe's soil. From victory here I proceed on to Paris to destroy and level and plant her ruins in thistles. Send Frederick at once to take his throne and build another capital.

"VON KRAL."

"That is all," she added, "proceed on your way; the powers for your safety made you the bearer of this message. Good-bye."

"Good-bye," I answered, and the circuit broke.

Mounting my horse I turned into the highway and hastened on to Berlin. I reached the capital and delivered my message without loss of time; indeed, my journey was made so quickly that I received the thanks of the king.

And now for two days I had been at the residence of Dr. Rankel, and during all that time had not heard a word from Iole. No response came to my repeated efforts to reach her mind; was anything wrong? Had she been injured? Calming my mind I determined to await developments; but that evening my fears were again aroused, for the startling news reached the city that the French had been overthrown with great slaughter, and Von Kral was pushing on, by forced marches, to Paris. All was excitement;

bands played, and salute after salute was fired throughout the city. Great bonfires lighted the streets and throngs of men and women filled the thoroughfares. Shouts of victory and triumph arose, and the name of Von Kral and the king echoed through the streets.

Was the report true? I asked myself, as I paced restlessly up and down the room. Did this explain why no answer had come from Iole? Had she been killed? Had St. Germain been wrong? Thus questioning and again giving way to doubt, I locked the door and continued pacing up and down my room waiting for the hour of ten to arrive. Determined to hear from the front, I had fully made up my mind to take the powder and communicate with Eral at Paris, if Iole did not answer. I remembered the warning, that death would be the result if disturbed, but felt secure for at least an hour in my present surroundings. Ten o'clock came at last, and taking an easy chair I concentrated all the energies of my mind on Iole, with the desire to speak. Thanks to a strong will and her willingness, she answered. The current commenced to throb in my head, and the words came plain and distinct front within.

"We have been marching day and night, and because of special communications I had to carry on with other parties, had to sever our relations for the time being. When important information and duty does not demand, there in no urgent need of it. I observe from your mental state that you have been under another rest for the last two days. Let me again warn you, never be disturbed or harbor doubt or fear; whatever happens you should take it calmly, and never become restless or give way to emotion. Now hear what has happened. We have overthrown the Germans and almost annihilated them. General Von Kral was killed and the entire army scattered. We are now pushing forward with all speed to Berlin. The reports you hear heralding our defeat are false, and send out for a purpose. Be not deceived, but warn all brothers to leave the city, for we have psychic information that the Germans themselves will destroy it when learn of our approach. Your mother is now a member of our secret council here, and communications to her from your father, who is in the eastern army, say that the Russians are victorious and are pushing toward the south six hundred thousand strong. Maximilian has been killed and Vivani is in command; all depends upon Napoleon, who seems, so far, to be the only fit instrument through whom the invisibles can work. St. Germain has him completely in his power, and gave him secret orders on the day of battle. The plan is now to subjugate all Germany, dethrone the king, and keeping in the country of the enemy, fall upon the Russians. We shall reach Berlin to0morrow night, and our victory will be known there by daylight, to the sorrow of the city. Warn all brothers and join our ranks; this is all tonight; my live, have peace."

The circuit broke and I immediately informed Dr. Rankel, who quickly sent word to all members. We were none too soon, for the sun had not risen over the city before the truth was known. The people, seized with a wild fear, became panic-stricken, and fleeing from the city fired their houses. That night a sea of flames met the triumphant army of Napoleon. The king had flown and with him Dr. Rankel and all royalists. The social democrats, who were the secret allies of the French because of their cry "All Europe one Republic," had tried to save the city, but of no avail. The torch had been applied almost everywhere at once, and before the night was over the city was in ruins. I joined the Napoleonic forces where they were encamped on the edge of the city. The secret council, now containing twelve members, occupied a house surrounded by a double guard, and no one was admitted without an order from one of the members. Proceeding to these quarters I was admitted by means of a letter from Iole, and was soon in her presence. She received me with a kiss and handshake and led me to her apartments. Each member had a separate room, and, while marching, a private carriage, so there should be no interruptions to their mental concentrations.

"Where can I see my mother?" I asked, recalling that she was a member of the council.

"All members are isolated from everybody except their mates, and it will be impossible for you to see even your long-lost mother," she replied. "Then she is your mother in an earthly sense no longer, for she is now a member of the great 'Third Degree.'"

Knowing the occult rules necessary for one to retain his individual, electrical condition, I showed no dissent, for I was convinced that everything the Masters ordered was for the best. That night I had the pleasure of Iole's company until a late hour, and in the morning w e proceeded on our march to the east. Napoleon, on a white charger, took the lead, and behind him came the twelve gilded palace carriages which contained the secret council. On each carriage was a coat-of-arms, and its central character was a five-pointed golden star, which showed that this army was, indeed, under the protection of mighty powers. A guard of officers rode on either side of the vehicles, and each contained only one occupant; but, at the order of Iole, I shared her carriage, which, by special request of Napoleon, was the first in line. To the stirring strains of "Liberty" we marched through the burned city. The Unter den Linden was lined with blackened ruins, and the beauty of yesterday was no more. Early in the march Napoleon rode up to our carriage, and seeing me, eyed me sharply, with what I thought was displeasure. "Ah! Mademoiselle has company," he said.

"Monsieur Colono," replied Iole, introducing me.

In reply he thanked me for my valuable services and complimented me on the possession of such powers and such an excellent companion.

"Give all thanks to the Brotherhood," I replied.

He eyed me keenly, but said nothing in reply; then turning to Iole with a rather tender look for his stern face, he asked:

"Will Mademoiselle allow me to ride with her sometimes when she is not engaged?"

"Ask St. Germain; I am under his rules," she replied, without hesitation.

A dark frown came over his face and he asked:

"And does St. Germain rule?"

"He does," she answered, not over-awed in the least by his clearly-implied superiority.

"Well, we will see," he answered significantly; "I think I rule here." As he spoke he rode to the front and Iole said:

"Will he, too, like his predecessor, be blinded by ambition, and in selfish egotism misuse his opportunity in the world? Does he think that he, himself, is great? No man is great in himself; he only becomes so by expressing the will of many. Only those who realize this are truly great. At this time the great majority of the people want liberty, and if he will but utilize his opportunity and be to the great mass what the head is to the body, his greatness is assured."

"Iole," I answered, not without a certain temporary pang of jealousy, "I believe he is smitten with you."

She looked at me with her larger brown eyes and answered:

"Never allow jealousy to contaminate your heart; keep it pure and good, for only thus will it be a fit place for he dwelling of the divine."

Late in the afternoon an officer handed a note through the window to Iole; passing it to me, I recognized the handwriting of my mother, and opening it read:

"Count de St. Germain, now in the eastern army, orders through father, who has just communicated with me, that you come by the quickest possible route to Vienna. You know your duty; lose no time. YOUR MOTHER-SISTER, NINA."

"Good-bye, Iole," I said, "I am off at once; and whatever happens duty shall be first."

"You are my noble brother," she answered with a smile, as she affectionately kissed me.

Leaving the carriage I sent the note to Napoleon, who, with a questioning look, came back to where I was and asked:

"Who is this Count St. Germain?"

"The King of Occult Adepts," I replied.

"Well, report to him at once, and tell him I say there will be no kings this time next years."

I immediately knew the hidden significance of his remark, but said nothing, and in an hour was hurrying across the country to the southeast. Arriving at the camp of the eastern army I proceeded at once to the isolated quarters of the secret council, where St. Germain met me with his usual stern and serious manner. Taking me into his private apartments he handed me two message he had written. The first read as follows:

"NAPOLEON MARLEON: Do you still hold yourself subject to those who have made you what you are, and whom I represent? Or do you aspire to an empire under the fictitious name of president? Allow not false pride or vain ambition to deceive you in this matter; we have made you what you are, and we can as quickly unmake. We have chosen you as our instrument, and it is our power that now sustains you; we will give you all the glory and fame any man can wish, and you had better serve our ends. We care not for fame or earthly power; we want results alone. We are content to work in secret and unknown if we can but bring the ends desired. Now, as our instrument, you must keep within set limits and be subject to our secret orders. All Europe south of the Baltic and west of the Dnieper must be one free republic, with its capital at Paris. All kings and thrones must go and the people reign. We will elect you first president so long as subject to our orders. Do you accept the compact? Yes or no. Yes, and your star still rises; no, and it sinks. —*Ipse dix*it.

"ST. GERMAIN."

The second message read:

"ALBAREZ: If Napoleon answers no, give him a stroke. —*Nyimayana*. "ST. GERMAIN."

This last message was written upon a peculiar paper, and had a mystic sign colored in the substance thereof.

"Take these forward at once," said St. Germain. "Albarez will be there when you arrive; he knows these orders already, but this message will be his official permit. When Napoleon answers report to him."

Without waiting I hurried back to the French army, now advancing on Warsaw and sweeping everything before it. The German king had made a stand in Poland, and reinforced by two hundred thousand Russians was awaiting battle in front of Warsaw. The English allies under Nelson were bearing to the north to take the Russian capital, while Napoleon, with new recruits, had four hundred thousand men and the enthusiasm which always follows victory. When I arrived and presented my message, instantly a change came over him. Turning to me with fierce sternness, he answered:

"Tell our leader no."

Message and new men from all over France and Europe had intoxicated him with vanity of victory, and he almost thundered the response.

"If I and he," he continued, putting the I first, "can be friends and allies, very well and good; but if we can be such only by my obedience to his orders, then our relations must be severed. I am ruler here."

"That is your official answer?" I asked.

"It is," he answered laconically.

"Very well," I replied, "it shall be so delivered;" and bowing, I was about to retire, when he recalled me.

"What do you know about this brotherhood?" he asked.

"All I know is that they possess powers superior death, and have a knowledge of the future; if they decree your downfall, no power on earth can save you." "And do you know that I have the lives of twelve of your members here?"

"And your life hangs but by a thread," I answered boldly.

He showed no change of countenance, but asked:

"And do they threaten me?"

"Not unless you threaten them," I answered.

"Well, take my answer to your leader and tell him I defy him. I hold his council as hostages to compel his peace, and she you love will be my queen. Go!"

Without a word I repaired to the quarters of the secret council, and was there met by Albarez. Giving him Napoleon's answer I handed him message No. 2. With an impenetrable face he told me to be ready for a call from the commander and not leave camp. That evening Napoleon was stricken with paralysis and I was summoned in haste. Repairing to his room I ordered every one to leave and sent for Albarez. The latter approached the stricken leader, and pressing his hands to his heart and head he returned to consciousness. Then taking a seat by has bedside, the adept calmly watched him. As the wonderful eyes of the adept remained fastened on those of the stricken leader, he turned restlessly and said:

"What does this mean? I am not subject to paralysis; have you, by your black art practices brought this on me?"

"Foolish ma," said the adept, "to thus defy the powers that regulate all destinies."

The fiery eyes of the commander looked at the adept long and intently, but the latter calmly returned his gaze.

"By what right do you claim relationship with God and assume divine prerogatives?" he asked the immovable adept.

"By the right of God enlightenment and thousands of years of work for man," replied the adept.

"Do you know that by my order you and all your members here would be executed in an hour?"

"You cannot give the order; and even if you should be permitted so to do it would never be executed. There are powers present you do not see; but, even though invisible, all your arms could not prevail against them."

"Charlatans make loud pretensions and speak with mysterious hints, but they never show their power," replied Napoleon.

The adept for answer leaned over the recumbent leader and moved his hands above his head. Probably for the first time in his life a startled expression came into his eyes, and he exclaimed:

"Man! What demon powers do you possess?"

"The powers of God," replied the adept, with deep solemnity.

The stricken leader moved restlessly and said:

"If your claims are true I will consider you demands; but can you prove them?"

"Partially," replied the adept.

"Then let me see your proof," said Napoleon.

"Sleep!" commanded the adept, with a sudden of this hand, and instantly the eyes of the future great Napoleon closed in sleep.

"Watch him," said the adept, as the commander commenced to breathe regularly; "when he awakes he will be well, and will change his answer to St. Germain. Tell him I have gone to assist in the ascent of his star, until, in growing splendor, he is proclaimed the Great."

The adept left, and the commander, with deep, regular breathing continued in his sleep for hours. According to orders I admitted no one, and watched him continually. About three o'clock a change came in his breathing; it grew lower and lower until there was no breath at all, and he appeared in a death -like trance.

"Ah!" I said, "he journeys afar;" and knowing the nature of his condition I gave strict orders that there be no noise about the house. In the morning, as his condition still continued, I sent for Iole; and she was present when, an hour later, he recovered. The first expression of consciousness showed a change in his manner. Looking at Iole with a pleasant smile, he said:

"Ah, my sister, I am well again."

All the effects of the stroke had disappeared, and rising he turned to me and said:

"Go at once to St. Germain and tell him all is well; Napoleon is convin ced. You can remain, Mademoiselle, I like your company," he added, addressing Iole as I bowed and left the room.

"Since you have joined St. Germain I am your sister and will not leave you," she replied, as I passed out the door on my way to the eastern army.

Five years passed; but why dwell upon these years of blood and carnage which washed away the accumulated sins of Europe at the beginning of the twentieth century? Suffice it to say that Napoleon, who now displayed greater genius than ever, pushed forward, met and overthrew the German-Russian allies at Warsaw. After three days' bloody fighting the king was killed, the city taken, and Napoleon, completely victorious, annexed Poland to the now proclaimed Republic of Europe. Then turning to the north he was about to follow in the footsteps of Bonaparte and march on Moscow, when, in compliance with St. Germain's secret order, he wheeled to the south, overthrew the Muscovites upon the Dnieper, and proclaimed that river the eastern boundary of the republic. The triumphant general was now called the Great, in order to distinguish him in history from his illustrious predecessor. The monarchial powers, Austria and Italy, who had joined with the Franco-English alliance at first for their own preservation, becoming alarmed at the great chief's growing power turned against him, but all to no avail. The secret order had placed all the commanding generals, and the armies, drawn from the masses, joined with Napoleon to fight for European democracy. Four hundred thousand French and English families were placed in the subjugated states, and the native families removed there from and scattered in homes over Europe. All people without property were given farms, and a wonderful industrial activity se t in. the English people proclaimed a democracy and joined with Europe; and in one great republic extending from the Dnieper and the Hellespont to Ireland's eastern cape, and from the Mediterranean toe the Baltic, liberty was proclaimed. In the cataclysm, while the church was not overthrown, yet the minds of men were changed; she lost her power upon the people, and a philosophical religion sprang up to take its place. Enormous schools were built at Paris, and thousands of wandering philosophers journeyed over the country, teaching without pay or price. Napoleon was proclaimed "liberator" and elected president by the votes of all the states. At the advice of St. Germain, who still kept in the dark, he for diplomatic purposes declined; but the people with one voice demanded his acceptance, and he was inaugurated at Paris during a convocation of all the states. A great parliament of Liberty was formed, and the new century announced by the constitution they proclaimed. In glaring headlines it was scattered over the entire world, while throughout the republic it was posted at every crossroad and corner and proclaimed by orators on the highways.

Thus it read:

PROCLAMATION OF THE TWENTIETH CENTURY.

All men are born free and all nature is their equal heritage; he who seizes more than his equal share must forfeit or render an equivalent.

Occupancy and use shall be the sole and inviolable title to land and all natural things thereon, and neither governments nor men can abrogate or set aside such title.

Taxes shall be levied to equalize all inequalities that spring from special privileges that men have seized, for there must be special privileges to none.

Men, women and children, singly or collectively, shall have the unqualified right to go, do, and act as they please, so long as they injure not their fellow-man or any harmless creature.

All proclaim—liberty, truth, justice, fraternity.

{Witness this THE PARLIAMENT

our seal.} OF EUROPE.

CHAPTER XVIII.
LHASSA.

ALL the time Iole, because of he influence she had acquired over the great chief, had been his almost constant companion. There was no concealing the fact; he was in love with her. I knew this to be the case, but quenching the fires of jealousy resolved to let things take their course. Although I loved her better than all else on earth, I trusted that the fates would give me my dues, and kept her never-to-be-forgotten warning—"to forget self" — constantly in mind.

During the five years of conflict I was now here and now there; now a communicating spy, and now a commander of forces. I had risen to the rank of general and was held in the highest esteem by my army.

Peace having been once more declared I was again at Paris—Paris of the twentieth century; Paris, the capital of the United Republic of Europe; Paris, with her four millions of people and her boulevards and palaces. Two schools, one of art and the other of philosophy, such as the world had never seen, fronted each other upon the Champs Elysee and students thronged their marble porticoes from all parts of the world. Lectures were free, and the long secluded teachers of the Orient discoursed on philosophy, while the Zerol school of mystic artists gave lectures on art. The municipal council decreed that all facades within the city should be of stone or marble, and a new interest in art having come with greater liberty of thought, the twentieth century renaissance made the city a dream of beauty and grandeur.

Once more I was at the palatial residence of Count Nicholsky, a residence whose classical exterior in pure white marble still ranked with the best in the city. There was to be a meeting of the council prior to the departure of St. Germain for the East. The war being over and the crisis which will ever mark the end of the cycle having passed, this mysterious personage had once more concluded to die, as it were, and return to his true station. Gathered around the council-table were the seven whom we had met at the opening of the conflict; but an eighth personage was also present. He was dark-faced, oriental looking man with black, piercing eyes and long black hair and beard. He wore a turban and sat close beside St. Germain, his eyes fixed upon the floor as though to avoid those around. Beside the council a dozen other members were in the chamber, among them my parents, Iole and Esmeralda. The most profound stillness reigned until St. Germain spoke:

"Brothers and sisters," he said, "the Karma of the nineteenth century has been expiated; once more the harvest has been reaped, the palaces adjusted, and inequalities made even. The golden age has been inaugurated, but our duty is not wholly done. The day for the people to rule has at last arrived; the days of kings and emperors are over, only the Muscovite, who has yet a destiny to serve, will for yet a little time be thus ruled. But remember, brothers, that rule by the people can only be successful when they possess intelligence and have true men to lead them. Now it is our place and duty to see that the leaders are not wanting, and the members of our Brotherhood must be ready to hold the places must be theirs, not as a reward for their services or to gratify ambitions, but because they are best fitted to fill them. Not a single place must be obtained by external force, only the powers of heart and mind, working in their proper sphere, must be used for this end. Scattered over the world, our members must by their constant labor for mankind, gain the hearts and minds of every people, and thus in a peaceable manner obtain the right to rule. Keeping the welfare of man in view, the invisible brothers and powers will aid them in their labors, if it only be pure and for the good of all. We have just passed through a great crisis, and I was sent forth to aid and assist you; but the conflict now being over, it is my privilege to retire from your midst and seek once more my wonted occupation. You have competent and worthy leaders, and they will direct you whenever outside directions are necessary; but let each one strive to reach that point where all directions come from within.

"Now, before I depart, I will consider the claims and merits of all applicants for the 'Third Degree;' let all except the council retire and await their call." At this command all except the council and the Oriental left the room. It was the first time Iole and I had been together for months; and as she walked along the hall with me, arm in arm, I asked:

"Iole, my virgin love, what is your aspiration?"

"To accomplish the end for which all souls exist, perfection and enlightenment," she answered with a sweet but serious smile.

"Then our paths still lie together," I replied, as we reached our waiting room. And now for the first time was I allowed to meet my father and mother; both received me with an affectionate kiss, but few words were spoken. Souls that understand each other need no recourse to speech, their thoughts reach each other's minds in silence. Hardly had they kissed my sisters, Iole and Esmeralda, who was also with us, when they were summoned by the council.

They returned no more. In an hour four couples had been called, but we, with Esmeralda and her blonde brother from Scandinavia, were still in waiting. Taking this opportunity, I asked how she and mother had escaped from the storm upon the gulf fourteen years before; and in reply she said:

"Albarez and another brother boarded the steamer just as it was leaving, and when we reached the first island, at their request, we were all landed. As though to conceal the fat, we were landed in a boat some distance from the harbor, and no one learned of our journey Albarez pledged us to secrecy, and in obedience to his orders we never communicated with you and father. I have since learned that it was a test, not unlike those through which you and I have gone. They tried his faith in his elder Brother by apparently taking his beloved wife and daughter to their death. Yet, through all these years he doubted not, and continued faithfully at his work. Truly, we can learn lessons from our noble parents."

"Alphonso Colono and his sister Iole," interrupted the caller, and as we passed out I said:

"Iole, be it life or death, ignominy or fame, all is for mankind."

"Most nobly said, my own true brother; if need be we will tear from our hearts the last thought of each other, and concentrate every thought for the good of man." As she thus spoke we paused for a moment before the door of the council chamber; then clasping hands and kissing each other as though for final separation, we entered.

"Brother and sister," said St. Germain, when we were seated opposite him at the table, "you have asked a high and more exalted privilege; a privilege few beings on earth possess; a privilege which can be given only after many lives of toil and labor for mankind's elevation; you ask for admission into the 'Third Degree.' If, heretofore, your duties have been arduous, in this degree they pass all comprehension and your lives become a ceaseless labor. Mark well this truth, I tell you now in time; this degree, instead of pleasure, bringeth pain, yet a pain that bringeth joy. For here you learn the ecstasy of pain when the result of efforts to bring happiness to others. This is the mystery of the suffering of Christ; this the reward of the Masters of compassion with whom pain, because brought in loving work for others, becomes the source of joy."

He spike in a deep, slow and solemn manner, and looking toward the Oriental who sat close beside him, I observed that his black, piercing eyes were resting searching upon us as St. Germain continued:

"Brother and sister, as you know, our great work is for man; and we therefore labor in every field that will assist in his uplifting. We have much to be done in the world, and you can both find abundant labor in the visible field of action; but if you enter the 'Third Degree' you must leave the world and labor in an altogether different manner. Now which do you chose to do?"

As if moved by a common impulse we both answered with one voice: "That which will make us the most effective instruments, and enable us to do the most good for man."

"Then two fields of action lie open before you; brother, let us first hear your choice. We see our way clear to make you Governor of Italy, in which position you can do much good; and after your term is served we will make you Napoleon's successor a President of Europe. Here, indeed, will your opportunities be vast for good. This is the first path. By the second you become a wandering monk with healing powers, and go teaching men the truths of life. Which do you choose?"

"Can you find others to fill the places of the first?" I asked.

"Our membership, though small, can ever meet all demands," he answered.

"Then let others take these places of fame and power, but let me humbly administer to mankind's wants and be a reliever of their woes. I choose path the second."

Without reply he turned to Iole and said:

"Sister, we have an opportunity for you to do much good, and have a request to ask; this request is not of necessity your lot, and you can, if you desire, refuse it."

"Any requests you may ask are granted in advance," she answered.

"Grant not before you know; what we ask may be more than you expect—so hear. Napoleon has found one worthy of his love; and, as a result, you possess great power an d influence over him. Now, although made great by us, he is no brother, and is selfish in his nature; but if you will be his wife your just and unselfish commands will be his laws. Through him you can do much good, and at the same time can purify and elevate his nature. Will you be his wife?"

Despite my utmost efforts, an agonizing pang tore through my heart; had she conquered all her heart's temptations, overcome all trials and spent her life for naught? Was she to be shut out of the Great Degree and linked to a man to save him? "Ah, God!" I muttered. "All for man!"

"If I can do good and be of benefit to my fellow -creatures, your request is granted and I will be his wife." She answered clearly and firmly, but there was a sad resignation her voice.

"And will you love him?"

"As I love all me," she answered, "but the love that comes to kindred souls it is not within my power to make."

"But all souls are kindred in the universal Soul," he answered.

"Truly, but vibrations make them different. If he should make the number of this soul the same as mine, then I would love, not because I willed it, but because I must; and he likewise would love, because sympathetic souls must from their very nature love."

"Most truly do you speak, my sister," replied the count; "if all men and women would attune their souls to the universal Soul, or the same vibration, all souls would love with purest love; not because they willed it, but because they, by their nature, must."

All this time the piercing eyes of the unknown Oriental had been resting upon s; but now for the first time he spoke, addressing St. Germain:

"This sister shall not marry, not even Marleon; I have other work for her." His voice was clear, yet half-suppressed, and it caused a thrill to run through my body. Evidently, even though half-suppressed, there was some strange power in his speech. St. Germain answered him with a low bow, and turning to Iole said:

"The Master's word is law, and from henceforth you are in his charge." Then turning to me, he said:

"Brother Alphonso, your sister Iole goes to the East; if you persevere and do your chosen duty it will be your privilege to join her later. Her labor from now on shall be through the invisible world of mind and soul. Although apparently separated from the world, she will impress and influence all creatures and men. The great hierarchy have adopted her into their inner lodge, and she leaves you until you have the power to join her; but remember that, though separate in body, you are never apart in soul." He ceased, and at his motion Iole, giving me one long, soul-communicating gaze left the chamber with the Oriental.

"Now, brother," said St. Germain, "you are under the jurisdiction of Eral and the western council, which you see here; meet them to-morrow morning at the chateau of Count Du Bois. Now you may go."

At his motion of dismissal I left the room and proceeded to the Durant mansion. Some time had elapsed since I had been at my old home, and in that time I had learned that the Durants were all twenty -year members, and that Camille was now Madame Callais. She was still at home, however, and welcomed me most cordially. M. Callais being a brother was no stranger, and talked with interest upon his chosen field of medicine. Having spent the day among my old friends and made some arrangements with M. Durant, I left the following morning for the chateau of Count Du Bois. I expected to see Iole no more; but when my carriage drove up was agreeably surprised to meet her at the entrance. Taking my arm she escorted me to our old rooms.

"My dear Cleo," she said, as we embraced again as lovers, "the great Master has given me permission to communicate to you more advanced instructions. The knowledge and powers we have so far possessed are, indeed, insignificant when compared with those that it lies within our power to obtain. In the morning I leave for the East and you for the West. We shall have the earth between us, yet we shall never be apart; for, while heretofore our distant communications have been mental, from now on we shall meet in the astral world. At last I have learned the secret which enables me to leave my physical body and go far away, fully self-conscious in the astral. For years I have been able to thus leave my tenement of flesh, but I could not make my astral carry my mind in full self-consciousness. This I now can do, and so can you, ere long. So while you are in the western world, I will be with you; and as you progress and carry on your labors I will instruct you through the world of mind. In that state called sleep we will every night be close companions; for I will be with you in the West during your day, and you will be with me in the East during min. but not even yet are all test over; our life is full of trials; for only by passing through and overcoming trials can we realize our strength and power.

"Trials and sufferings bring us to a full self-conscious realization of our might and unfold our undiscovered possibilities within. We never know and feel our strength until we are tried. Two years of trials and arduous labor lie before you; then will your seven years of probation have expired. During these years you must labor in America, the land of the ancient Atlanteans, and bring light unto the souls unfolding there. In this work you must go alone, a begging mendicant, without home or wealth; from place to place you must journey, doing good and shedding light. The strength here needed will not be strength of mind and soul; for the people there are deep in the mire of earth and blinded by the lust for power and gold. When they find you do not work for money and seek not gain, their minds, failing to comprehend your actions, will brand you as a fraud; and when you alleviate the misery of the suffering you must suffer as a charlatan, for they know not the powers of occult medicine and will ridicule you as a quack and punish you as a pretender. As a beggar you become a vagrant and subject to their laws of slavery. No matter how much moral or subjective good you do by thought and teaching, you have no visible means of support and cannot justify your actions. But ever persevere, and never lose your faith in truth and duty. Remember that the Protectors are ever around you and you need fear no harm. Amid all these trials and sufferings you will find an inner peace, the joy and ecstasy that comes from a knowledge of duty done. Ask no justification from the world; let your conscience be your justifier. Ask no praise from those around you, let your praise come from within. Mind not the scorn and sneers of the world's deluded ignorant; pity their mistake and continue in your labor. All teachers of the truth must suffer; but this suffering is the fire of sublimation. Slander, misrepresentation, calumny and abuse will be heaped upon you, and you will become the target for every vile tongue; but know that their suffering souls condemn their actions, and pity but heed them not. Let your life be an example for all men to follow, for the example of life is more powerful than all men's teachings. You have chosen the path of renunciation when fame and power were offered you; you have sacrificed your individual love to labor for mankind; your trials will indeed be great but the end is greater. Like the Buddha, you renounced the throne and loving wife to labor for mankind; and, like the Buddha, peace and enlightenment will come to you. When your time has expired, either you will be called or I will join you; duty will determine which. Now let us part; go to your duty in the West, and let no darkness blind you to the light or lead your footsteps from the path."

Thus her final lecture closed, and with a farewell caress she left the room, and I was alone in her apartments. For over a year I had perceived a change in my body; it was filled with lightness. I seemed never to tire, and, strange to say, day after day required less and less food. But as I was now left alone a still greater sense of bodily freedom came to me; being filled with a tingling sensation I seemed to have no weight, and almost before I knew it fell into a dozing sleep.

The next morning, with nothing but my wearing apparel and

a long cape cloak of indigo color, I commenced my pilgrimage. In this attire I passed through the city without being recognized.

At Havre I read a copy of "Des Mondes," and there learned that Alphonso Colono had mysteriously disappeared, and nothing could be learned of his whereabouts; but it war rumored that he had been taken away by the occult society that for a time was supposed to exert such an influence over Napoleon. This same mysterious fraternity, it was said, took Princess Louise of England some years since. Princess Louise and Colono had both spent much of their time in Paris, and were known to have associated with so-called occult adepts. It was said that the princess owed her life to one of these, who saved her in a runaway in the streets of London many years ago. Then followed a long article on mysterious disappearances and occult societies, the editors commenting upon the large number of prominent persons who had thus disappeared without known cause. Boarding a steamer I continued on my way, thinking how many mysteries the Brothers could explain in the history of the world and prominent individuals.

After fourteen years I again crossed the Atlantic and arrived at New York. Here, without revealing identity, but on the strength of my otherwise evident position, I called together the American council, and asked their co-operation in the formation of a "League of Justice and Mercy;" justice for the innocent and mercy for the suffering and helpless. Visiting all the lodges I went from city to city and doctors and lawyers were the men whose co-operation I in particular sought; for these two professions, when rightly used, have wonderful power for good. Every one in these professions, whose heart was not atrophied by the lust for self and the dross that men call gain, were organized into a brotherhood to work for justice, mercy and the alleviation of suffering, without pay or price. No case of misery was to be left unattended, no case of injustice allowed to pass unnoticed. Even in the smallest things, justice and humanity, and at heart are good. When it became evident that we worked unselfishly for the good of man, the floodgates of accumulated stores were opened to us. Men, indeed, had lost nearly all confidence in their fellowmen, and universal selfishness and distrust was threatened; but we restored their confidence and aroused the flickering light within them. Having with glad heart seen this work successfully established, I once more disappeared, and in the garb of a monk continued my pilgrimage. From town to town I wandered, healing the sick and alleviating suffering. From place to place journeyed, teaching the great truths of love and duty and the fellowship of men. Universal religion I proclaimed, never ceasing in my efforts to break down the barriers of nations, creeds, wealth and races; but what would one expect to meet if he proclaimed that the essential truths of Krishna, Zoroaster, Buddha and Christ were all the same? I thought it would be violence, but no; the simple-hearted masses were nearer the truth than many then expected. Narrow-minded teachers had, indeed, perverted their heart's judgments, but the seed sown found nourishment and brought its fruit. Only the narrow-minded and deluded bigots feared and fought my words and labor. With ran-cored hearts they ridiculed the beggar and drove him from their doors; but through all these trials I felt an over-shadowing presence, and every night, freed from my corps of flesh, journeyed to the East. As I labored on my powers grew stronger, and became more manifest. Sometimes, in the intense enthusiasm of my discourse, going into transports, the veil of mater would be rent. One day while thus speaking to the vast throng that had gathered around me in the streets of New Orleans, I entered into one of these higher conditions and saw a form, like unto my sister, standing beside me, but invisible to the multitude around.

"Brother," she said, as plainly as voice could, "Let me speak." Silently I yielded; the next moment I was a spectator and the voice of Iole spoke from my form. In amazement and rapt attention the multitude stood around and listened to her words. Suddenly a voice commanded me to come with him, and at the same instant I saw St. Germain beside me. Without question or even surprise I obeyed, and felt myself going through space with the rapidity of thought; my body had no weight and was connected to that of St. Germain by a violet thread of misty substance. All around was a world of substance, but the earth I could not see. Suddenly all became a black, and when I returned to consciousness I found myself—another being? At first I knew not; I was in a strange locality and had another body. My masculine hands were no longer, but instead the delicate white hands of a woman; and dressed in a woman's robe of white I felt as never before. Recovering from my amazement, I looked around to find myself in a columned court that somehow looked strangely familiar, although I could not recall the place; then turning I saw St. Germain of France; his features were the same, but now radiant with a divine light and beauty. His kindly smile at my astonishment reassured me, and I asked:

"Where am I, brother?"

"By request of your other self you have been granted some experiences in the 'Third Degree.'"

As he spoke he held a mirror up before me, and to my increased astonishment I beheld the features of my sister Iole. Smiling kindly at my surprise, St. Germain said:

"By a change of polarity you have assumed the body of your sister and she has assumed yours. Your soul and individuality are the same, but another aspect of it is now manifest. You now feel as your sister felt, and she now feels as you did. This change would not have been permitted but that your souls are one, that is, their number and vibration is the same."

"And where is Iole?" I asked.

"She is in New Orleans, and you are now in Lhassa."

"And how long will this exchange continue?"

"Until you both consent to re-exchange."

"And did I consent to this transfer into her pure and holy body while she takes my impure form?"

"Most certainly you did, or it never could have happened. The soul is master of the form it tenants, and no power can drive it there from or replace it against its will. Your body has by your labors been made pure; otherwise Iole, pure soul, could not have entered it."

"And are such exchanges always good?" I asked.

"All we sanction, yes; many others, no," he answered. "Many people by becoming passive and surrendering their will, or by degrading their forms through sensuous passions, allow elemental spirits or disembodied demons to enter their bodies. These make the world's insane and demoniacal possessed. Sometimes, not often, the Masters use these passives, but not unless the form is pure and they can accomplish good through using it."

"And whence all these strange memories and this wonderful knowledge and light now breaking on my mind?" I asked, as a train of ceaseless thought throbbed through my brain.

"As member of the 'Third Degree,' it is within your power to recall your past existences extending back through the vast and shoreless sea of time. These memories, registered deep in the immortal soul, are locked and withheld from untrained minds, for, with memory limited to one short lift, how many precious hours are spent in useless lingering on scenes gone by. Only those who realize their soul and sink their minds into its depths, can read this endless record. To us who can control our minds and attune them to our souls, these memories, and the vast store of knowledge gathered through many lives gone by, are not withheld. Dim and uncertain is the memory which comes through the brain alone; the greatest portion of most men's lives is blank, and what they are conscious of to-day is lost to-morrow. Within the eternal memory of the soul are stored the vast accumulations of an endless evolution; and you have now, by your superior development, become conscious in this memory of your unborn and uncreated self. But control your minds. He who cannot control his mind cannot control his thoughts; turn loose this awful torrent in his brain and he would soon succumb and be a madman. They who, unprepared, play with the occult, play with an awful fire and mind-shattering powers. Now, with thy mind controlled, gaze into and read thy past."

As he spoke the mystery of Iole's words about past lives became explained; for, carefully watched by St. Germain, my mind went back into the past. Once more I was a Benedictine monk, laboring on the fields of Poitiers, and all life was recalled.

"Suffer not regret to disturb your mind," warned St. Germain, as I saw myself once more in the convent on the Pyrenees; "the past is beyond recall; go back."

And, as by the magic of his words, I was again Cleomedes in beautiful Attica.

"Suffer not emotion to disturb your mind's serenity," warned my guide, and once more I proceeded backward. And lo! An Egyptian priestess in the halls of Thebes; then another lifetime back, and still a priestess in the land beside the Nile. "Go on," commanded my guide, and—now a Brahman woman in ancient Aryanvarta; then a Brahmin monk; then a Kshatriya; and then a dark-faced citizen of that great country where the north Atlantic rolls. "Return." Said St. Germain, and once more I was in the columned court.

"Now fix thy mind upon the yellow chakram and read and see; go to any place on earth thou wilt."

No sooner had the adept spoken than my vision seemed to ignore the quality of place, and I was looking at a sleeping form reposing in a little cottage room in New Orleans.

It is myself—no, my former temple, now in charge of sister. "Hasten!" commanded my guide; and from place to place, continent to continent, even to the impossible and secluded places do I fly; all the world is open to my vision.

"Cross not the depths of space, thy will has not sufficient strength; much higher yet must thou go before thou canst its mysteries know, unless thou learnest them from their presence in the world, and that little world—thyself. Return!"

Again I came back to consciousness within the court.

"Brother," said St. Germain, "you have seen a few of the mysteries of life, but only the smallest portion of the whole."

"O that men could realize the grandeur of life and the sublimity of his nature!" I exclaimed, as my thoughts recurred to the blind and deluded world.

"All will in time," replied St. Germain.

"But how vast the time, how slow the progress," I replied.

"Yes; but little by little, one by one, we gather them into the Great Brotherhood."

"But how many new souls come for the few we gain," I said.

"The number of souls in the present universe is fixed; no new ones come. The transmigratory flow from the universe before us has ceased. From now on every brother we receive is a net gain. Do not for a moment think that souls are created for every newborn body—'tis not so. The body cannot be the cause of soul, the low cannot cause the high. Can the temporary cause the eternal? Can body cause spirit? No. Spirit, perverted as desire, prompts the formation of bodies. If God had to create a soul for every body, He would be subject to the lusts and caprices of men, a subservient maker of souls for bodies; whereas the reverse is true, and bodies are made for souls. If the soul was made for the body, and the body was the cause that called it into existence, then does death of body end the soul's existence. But the reverse is true; the body is created or formed for disembodied souls."

"But," I asked, "can the spirit or soul prompt the low and lustful acts which produce some bodies?"

"Pure spirit—no; pure souls—no; but spirit perverted as desire and lost souls—yes. You must remember that those who have damned themselves in former lives continue to seek new forms, and they prompt these monstrous deeds of vice. Woe to those through whom these lost souls work, for they only seek those who have like natures.

"But, brother," he said, changing the subject, "your seven years of probation are up, and it is your privilege to be initiated into the 'Third Degree,' a few of whose mysteries you have just seen. Now, as in the lower degrees, even here there are two routes, and you must choose which you will take."

"Has Iole chosen?" I asked.

"She has chosen and passed on," he answered.

"Then let me as her companion choose the same."

"No one can thus choose; the paths I state, and you must take your choice. The first is that you continue your labors in the world until the time arrives for the natural dissolution of your body. The second is a trance interment and continued life in a self-conscious astral. Which do you choose?"

He paused, and for a moment I hesitated; then thinking it was selfish to wish to get rid of my body before its natural time, I answered:

"I take path the first and continued labor in the world."

CHAPTER XIX.
BROTHER OF THE "THIRD DEGREE."

EVERYTHING else being equal, the more thought a man has given any subject the more apt is he to be right thereon. But far more important than thought itself is an honest desire to know the truth, free from bias and without preference. The man who seeks for truth with a selfish motive will never find it. For his desires will pervert his judgment and befog his reason. Truth is pure and undefiled, and none but the pure in heart and mind can see it in all its beauty. The greatest cause of error in the world is that prejudice which distorts facts to make them fit with preconceived opinions, and prejudice has its root in self. Remembering my motto —"Forget self," —I had instantly chosen the path which seemed to bring more arduous labor. Trusting to the love of truth and right within me, I had chosen with hardly a second thought. Had I chosen right? St. Germain soon dispelled my doubt by saying:

"Brother, you and your noble sister are most truly one; you have chosen the path on which your sister now precedes you, and without delay you shall join her. Two souls like yours should work together until the end. But before we send you forth, we will help you to unlock the mighty powers within your soul. These powers, so long withheld, can be but faintly realized by what I now tell you. Power will be given thee to surround thyself with an impenetrable shield, to become invisible even though present, to project you conscious astral to a distance, to transmute metals, to read the past and the future so far as determined; to read the hearts and minds of men, to influence their thoughts unknown, to control the elements, to cast out demons, to heal the sick by power of will, to mould into visible forms the astral substance, and to master all the powers of nature by the God-power in yourself. I say these powers will be given to you; but, more correctly, you give them to yourself, for you even now possess them though you know it not, otherwise you never could; for nothing can be added to man from without, all comes from within. Before I give you the secret which enables you to unlock yourself, must be convinced beyond all shadow of doubt that you never will use them for selfish ends, even though to save your life or those you love. Of your unselfishness I am now convinced, not only by your soul a s visible to the spiritual sight, but from your life for seven years. But one duty you have yet to perform before I can give you the sacred word; your body must received a complete and final purification, and that necessitates your return to it in the West.

"Iole will return here and wait for your life-term to terminate, which is not long."

"And has every man a fixed time for its dissolution," he replies, "but as man changes is organism, so also does he change the time for its death. The astrological conditions which meant death to your constitutional combination previous to the time when modified by your will, have no power over you organism as it now is. During life you have, by the power of will, so modified your form that its dissolution comes under different planetary aspects. Esoteric astrology does not preclude free will or the power of man to modify his nature."

"Then destiny is a variable quantity?" I asked.

"Every conscious act of will brings a modification in you so - called destiny; but only a few men consciously will, most following blindly the impulses or tendencies of their nature. Therefore, most men's lives are fixed and subject to only slight variations. But there are exceptions, and if you take a man of powerful mind and will it is difficult to cast his horoscope; for he can in a few short hours modify his course in life, and his predominant quality to-day may be replaced by another to-morrow."

"And you say my life-term is short?" I asked.

"Your bodily combination of early life would not have come under death -dealing influences until it had reached its sixtieth year, but your body, as it now is, will meet the influences which mean its dissolution in four years. It so happens that it will then be at the mystic age of thirty-three. You have shortened your earth life, but you will enter that much sooner into the higher life."

"Only four years to labor, yet, oh! So much to do!" I exclaimed, as an all-encompassing love welled up in my heart.

A loving smile lit up the face of St. Germain, and he said: "It will then be permitted you to labor as an invisible or be reborn; now turn thy mind within."

As he uttered this command a heavenly rapture filled my soul, it seeming to expand until all beings and creatures were included in ties wondrous love, and an unutterable peace took possession of me. Looking at St. Germain I saw that his face was radiant with light, and his features seemed angelic in their beauty as he gave the command— "Return!"

In obedience to his command, I threw my consciousness within, a numbness came over my body, and an outward suction commenced in my left side; then there was a moment's blank, from which I awoke to find myself looking at Iole's body, now in deep trance in a chair before me. Wondering what I was I tried to see my form, but my mind and consciousness seemed to be in nothing but a nucleus of substance. As I longed to see, I again took form, the transparent ether obeying my desire. St. Germain had evidently gone through like transformations, for he floated in like form beside me. "Come!" he said in mental speech, and again with the rapidity of thought we passed through space. Through clouds of floating substance of many hues and colors, which scintillated with life and seemed to be in one continuous transformation, we flew. I had no breath or sense of weight, and my transparent form seemed carried by my will. Suddenly I was drawn down as by a suction, and the next instant was beside a bed on which lay my sleeping form; and beside me, in body like my own, stood or floated my sister Iole.

"Hast thou returned?" she asked in thought, for no words were spoken.

"Yes, sister, go thou with the Master to the East; when my life-term is up we will meet again."

Thus speaking I saw that a thread of violet light formed a circuit through our bodies and that of St. Germain. It formed a loop and passed from Iole to me through my sleeping body, and then two strands reached from St. Gemain's transparent form and mine to a misty cloud behind us. A current of life was throbbing through this slender wire from Iole to my sleeping form; but as I spoke the current changed, and I was drawn toward my form and sank into unconsciousness.

When I awoke I was in a little cottage in New Orleans, once more embodied Alphonso Colono; but an awful change had taken place. I was not then conscious of the experiences just written, they have since been recalled. My mind was almost a blank, a horrid blackness was around me. I had a faint recollection of lost knowledge, but in vain I pressed my head in effort to recall it; all was gone! Had my brain been shattered? Had I lost my mind? My God! What did it mean? Who was I? Iole! Who was Iole? Masters! Who were Masters? Ha! Ha! It is nothing but a delusion produced in the brain. Soul! Soul! There is no soul! It is a superstition for which we have no proof. Who ever saw a soul? What is it like? Has it shape or form? Is it a body? Ha! Ha! Who ever saw anything without a body? Thus I raved. My God! Where did these thoughts come from? Strangely unlike myself I arose and dressed. Feeling like some one I did not know, I walked to the mirror. "My God! My God!" I cried, "What demon is it!" The face of Alphonso Colono, but strangely distorted and evil. I turned away; I was abnormally sensitive, and everything I touched appeared to move. My ears thumped and I could hear constant rappings through the room; cold currents touched my face and slimy hands grasped me. In trembling terror I strove to drive them away, but all of no avail. I put on my hat and left the room, but the horrible sensations followed me. Along the street I hurried, hardly knowing what I was doing and ignorant of where I was going. As I passed by people stopped and in horror shrank back; while now, to add to my torments, a demoniacal voice laughed in my ears, ha! Ha! Ha! Ha! Ha! They are afraid of me! Seeking relief and finding none, I returned to my room. All day long I paced restlessly back and forth before the mirror, dimly conscious that I was something, yet lost to myself. The evening grew apace and nigh came on; it was a dark and sultry night, and the oppressive stillness around only made the rappings and invisible voices more awful. As though seized by an insane idea, and despite the oppressive heat, I built a blazing fire upon the hearth, and sitting down before it gazed into its red flames. As I did so the licking flames grew higher, and leaping up seemed to lean forward toward me; then I became as though entranced and lost the power of motion. At the same moment the horrible creature I had seen at the Durant mansion formed in the flames before me; but this time instead of repelling, it seemed to fascinate, and as I leaned forward I recognized its evil and malignant features as my own. It smiled hideously, and continuing to look, it became attractive. As I did not repel, it came toward me; but now, my God! What is it? It shapes into a living skeleton, and its bony form, covered with dry and wrinkled flesh, shone with a greasy gloss of reddish-green. It extended its bony hands to embrace me, I felt them on my neck and shoulders, I inhaled its sickening, poisonous breath; then, as its bony fingers clasped me around the neck as though to choke me, a faint ray of light dawned upon my mind, and I uttered the one word—"Iole!"

An awful, demoniacal shriek rang in my ears; a groan of despair, and the form was sucked back toward the fire. It struggled and pulled toward me, its fiery eyes looking from their sunken depths with a wild, satanic glare; but a white form now stood before me, and with outstretched hand pushed the monster into the flames. With one last wild shriek, it fell into the fire, and as though made of pitch was consumed by the lurid flames. At the same moment, as by an instantaneous change, my soul was filled with light, and looking up I beheld the radiant form of my glorious sister.

"Iole, my savior!" I cried.

"Only the Iole in thyself can be thy savior; only the Christ, Krishna, God or Master within can save thee," answered her mind to mine.

"Thou hast just now slain the last shadow of thy demon nature formed in lives gone by; and now thou art absolutely pure. All men must meet and slay their demon before they can pass on, for this demon shadow ever awaits them at the threshold, and unless they conquer they cannot pass through. When you called for me you called upon your God, for I am but a symbol of the God within your soul."

"With this, thy last experience, thou canst realize the condition of those men who are completely imbued in matter," interrupted another voice-mind, and St. Germain stood before us.

Before I could reply he continued:

"The great hierophant sends me to call thee to the East, and as

I leave with thy sister, in peace retire to sleep; when the morning comes start on thy journey. Thy sister will meet thee at Calcutta and journey with thee through the forbidden passes to Teshee Lumbo."

"We leave you wit hour bodies, but we are with you in our souls," said Iole, and as she spoke a misty cloud enveloped them and I was left alone. No, not alone this time; the ecstasy of God was in my soul, the spirit filled my being. That night I slept the sleep of pence, and in the morning, with my heart as light as the spirit can make it, commenced my journey to the East. What joy I had en route! What peace and happiness I spread along my path! The soul illuminated with love spreads peace where'er it goes. When I reached Calcutta Iole met me robed as a Buddhist nun, her face being veiled to hide the radiant beauty of here features. We reached Darjeeling, and from there journeyed as pilgrims on to Lhassa, the secluded city from which all foreigners are debarred. Here St. Germain, the St. Germain of France, once more in body, met us to lead us across the unknown country to the sacred home. For many days we traveled, but without weariness or haste, and our journey was one continuous discourse on al that is grand and beautiful. The towering Himalayas and the bleak ranges to the north impressed us with feelings of sublimity, while the azure blue of heaven, filled with rainbow-colored clouds at day and the starry constellations at nights, turned our minds and conversation to only the beautiful and good. At last we passed the guarded valley and reached the isolated monastery of "Him Who Knows." Far up the mountainside, reached only by a narrow path, this massive structure, built in cyclopean style, was beyond the reach of the despoiler's hand. All around were deep gorges and ranges of snow; but no sooner had I entered into the inner court than I knew that I had seen the place before. But where or when? Ah! I had seen it in my visions both in Mexico and France, as also in my astral voyage in the care of St. Germain. I thought of the initiations of father and mother, and as a questions arose I my mind, as though she read it, Iole said:

"Your father and mother are members of the 'Third Degree' of Lhassa, and are now head teachers with Kind Eral in France. Your sister, Esmeralda, has gone with her brother Henrie to teach in Scandinavia. Your friend Garcia is a high teacher in California, and Dr. Rankel is Governor of Germany. Seg. Parodi is Governor of Italy, and Albarez makes the world his home."

"And Napoleon?" I asked.

"He lives for many years yet, until, by his now mighty genius, the republic makes all past ideals a fact."

"And may I now ask you of your parents?"

"That I will answer," interrupted St. Germain. "But for your sister you would not have passed beyond Lhassa in this life. Iole has made several incarnations in one life. When the Princess Louise of England died, before her body was marked for dissolution, she whom is known as Iole incarnated there. When she had served her purpose there, she discarded the former form of Princess Louise and took another, which she now has. She has given her past history, but has by her powers ever veiled the present. It was through her that you were recalled when I sent you forth for four more years' labor in the West, and as she is the adopted daughter of the Great Lama himself, she had a right to give the order, for she knew your past existences. When you, with the powers you now have, recall these prior lives, the reason of your present elevation will be made clear."

"Yes," I replied, "I see that far back I was a Brahmin monk of adept power, but for lack of certain experiences I took western incarnations."

"All things are then made clear, are they?" said Iole.

"The past is now an open book." I answered; for all my lives were now linked into one.

"Then we are ready for our great labor," she replied.

"And can I accomplish more here than in the West?" I asked.

"Much more," she answered, "for here we labor day and night; in the day-time in our material bodies, and at night, in that natural trance called sleep, we labor invisibly in our astrals among our brothers in the West. The superficial world thinks we have left them for selfish solitude, but we work through the world of mind and never stop for rest."

We now entered a cyclopean-like chamber of white granite, and were in the presence of the dark Oriental we had seen at Paris.

"Brother," he said, addressing me, "after my weary incarnations the wanderer has returned; gladly we welcome his now purified and illuminated soul. He has seen misery and suffering; he has seen and experienced pain and woe; now can his soul realize divine compassion and labor for mankind. Go with our sister Iole and learn to employ the powers it is now your privilege to use. Another crisis is approaching in the new Atlantis of the West, and as we never idle, you must be prepared. No, the question in your mind concerning your approaching disembodiment will not keep you from this labor. You have joined the immortals, and if your body is deemed fit for another life, when its hour of dissolution comes we will place it in a trance-like state in which life and its inimical influences cannot act; for life is death, and the vital activity disintegrates the body. That which in life works as a unit in all the atoms of the body, at death assumes an individual and separate activity in each. No, you will not die; both you and Iole shall have self-conscious astrals and live immortal in the world of mind and ether, until you choose to pass into the two degrees that lie still higher on. These two most superior degrees are too high for earthly mind to comprehend, and even you can but dimly realize. In the next degree there is no fixed form or body. Each being, in a flame of the universal Spirit, and with its creative power, can make a form to suit its wants or needs in any portion of the boundless universe. As a spirit spark, a center without form, it can dart through the universe of space from star to star, and system to system, and there make a form of vehicle to suit its sphere. This form it can at will cast off, disperse, and then through space pass to another universe and build again. For these beings or spirits are in essence God-spirit, and possess all the powers therein. Of the First Degree, it is not permitted us to speak, all words degrade; the conception is too grand for any but the gods to realize. Now to your chamber with your sister; your initiation comes this evening."

As he finished, Iole led me from his presence.

"Brother," she said, "we hold the thought in common; can we not cloak the mysteries and reveal up to a certain limit?"

"Yes; tell the world our lives, but conceal well the secret teachings. The great truths are open to all who seek the light and allow their minds to become illuminated by a pure, unselfish heart; but everything must come in its right order."

"Then I will veil the teachings, but so lightly that the seeker cannot but find; the ignorant we cannot reach; they will but laugh and scoff. Their ignorance we pity, they must abide their time."

That evening the initiation of my visions was reenacted, and I was principal. Clothed in a gauze of silken threads I was led before the throne. The God-man gave me the "magic kiss," and the slumbering Christ awoke to liberate the virgin from the tomb.

Awake!
Thou that sleepest,
Arise from thy tomb,
Descend from thy cross,
Rend the veil of the Temple,
Stand out in the light,
Let the Holy of holies
No more be in night.
Join hands with the Masters,
The Great Brothers above,
Who labor forever
Through greatness of Love.
Man! Know thy Redeemer,
He dwelleth within;
Buried deep in thy body,
Now gross from thy sin,
Is the only true Savior,
The Christ-spirit-within.

Four years, or what men call years, went by; years of divine love and the ecstasy that come from labor for mankind; years of celestial rapture in which the soul realizes that it is all and lacks nothing. It was in the "sacred chamber," and Iole and I were seated by each other in great pearl chairs beside an emerald table. The great hierophant with his council, St. Germain and the dark Oriental among them, sat around.

"Cross thy hands," said the great Master.

We obeyed, and with reclining forms crossed our hands upon

our breasts.

"Now breathe together deeply," came the order.

We obeyed, and at once became identified with each other and all in the chamber.

"Now turn thy mind within and place it upon the seat of Brahma."

And as the mind sank into the spirit's center, a sacred mantra filled the room, and then the sacred word; then our soul, both now merged into one, became filed with celestial music made by the universe of sphere, and we entered the eternal.

Now did we realize that "there is no death;" with bodies cast aside we live immortal in the pearly essence capable of a higher form. We now overshadow all who seek the light, and in time will come again to assist you with our love.

Om, mand padme, hum.

VOCABULARY.

OCCULT SCIENCE.

The secret or esoteric science of the ancients and the medieval Rosicrucians; the science which deals with the invisible essence of things and explains their mysterious nature.

ASTRAL.

Pertaining to the stars, or a subtle and ordinarily invisible substance which surrounds the earth and stars and pervades all things; a vapor-like ether which pervades and holds together the molecules of all things.

AKASA .

The primordial, homogeneous and all-pervading substance or essence out of which the universe and all differentiated matter are evolved. The highest ether, but not the luminiferous ether of western science.

ELEMENTALS.

Invisible, but intelligent centers of force; atomic lives; the beings that live on astral plane.

CHAKRAM.

The eastern name for certain centers of force in the human organism.

KARMA.

The eastern name for the universal and all-inclusive law of cause and effect, action and reaction; it includes all rewards or punishments that may be due us because of good or evil deed we have done, either in this life or some or many past lives.

KRIYASAKTIL.

The power of adept will which can condense, control, and

mould into forms the astral substance around the operator.

KASHATRIYA.

The warrior cast of the four into which the people of ancient India or Aryavarta , were divided.

MANTRA.

An eastern chant of peculiarly intonated sounds which, when rightly uttered, awaken certain occult forces in the ether.

MASTER.

(1) The divine self or God in man.

(2) Those perfected men in whom the divine self is fully active and supreme ruler.

YOGI.

The name given to the mind concentrators of India, both high and low, but not necessarily a fakir.

END

More Masonic Books from Cornerstone

The Freemasons Key
A Study of Masonic Symbolism
Edited by Michael R. Poll
6 x 9 Softcover 244 pages
ISBN: 1-887560-97-1

Éliphas Lévi and the Kabbalah
by Robert L. Uzzel
6 x 9 Softcover 208 pages
ISBN: 1-887560-76-9

The Teachings of Freemasonry
by H.L. Haywood
Edited by Michael R. Poll
6x9 Softcover 144 pages
ISBN 1-887560-92-0

A.E. Waite: Words From a Masonic Mystic
Edited by Michael R. Poll
Foreword by Joseph Fort Newton
6 x 9 Softcover 168 pages
ISBN: 1-887560-73-4

Freemasons and Rosicrucians - the Enlightened
by Manly P. Hall
Edited by Michael R. Poll
6 x 9 Softcover 152 pages
ISBN: 1-887560-58-0

Masonic Words and Phrases
Edited by Michael R. Poll
6 x 9 Softcover 116 pages
ISBN: 1-887560-11-4

More Masonic Books from Cornerstone

Masonic Enlightenment
The Philosophy, History and Wisdom of Freemasonry
Edited by Michael R. Poll
6 x 9 Softcover 180 pages
ISBN 1-887560-75-0

God's Soldiers: Roman Catholicism and Freemasonry
by Dudley Wright
6 x 9 Softcover 148 pages
ISBN 1-887560-71-8

Masonic Questions and Answers
by Paul M. Bessel
6 x 9 Softcover 144 pages
ISBN 1-887560-59-9

Our Stations and Places - Masonic Officer's Handbook
by Henry G. Meacham
Revised by Michael R. Poll
6 x 9 Softcover 164 pages
ISBN: 1-887560-63-7

Knights & Freemasons: The Birth of Modern Freemasonry
By Albert Pike & Albert Mackey
Edited by Michael R. Poll
Foreword by S. Brent Morris
6 x 9 Softcover 178 pages
ISBN 1-887560-66-1

Robert's Rules of Order: Masonic Edition
Revised by Michael R. Poll
6 x 9 Softcover 212 pages
ISBN 1-887560-07-6